Longarm and Jessica Starbuck—
One hell of a team!

Jessie came out of the bath running a comb through her golden hair. Longarm said, "That was sure fast," and she said, "I didn't take time to tub. I just sponged that train trip off a mite. It's dark out now, so what are we waiting for?"

Longarm started to unbutton his clothing. Jessie laughed and said, "Not that, you sweet fool. We have to go save Ki. Let me get dressed."

Longarm pulled her down on the bed beside him and as she began to struggle he said, "Hold it! I come in peace . . ."

TABOR EVANS

LONGARM

AND THE
LONE STAR MISSION

A JOVE BOOK

LONGARM AND THE LONE STAR MISSION

A Jove Book / published by arrangement with
the author

PRINTING HISTORY
Jove edition / February 1987

ISBN: 0-515-08880-3

Chapter 1

The Justice Department might not have approved. So it was just as well nobody else on its payroll knew why Deputy U. S. Marshal Custis Long was more apt to get to work on time after a night in bed with the widow woman up on Sherman Avenue than if he spent the night alone in his furnished digs on the unfashionable side of Cherry Creek. It was all too easy to oversleep when there was nothing more interesting than a battered brass alarm clock saying it was time to rise and shine.

He gazed fondly down at the part of her light brown hair and said, "I'm sure glad to wake up with you, bless your sweet hide."

She grinned at him like a mean little kid and said, "I'd hate to make you late, but how do you feel about one more time?"

She didn't wait for an answer. She knew her overnight guest was still a mite sleep-drugged. So she simply settled down atop him, hissing with pleasure.

In addition to how good it felt, the widow woman's

junoesque naked body was exciting simply to watch in motion.

She was perhaps a little older than Longarm. He'd never asked such a delicate question and she'd never asked him to make a more honest woman of her. That was no doubt why they were still good pals. A late husband Longarm didn't really want to hear about had left her well off. She'd once told him a rich widow woman had to be sort of careful who she associated with, and he sometimes wondered if she admired him more for his muscles and moustache or the fact he was too far down the social totem pole of Denver to try to marry her for her money.

Meanwhile, whatever their relationship was, it sure felt good. Longarm rolled her over to finish right and, as always, it was even better that way. But when he attempted to keep going, she shook her head and protested, "I promised to get you to work on time, and I want to talk to you about something else before you leave, dear."

He glanced at the dawn light coming through her lace curtains. "Hell, it's early, and I'd rather skip breakfast than you, you sweet little thing."

She sighed and began to move under him again. "All right, just one more time, then," she murmured. "But you told me it was payday at your office and made me swear I'd throw you out early even if you didn't want to go."

He kissed her pale throat. "I ain't going nowhere right now. But what else did you want to jaw at me about, honey?"

"Good Lord, you expect me to hold a conversation and do . . . *this* at the same time?"

He laughed. "Why not? Neither one of us has his or her *mouth* filled right now."

She chuckled. "Mmmm, nice. What I wanted to ask you was what you'd planned on doing this coming weekend."

He kissed her again and said, "That's a mighty dumb question, unless you was fixing to have other house guests in the near future."

She sighed. "It's worse than that. I have to attend the

2

opera and a social gathering after, dear. You know about my box at the opera house, don't you?"

He did. The Denver Opera was something he tried to ignore unless he had a warrant for some tenor's arrest. She dug her nails into his bounding buttocks and moaned. Then she told him, "I don't have an escort, and if we tidy you up and one of my late husband's formal outfits will fit you . . ."

He withdrew and rolled upright, swinging his bare feet to the bedroom rug as he told her, as sincerely as a man who was fibbing could, "I got my own boiled shirt and claw hammer coat, honey. But I just remembered my boss, Marshal Vail, said something about one of the James—Younger gang being spotted here in Denver by a soiled dove I'd never want a lady like you to meet."

"In other words, you don't want to take me to the opera, you mean thing?"

He rose to grope for his duds as he assured her that wasn't it. He'd be proud to take her to the opera and anywhere else she wanted to go, if it was all right with his office. He said he'd let her know later, after work. As he'd hoped she might, she said that would be too late and that she would have to ask someone else. He tried to look disappointed as he kissed her goodbye, put on his Stetson, and left. It wasn't easy.

Twenty minutes later Longarm was down at the federal building, well before even sissies were supposed to get there. As he banged on the big bronze doors for the night watchman to let him in, Billy Vail joined him there, his own key ring out, to growl, "I give up. Did a husband come home early, or is the South Platte flooding and you come to save the furniture?"

Longarm grinned sheepishly. "It's payday, in case you forgot. Will you and your wife be going to that new opera this weekend, boss?"

Vail unlocked the door and led the way in. He sighed and said, "I can't get out of it. My fool wife bought a season's ticket behind my back. I sure hate Italian singing.

3

It seems to me that for *that* kind of money they could teach the singers to speak *English* like everyone else."

As they moved up the interior stairwell together Vail asked Longarm, "How come you wanted to know, old son? I couldn't sell you a couple of tickets, could I? My wife already knows the story of this one, and even she thinks it's sort of depressing. The fat gal as yells all through the infernal show up and kills her fool self in the end. But if you want to go with some little gal as enjoys a good cry..."

Longarm shook his head. "I want you to tell a certain lady you sent me out of town on serious business, should you meet her there, Billy. You mind that handsome widow woman who lives on down Sherman Avenue from you?"

Vail unlocked the frosted glass door of their office. "I do, and you ought to be ashamed of yourself. You know I don't lie to gents, let alone ladies, Longarm."

"You don't? I know you used to ride with the Rangers and I've seen you hold your ground in more than one shootout. But when did you pick up such a disgusting new habit, Billy?"

Vail smiled crookedly and explained, "I only lie in the line of duty. Your widow woman is a neighbor and it's a good thing my wife don't know about you and her, for I'd never hear the end of it. Don't ask me to cover up for you. If I had jurisdiction over your love life it wouldn't be so interesting. By the way, you sure look stupid with that face powder on your lapel."

Longarm wiped the rough tobacco-brown tweed sheepishly with his fingertips as he followed the marshal into the inner sanctum. Vail sat down behind his massive cluttered desk and waved his deputy to the leather guest chair as he reached for a cigar saying, "Matter of fact, I do have a matter I want you to look into. Lord knows why I'm sending you instead of Smiley and Dutch or maybe Guilfoyle. The State Department says it's delicate as hell and wants me to handle it with kid gloves."

"I can be delicate as any kid, boss. But before we put

4

me to work, could we discuss some back wages? Like I said, it's payday, and I was out in the field the last time you saw fit to part with any money. So that's close to a hundred dollars we're talking about."

Vail growled, "You get paid the same as the others, when Henry makes up the payroll out front, later in the day. You'll be interested to hear the department disallowed most of that expense account you handed in. So we're talking more like eighty than a hundred. Here, read this— it may cheer you up."

Longarm reached for the yellow Western Union form the older lawman held out to him and settled back to scan it. The words were, of course, in Roman block lettering, but after that it was all mysterious. He knew Billy Vail had a twisted sense of humor. So he fished out his own smoke and lit up before he said softly, "No offense, Billy, but this wire don't seem to be written in English or anything else sensible."

Vail looked pleased with himself and replied, "That's 'cause it was sent by the Japanese Embassy in Washington. Lord knows why. Mayhaps it's a follow-up to the instructions from State. I can't show 'em to you. Orders. The Japanese have asked us to pick up a renegade embassy official who deserted his post and now seems to be following the owlhoot trail. State says they are afraid their emperor's face is about to fall off, silly as that may sound, so they want us to catch the rascal discreet as hell. I can't even show you the official dispatches. There's things the grown-ups may not want you children to know, see?"

Longarm took a thoughtful drag on his cheroot, let it out, and decided, "If you're not just funning me, I feel so discreet I don't see what in thunder I can do about the emperor's face, boss. I hate to have to admit this, but I hardly ever catch a want unless I know his fool alias and have some notion as to what he might look like."

Vail nodded. "I reckon I can tell you that much. They calls him Nakamura Sam and he looks Japanese, of course. Some other Japanese as lives here in Denver spotted him a

5

few days ago, wired the embassy in Washington, and the rest you know. So why don't you go out and scout around for the cuss? How many Japanese called Nakamura Sam could there be in Denver to begin with?"

Longarm swore softly and said, "I think his name would be more like Nakamura-San or Mr. Nakamura, Billy. As to how many gents of the Japanese persuasion we may have in our fair city at the moment, I can't tell you. How in blue blazes am I suppose to find an undescribed one?"

"Well, hell, you just said you understood some of their talk. How did you know Sam means Mister, anyway? What other words do you know, and who taught 'em to you in the first place?"

Longarm shrugged. "I know more Cheyenne than I know Japanese. Somehow it's always seemed more important out this way. I picked up the little I know from Jessie Starbuck, down Texas way. You remember her, don't you?"

Vail looked incredulous and replied, "Remember her? Hell, if her late father hadn't been an old Texas pal of mine *you'd* have never got to know her. I mind when I was in the Rangers and we'd stop now again at the Circle Star for shelter. That pretty little gal was just a toddler the first time I bounced her on my knee. Even then she knew how to get her own way with us dumb men. Longarm, why are we talking about Lone Star?"

Longarm said, "You asked where I learned a mighty few words of Japanese. Starbuck Enterprises deals in more than beef these days. They export and import all sorts of stuff from all over. But even before they got so big they were trading with the Orient a lot and Jessie was raised by Oriental servants, so—"

"Yeah, yeah, I noticed how good the tea was when I stopped by in my Ranger days," Vail cut in. "Forget about Jessie and her spooky breed bodyguard—what's his name?"

Longarm said, "They call him Ki. *I* think he's sort of spooky at times, too, but he's half Japanese and knows

6

more about such folk than even Jessie does. If we wired them, and they had nothing better to do, seeing as it's between roundups . . ."

"I said no!" Vail snapped. "We're under orders to walk on eggs and take this renegade official so quietly the newspapers never print a word about it."

"Jessie can be very discreet, boss."

"The hell you say. What sort of a tomboy gal puts on pants and guns, calls herself Lone Star, for God's sake, and goes whooping and yelling after outlaws?"

Longarm had to smile fondly at the picture, but he insisted, "That's all in the past, Billy. You know the Lone Star legend as well as me. It was natural for the little gal to feel upset when business rivals murdered her dad and tried to take over his business empire. It was their misfortune that the dead man's daughter and a mighty dangerous breed her dad had left with her had a list of her dad's enemies to work with. So, sure, she got sort of wild for a spell."

"Sort of wild?" Vail raised his eyebrows. "You know I've always been fond of the little gal. You know I've sent you to help her more than once. But this department don't need no help from a self-appointed female vigilante and a Japanese breed who kicks through walls with his fool bare feet! I thought of them right off, as soon as I got the delicate mission from Washington. I can see as well as you can that a couple of folk who can talk the lingo and might know a Japanese from a Shoshone or, hell, Eskimo, could offer some helpful hints indeed. But, like I said, we don't have anyone called Lone Star or Ki on the federal payroll, and we'd best do this ourselves, discreet."

Longarm blew smoke out his nose like an annoyed bull. "You sure like to make me do things the *hard* way. I don't even know where to begin or who to talk to if you won't let me talk to the only people I know who speak one word of Japanese!"

"Well, you ain't likely to find Nakamura Sam here in this office. So what say you start by looking somewhere else?"

Longarm got wearily to his feet, not daring to say what he was thinking if he wanted to get paid that afternoon. Instead, he said, "I'll start down around the Union Depot. Ticket agents and porters tend to remember anyone unusual getting on or off a train, and it might help if we knew whether the son of a bitch could be here in town or not."

Vail nodded. "What about Chinatown? I know the rascal is a Japanese, but he might know he'd attract less notice in that part of town."

Longarm grimaced. "The Chinese would notice. We're sort of short on *any* sort of Oriental here in Denver since those last riots. The ones left are too spread out to call any part of our Cherry Creek slum a Chinatown. But I'll ask a laundryman I know. He *might* tell me if he knows anything. I saved him from a lynch mob the last time the Great Unwashed were trying to prove any two dozen white men could lick one skinny Chinaman fair and square. Don't bank on it, though. If I was living in the Far East and me and my kind was getting picked on regular, I ain't so sure I'd tell even a friendly Oriental lawman where he could find another white man I had no reason to be sore at."

He made it to the door, but paused as Vail cleared his throat and said, "I'm glad you told me Jessie Starbuck ain't playing at being Lone Star no more. She was ever such a sweet little gal, growing up. You didn't say what she might be doing these days, Longarm."

Longarm turned his face away, knowing how good his boss was at reading his eyes, before he muttered, "Just acting more ladylike, I reckon. Without her dad's old enemies to worry about she just has to run Starbuck Enterprises, raking in more money than you or me will ever see, even if we solve a mess of bank robberies."

"Yeah, the Starbucks was quality, even when I first met 'em in my Ranger days of yore. You reckon she'll get married up, now that it's safe for her to act more sedate?"

Longarm shrugged. "Most ladylike ladies do, sooner or later. It won't be to anybody we know, however. So do we have to dwell on such dreary matters, Billy?"

"I was just asking. A man who's bounced a pretty girl child on his knee has a right to wish her well. I confess more than once I expected you and her to get serious-like. You can't tell me you ain't fond of her, Longarm."

Longarm sighed. "I'm fond of her. I think poor old Ki is head over heels in love with her. But, like you said, she's quality and, even if she'd have me, I'm more likely to get a bullet in the back than a thousand a year, no matter how long I stay at this fool job."

Vail sighed and said, "I keep telling 'em good help is hard to find at five hundred per annum. Old Ki would be out of the running because he ain't a white man, right?"

"Not exactly. Jessie ain't down on Orientals and Ki could pass for white if he put his mind to it. He's out of the running for the same reasons I am. What kind of a man would propose to a gal so rich? I'm having enough trouble with a gal here in town as wants to spend her own damn money on me."

Vail chuckled. "I sure feel sorry for the way they pick on you, Longarm."

Longarm grinned sheepishly and met his boss's eyes some more as he said, "We're both too ugly to take up pimping or fortune hunting. Do you want me to go get that Nakamura cuss, or do you want to gossip about gals some more?"

"Powder River and let her buck! Bring that one in before we close the paybook for this month and I'll allow you that double pullman expense voucher no matter what they say back East."

Longarm sighed. "Easy for you to say, since we both know what the odds are. By the way, you never told me what the Denver Oriental who spotted Nakamura in town was called."

"That's because nobody saw fit to tell me. It *could* be in that wire they sent us in Japanese. But the case is so delicate both the embassy and State seem to be playing it close to the vest as hell."

It was safe to say what *he* thought about the pencil

pushers at State, so Longarm did. Billy Vail complimented him on the originality of his cursing and agreed, "I don't expect us to pick the bastard up without more to go on, either. But they won't be able to say we never tried."

Longarm nodded. "I'm off for the Union Depot, then, on one condition."

Vail frowned and answered softly, "I don't like my deputies making conditions, old son."

"I don't like being sent on fool's errands, either. If you won't let me hunt Nakamura my way, with sensible help from old friends, I'll try it your way, dumb, provided you, me, and a certain widow woman understand I'm likely to be tied up all weekend with overtime. Do we have a deal?"

Vail hesitated, smiled wickedly, and said, "Deal. But remember that if I have to fib to a lady, you don't get the overtime *pay* for real."

Chapter 2

Down in Houston, Texas, about the time Longarm was asking dumb questions and getting dumb answers up north at the Denver Union Depot, the man called Ki was pacing the floor of his hotel room like the big cat more than one friend or foe had noticed he resembled at times.

The tall Eurasian was resisting the temptation to consult his watch again, knowing it had been less than a dozen times across the rug since he'd last looked. He knew he was on edge with less reason than usual. His friend and employer, Miss Jessica Starbuck, had warned him she might return a little late from the business meeting she was attending a few blocks away. Ki knew she'd been properly introduced to the businessmen she was with, and he'd taken the liberty of checking their credit by wire early that morning. Wall Street vouched for them, and Ki knew all too well why Jessie hadn't wanted him to tag along. The business deal was delicate, and they both knew Ki tended to intimidate people.

Sometimes, catching himself unaware in a mirror, Ki

scared himself. It wasn't that he looked ferocious. Ki could smile as pleasantly as anyone else, when he wanted to. It was simply that he was harder than most to size up at first glance, and many men of any race were afraid of what they didn't understand. As he recrossed the rug Ki paused before a full-length pier glass to see if he could make himself look less sinister.

He didn't know where to begin. Since he and Jessie had come to Houston on business, he was dressed as much like a white Texas businessman whose business tended to be cows as any other male guest in the hotel. He had on a three-piece suit over his weaponry and riding boots. His pearl-gray Stetson was hanging from a bedpost across the room. He was tall even by Texas standards, and the white blood that had given him his athletic build had blurred his facial features to a visage that could seem white or Oriental. His long black hair and somewhat drooping moustache neither added nor subtracted from the exotic cast of his features. His skin was tanned and his wide-set, rather feline eyes tended to spook strangers most. They didn't look quite Oriental, they didn't look quite Caucasian, and, when Ki was on the prod, they often didn't quite look human. In a pinch he could and in the past he had passed himself off as an Indian or a Mexican with plenty of Indian blood. Nobody would argue with Ki no matter what he told them he was. Ki was not the kind of man most people felt up to arguing with.

Ki turned from the mirror as he heard a timid rap on the door. It was not a familiar knock. Ki slipped a thoughtful hand inside his frock coat as he moved to the door with panther-like grace and opened it, braced for almost anything but what he found himself staring down at. Had Ki's facial muscles been less under control he would have had to laugh.

The diminutive Oriental bowing at him was dressed in striped pants, a black cutaway coat, and owl-eyed glasses. He clutched his stovepipe hat to his breast as he hissed politely and announced, ''I shall be Higasi on Houston consulate. Have me honor to talk on foreman of Circle Star Ranch?"

His English was hard for even Ki to follow. The Eurasian bowed back at him and introduced himself in fluent Japanese, explaining that he was indeed the foreman of the Circle Star. Then he asked, "In what manner may I satisfy your desire, Higasi-San?"

The little consular official gasped with pleasure and replied, "This humble servant of the Divine Chrysanthemum was told you spoke Japanese, but not so well, with such an aristocratic accent. But I beg you to tell me, is my English as dreadful as I fear it might be?"

"Not at all," Ki lied, politely. "I merely took the liberty of assuming Higasi-San might find it more desirable to converse in his own language. I mean no disrespect, but Higasi-San has yet to tell me to what I owe the honor of this visit."

Higasi sucked his teeth politely and said, "My government is most anxious to learn the whereabouts of a very deluded person known as Hideki Nakamura. My superiors thought it possible you might know something of his present whereabouts."

Ki looked sincerely confused as he tried to connect the name to anyone or anything he knew, failed, and said so, adding, "Why would your honorable government assume I knew such a person? I am not, as you see, a true son of Japan. I am half American, and so almost everyone I have known for quite some time would be American, if not Mexican or Indian. I meet very few of my honorable mother's people these days. So I am sure I would remember the name if I had ever met this Nakamura person. I can assure you I have not."

Higasi sucked his teeth some more. "Forgive me, but as there are so few in this country with any connection to Japan, we take the liberty of keeping track of them. Thus we know you have some connection to the Tokugawa clan, as does your no doubt remote kinsman, Hideki Nakamura. Like you, he has turned his back on the Center, although in

13

your case this is understandable, and thus less a reason to feel shame."

Ki's eyes went cold as the snows of Fuji, but he kept on smiling as he murmured dangerously, "This person sometimes feels confusion as to his true identity. I assure you he has yet to feel *shame*. As to being in any way related to the leaders of the former shogunate, I humbly assure you someone is full of shit. Nobody on the Japanese branch of my family tree was a member of the Tokugawa clan. My honorable mother's family was of the two-sword class, but hardly Tokugawa!"

"In that case, would you find it desirable to inform me just what clan we *are* talking about?"

Ki bowed stiffly and replied, "I do not desire to discuss the honorable but tragic circumstances of my birth. The marriage of a high-born Japanese maiden to a barbarian caused great pain to some of her people. As they disowned her—and me, of course—they have the right to enjoy family secrets, and I must respect that right. I simply give you my word, for what it's worth, they were neither Tokugawa nor allied with the Tokugawa. What made you think a Tokugawa would contact *me,* in any case?"

Higasi looked as if he were about to cry. "Oh, this is all so delicate as well as confusing! Perhaps if you found it possible to come back to the consulate with me we could clear the matter up with my confused superiors."

Ki shot a glance at the clock on his bed table before he told Higasi, "I find it possible but improbable. I await the return of my employer, and escorting her back to the Circle Star seems more important to me than discussing people I have never met with any people I can't help." Then his curiosity got the better of him and Ki found himself asking, "Just what did this Nakamura do to attract such great interest and displeasure from his government?"

Higasi sighed and said, "He apparently went insane. As you may know, some samurai of the old order were not too pleased when the shogunate was overthrown in 1867. Many were, as the Americans say, put out of business when Japan entered the modern age and it was no longer desirable for each great house to retain its own private army. But, of course, most gentlemen of the two-sword class in time adjusted, and many found honorable positions with the new government as commissioned officers. Nakamura was posted as security officer at our San Francisco consulate, with the rank of captain. Apparently he did not find this enough honor for a noble of a deposed ruling class. He deserted his post, along with thirteen of his bushi. They must all be brought to justice. Orders regarding the undesirable situation come from high places."

Ki frowned. "Why? What damage could it do to Japan if a surly samurai and his family retainers want to try their luck as railroad workers or dishwashers? Speaking from sad experience, I can assure you Orientals have a hard time convincing many an American they're high-born gentlemen."

Higasi sighed. "We are not worried about their position in American society. We are more concerned about our loss of face should American justice catch up with them before we do. The Americans have no mercy. They do not allow a disgraced gentleman the honorable way out. They insist on public hangings. Oh, the shame of it, to think of a two-sword samurai dancing at the end of a rope with barbarians laughing at him!"

Ki said, "They don't dance much when it's done right. But, again, I must ask why. Americans frown on their own military deserters, but I can hardly see them arresting a Japanese for going over the hill, as they put it."

Higasi shuddered. "Nakamura and his band have done more than that," he explained. "As warriors, they have no other trade to follow and, since they regard all Americans as mere barbarians, they feel free to rob, rape, and kill. That is what they have been doing for more than two weeks now!"

Ki whistled softly. "In that case, you don't need my help. Speaking again from experience, I know something of the way American lawmen deal with such matters. With

15

all due respect to Nakamura's martial skills, he won't get far. Orientals have a hard enough time getting served a drink out here in the American West when they're *behaving* themselves. Fourteen wild Japanese are going to have a hard time blending into the scenery of a country they don't know."

Higasi sucked his teeth and said, "Just so. We agree completely about that. I would find it most desirable if you could come down to the consulate and give your views on the matter to my superiors. You are, as you say, more experienced about the methods of the police officers of this wild West. Perhaps if we all put our heads together we might be able to discover some way in which the foolish sons of Japan can be captured before they disgrace their country in the barbarian newspapers!"

Ki glanced at the clock again, moved over to open a drawer under it, and said, "I suppose I can spare a few minutes, even though I doubt I can be of much help. Let me leave a note for my employer and we'll go down and clear this matter up. I do not find it desirable for your government to bother my honorable mother's people back in Japan and, with all due respect, I know the methods of your Thought Police."

He got out a notepad and pencil to jot a few hurried lines to Jessie Starbuck, telling her he would be back within an hour or so. Then he left the hotel with Higasi. A coach and four with a Japanese driver was waiting out front. It only took a few minutes for them to get to the consulate near the ship's channel. A brace of Imperial Marines offered them rifle salutes as Higasi swept past them rather grandly, with Ki in tow.

They crossed a courtyard and paused before a sliding paper shoji. Ki had a little more trouble removing his riding boots than Higasi had with his high-button shoes, but he managed. His guide slid the screen open and led him into a cavernous room furnished only with straw floor mats and a small tea table. Behind the low table knelt an older, larger man in a black kimono. Higasi introduced him to Ki as Moto-San. Ki didn't argue, but he had to wonder. Higasi was as common a Japanese name as Jones, while Moto made a good substitute for Smith. Ki knelt beside Higasi across from Moto. They had to share some tea and saké before getting down to business. The official calling himself Moto was not as pleasant as the little man he had sent to fetch Ki. He listened impassively as Ki explained he had never heard of their renegade officer until just now. Then, in better English than that of Higasi, Moto said, "I do not desire to be overheard. Your accent is silly, in any case. Tell me, how is it that a mixed-blood effects such a high-toned accent in the first place? What sort of a two-sword aristocrat would sleep with a mere barbarian?"

Higasi had the grace to suck in his breath with dismay at the insult. Ki smiled wearily and replied, "My honorable parents were married. Were yours, Moto-San?"

"You imply I am a bastard? You dare?"

"I know nothing of your ancestry, Moto-San. I did not come here to buy any salve, either. So can we confine this conversation to more seemly matters?"

Moto blinked his eyes rapidly and lapsed back into Japanese to marvel, "First he calls me a bastard and then he calls me a salve seller! Are you going to allow this, Major Higasi?"

Higasi soothed, "Perhaps he did not mean that last the way it sounded. In any case, the drug should be taking effect any moment now."

The hairs on the back of Ki's neck rose as that sank in. He started to rise as well. But his legs didn't seem to want to move and it didn't help at all when the small but treacherous Higasi chopped the side of Ki's neck with the horny edge of a hardly diplomatic hand.

As Ki found himself diving headfirst into a spreading pool of India ink where a tea table had once been, he felt Japanese enough to know he'd been caught in a standard trap and American enough to wonder why. By the time he crashed all the way, he no longer felt anything.

• • •

As they were binding Ki hand and foot at the consulate, Jessie Starbuck was having her own problems in another part of Houston. It was getting late. She'd already said no more than once, and the fat smooth talker across the table from her still kept trying to phrase his proposition another way as he blew cigar smoke at her. Jessie wasn't usually offended by tobacco smoke. She had fond memories of her late father's brand and the three-for-a-nickel cheroots of a certain deputy marshal had been surprisingly pleasant to share on occasion. But this smug idiot's more expensive reek simply served to make her dislike his company more. So the next time he stopped for breath Jessie made a point of consulting the watch-brooch pinned to her blue silk bodice and said, "I really must be going, Mr. Skane. It's very late and my foreman will be worried about me."

The fat man regarded the sedately dressed but athletic blonde knowingly. "Don't worry about your pet breed, Miss Jessie," he said. "We've still got some dealing to do, and I suspect you don't savvy where I'm coming from."

Jessie had been brought up too polite to tell him where she wanted him to go. So she smiled demurely and replied, "I understand your business proposition perfectly, Mr. Skane. You have to understand *my* position. As I said, it's true Starbuck Enterprises does trade beef and lumber to the Orient, and we do import some Chinese cotton textiles as well as Japanese silk. The blue denim from China is in demand for jeans made in San Francisco. A New York firm takes most of our silk. We import a little finished textile here to Texas, but no raw cotton bales. It's hard enough for our East Texas cotton growers to make a living without having to compete with coolie labor. I don't see why you approached me to begin with. Why would I be interested in buying raw cotton from your firm? I have my own established sources of supply and, no offense, I prefer to do business with people I know."

Skane chewed his already sticky cigar and growled, "You must have wax in your pretty little ears, Miss Jessie. I haven't been *asking*. I've been *telling*. Certain pals of

18

mine has built them a swamping cotton mill in Japanland on borrowed money they has to pay back at considerable interest. Them Japs ain't half the businessmen we is. To pay back anybody they have to show a profit, and you're right about Chinese denim being better. Poor Japs would as soon buy cheap hemp cloth, and rich Japs prefers Chinese cotton. So there my pals is in Osaka, with all them machine looms working half-time and all that raw cotton piled up on the docks. Me and my American associates has contracted to take said cotton off their hands, cheap."

Jessie cut in, "You didn't quote me a cheap price."

"Shoot, a middleman's entitled to *some* profit, ain't he?" Skane asked.

Jessie shook her head. "Not that much. I told you I don't like to compete with Texas cotton and, even if I did, I told you your price was way out of line. For heaven's sake, I can buy all the raw cotton I want, cheaper, here. I would, if I had any use for it. But I don't. Shipping it around the Horn to San Francisco costs more than importing it from China. That's why I can't help Texas growers I know a lot better than you."

"Now what's all this stuff about *knowing* folk, Miss Jessie? Are you a businesswoman or a charitable organization?"

Jessie knew she was wasting her breath, but she shrugged and said, "I know this may come as a great surprise to you, sir, but it's possible to make money, a lot of money, without hurting old business partners. I still deal with old gents in Shanghai and Yokohama my late father dealt with before I was born. It wasn't easy for my dad to get them to trust a barbarian—which is what they call us, with some justice. You've heard, of course, of the Opium War and the Great Black Ships steaming into Tokyo bay uninvited?"

"Hell, we had to teach 'em modern ways, didn't we?"

"Whether we had to or not, we did, and I'm not sure we won't regret it some day. Meanwhile, I get by just fine without hurting honest merchants of any country. I might

19

have to, if I took you up on that raw cotton. I know Starbuck Enterprises would lose money on the deal. So it's
been nice talking to you, but I really have to go now."

Skane said, "No you don't. Stay put, Lone Star. Like
the Indian chief, I'll tell you when I has spoken."

Jessie regarded the fat man with renewed interest. "Why
did you just call me that, sir? I thought you invited me here
to discuss doing business with Starbuck Enterprises."

The fat man chuckled knowingly and said, "I did. I
checked you out some before I decided you needed our raw
cotton and had the cash reserves to take it off our hands. I
know all about your tomboy ways, riding astride like a
man as you and your Jap lover play vigilante games like
you was real American he-men."

Jessie smiled thinly. "If this is a blackmail ploy, you can
stuff it where the sun never shines, you silly lard-bucket!"
she said. "You have your facts twisted, but for the sake of
argument, what could you *do* with the information if you
could prove I was a camp-town harlot and Ki was pimping
for me? Feel free to go to the law with fable or fact about
me and mine, fat boy. For I was bounced on many a Texas
Ranger's knee before I learned how to stomp on bugs like
you, and one at least is now a U. S. marshal. Whether I'm
Lone Star or not, I'll have you know I *own* half the state of
Texas and have some say in the parts I don't, so—"

"We got your Ki," Skane cut in flatly.

Jessie blinked in surprise. Before she could ask, Skane
said, "That's right, Lone Star. We got your domesticated,
dangerous whatever under lock and key. So it's just little
old you and big old us, now."

Jessie smiled sweetly, said that sounded fair, and the
next thing Skane knew he was staring down the muzzle of
her .38.

Skane paled but managed to grin as he observed,
"That's the .38-framed .44 they said you might be packing
under them pretty blue skirts. How do you manage that?
Garter holster?"

"I carry a derringer in my garter holster. I'd show it to you, but I think this gun in my hand should do the trick. It has five in the wheel and you'd be a hard target to miss at this range, fat boy."

"Aw, is that any way for a lady to talk, Lone Star? You know we can't shoot one another in this fancy office building."

Lone Star cocked her big revolver just to make her point and asked demurely, "How much are the table stakes in this wager?"

"Ki's life, for openers," Skane said. "I was picked for this job because I'm good at poker. The gents holding your friend ain't as easygoing as me. So if you harm a hair on my handsome head they'll treat old Ki ugly as hell and, for all I know, send his head to you in a basket. You know how disgusting some gents can act, even when they're as white as us."

"You have some Orientals working with you, then?"

"Now, did I say that, Lone Star? Never mind who might or might not be sitting on your Japanese houseboy right now. We come here to talk business."

Jessie Starbuck was on her feet, moving around to his side of the table with a look in her eye that wiped the grin from Skane's face and made him cower back in his seat as he warned her, "Take it easy, little darling. I bruise easy, and we gotta think of old Ki!"

Then he was sitting on the floor, a pudgy hand to his pistol-whipped face, as Jessie kicked him in the ribs with the pointed toe of her sturdy Justin boot. "You're right about this being the wrong place for gun play, but don't bank on it. For even if you live, I can always say you tried to rape me, and the law in this town figures to be on my side."

He protested, "Carrying on so mean ain't going to get old Ki back, damn it! If *I* don't report back soon, they'll start to treat him even meaner!"

"Maybe. I couldn't help noticing you were the one who

21

seemed to have all night. So that gives us a little time, and you won't be going anywhere, alive, until you tell me who has Ki and where!"

Skane rolled upright on his fat rump, stared at his bloody fingertips morosely, and heaved a great defeated sigh before he said, "All right. Nobody never told me you poker-bluffed so rough. I was bluffing more civilized. Nobody's grabbed your infernal old Jap. Right now he no doubt feels a whole lot safer than I do."

"Where *is* Ki, then?" she demanded.

"Where did you leave him?" Skane asked. "Me and my pals are only honest businessmen. Did you really think we'd go up against a gent as can kill a man even without a gun? I told my pals we was playing with fire, fibbing to you. But they figured it was worth a try if we couldn't get you to see things our way. We all know how *that* worked out. So can we call it a draw, Lone Star?"

She said, "Not yet. On your feet. I'm taking you back to our hotel and then, if Ki's all right, you can go to the devil for all I care. If he's *not,* well, I may start with your knee-caps, after hanging a 'don't disturb' sign outside, of course."

Skane grunted to his feet, casually slipping a pudgy hand inside his coat but removing it fast, empty, when Jessie shoved her cold steel muzzle into the fat of his neck and said, "Don't," in a hardly ladylike tone.

Skane sighed and said, "I know when I'm licked."

"Sure you do. Place your hands against that wall and spread your feet so I can see how licked you might be," Jessie ordered.

He did as she commanded. She removed the .45 from his shoulder holster and said, "Shame on you," as she got his vest-pocket derringer as well. She placed them on the table by the overflowing ashtray and said, "You go first. You know the way to my hotel and it's not too far to walk."

"Lord have mercy, Lone Star. Do you aim to frog-march me through the streets of this great city at gunpoint?"

"That's for me to know and you to worry about. Just do

22

as I say and don't look back as you lead the way. You won't get hurt if you do as I say and we find Ki alive and well where I last left him."

Skane couldn't do anything else, so he did as he was told. They moved down the stairwell without meeting anyone this late in the business day. Outside, the walks were crowded with people on their way home from work. Jessie stayed as close as she could with the gun discreetly hidden by her dainty but large silk purse. They made it to the corner and Skane swung the right way. As they approached the gaping mouth of an alleyway she told him, "Forget it. Keep going."

Skane did, for perhaps three more steps. Then a rifle squibbed somewhere down the alley and Skane's derby and half Skane's head sailed out into the street as the rest of him crumpled to the dusty walk.

Jessie cursed, drew her .38 out of hiding, and headed for the alley entrance until she wondered why on earth she would want to do a dumb thing like that. So she had her gun tucked away again as a uniformed policeman tore up the walk behind her, blowing his whistle for help. He stopped to ask Jessie what was up as he got to where she was standing near the corpse. Jessie told him, "Somebody just shot that gentleman, Officer."

The Houston copper badge said, "I can see that, ma'am. The question afore the house is who done it."

"Don't look at me," she said. Another innocent bystander, bless him, called out, "I seen it, Callahan. That little lady was walking just ahint him. He took a rifle round from that alley. *Had* to be a rifle, from the way it sounded and the way it tore his head apart!"

The copper badge lost interest in Jessie as he stared morosely at the alley entrance and pondered the wisdom of sticking his head in it. He decided, "My wife and kids will never forgive me if I don't wait for some backup. I'll just make sure nobody can get out *this* end and, as long as I'm here, get a statement from one and all as seen the dirty deed take place."

23

But as he got out his notebook Jessie was already out of sight. He didn't worry about it. What could a fool woman tell the law about such manly matters? The poor little thing was likely scared skinny.

He was right, in a way. Jessie was plenty scared as she made it the rest of the way as fast as she could without a horse. The sight of gore hadn't upset her half as much as what it might mean. For people desperate enough to gun a confederate to keep him from talking would hardly stop at kidnapping, and Skane had warned her they would take it out on Ki if anything happened to him.

She entered the hotel via a side door and took the stairs two at a time, muttering, "You had to be so smart! You thought you had the drop on that poor pawn, and *now* look what you've gone and got yourself into!"

She entered the suite she had hired for the two of them and tore into Ki's room without knocking. There was nobody there, and no sign of a struggle. As she stared about she spotted the notepad on Ki's bed table and moved over to it eagerly. But the top page was blank. Or was it?

Jessie held the notepad up to the slanting rays of the sunset outside. There were indentations left by someone having written on a torn-off page. She frowned and murmured, "Get smart with *us*, will you?" as she carried the pad into her own bedroom. At home or on the range, Jessie Starbuck had no use for makeup. But dressed for the big city a lady had to look her best and even a perky suntanned nose looked shiny in a fancy dining room. So she packed a makeup kit as well as her guns in town. She sprinkled some light rouge on the apparently blank sheet they had left her to work with. With a little rubbing and a lot of squinting she could just make out what Ki had written before leaving for the consulate.

Jessie frowned, read it over again, and muttered, "What on earth could Ki be doing at the Japanese consulate, of all places? I thought he'd broken all ties with that side of his family?"

There was only one way to find out. She checked her

hair, decided it looked good enough, and went down to hail a cab to take her to the infernal place.

But as she climbed into the one-horse cab she reconsidered and told the driver she wanted to go to the nearest Texas Ranger post.

He didn't argue, and it wasn't far. By the time she got out to pay him she had composed her thoughts and knew what she was doing.

Inside, she told the crusty old desk sergeant on duty what she wanted of the Rangers. He stared up at her dubiously and said, "Let's see if I got this straight, Miss Starbuck. You suspicion the Japanese of kidnapping your segundo? Now why on earth would they want to do that?"

She said, "I'm not sure. You give me two Rangers to back my play and I mean to find out."

He shrugged. "Wouldn't take *two* Rangers. If I saw any call to send one after anybody, ma'am. But let's eat this apple a chaw at a time. How do you know your segundo is even at that consulate? Have you been there to ask?"

"Alone? Surely you jest. What chance would I have against an outfit tough and slick enough to take poor Ki? It's *me* they're after to begin with. Give me two Rangers and I'll make them work at it, though."

"I wish you wouldn't mean-mouth my boys, ma'am. One Ranger is tough as anything."

"So's my foreman. I'm not sure they took him alive. But, dead or alive, I have to find out where they're holding him."

The old Ranger took a paper-covered booklet from a desk drawer as he told her, "We'd best study on your notion, some. It do seem to me we might not have *jurisdiction* in this here dumb situation."

He found the entry he was looking for and sighed. "Yep, I was right. Them consulates has diplomatic immunity, ma'am. I couldn't arrest any of 'em for you if I knowed for *sure* they was busting Texas law and, no offense, I don't. You're asking us to invade Japan for you on no more than a guess. Ain't no lawman ready to violate diplomatic immunity without a better reason than a pretty gal's suspicions and, even if they was more sure, it'd take a writ from at least the Supreme Court."

Jessie stamped her foot and said, "Pooh, I'll just go to the Houston police if you Rangers are scared."

It didn't work. He didn't even look insulted as he told her, "The Texas Rangers ain't scared, Miss Starbuck. They're just not damn fools. We just got rid of the infernal Reconstruction. We don't want President Hayes sending more federal troops down here, telling us we ain't tame enough to do our own policing. That's what they'd surely do, with some justice, did Texas declare war on Japan on its own." He struck a match to relight a burned-out cheroot as he added, "Shucks, they won't even let us invade *Mexico* no more, to recover Texas cows, and you want us to shoot our way onto the grounds of a *friendlier* country? Go ask the local law if you've a mind to. While you're at it, tell Houston us Rangers would feel duty bound to run 'em in if the Japs called on us Rangers for help. According to these federal regulations, they can. The guest country is honor-bound to protect a furrin legation if it's own armed guards can't manage."

She started to say something nasty. Then she stared thoughtfully at the thin cheroot he held gripped in his grin. She asked where the nearest telegraph office was.

"There's a Western Union just up the street, ma'am," he said. "You figuring on wiring someone?"

She nodded grimly and said, "Yes. The one lawman I know who's not afraid to help a lady, come what may!"

Chapter 3

Longarm never got the urgent wire Lone Star sent him. She didn't know the address of the widow woman on Sherman Avenue, just as Longarm didn't have the names of some good-looking gents she was friendly with. So the wire was sent to Longarm's office in care of Marshal William Vail.

Because he hadn't spent the night with the widow woman on Sherman Avenue, Vail arrived at the office way ahead of Longarm. Vail opened all wires sent to his office, no matter to whom they were addressed, so he had plenty of time to read it and worry about it long before his wayward deputy turned up.

Bill Vail was not an evil man, despite the impression he tried to give his hired help, and he was fond of little Jessie Starbuck. But he knew federal law even better than a mere Ranger sergeant, and what Jessie was asking was impossible or worse. It was impossible to help her lawfully, and no doubt just the crazy sort of thing Longarm would try.

It was too bad that odd segundo of Jessie's had been run in by the Japanese law. But the Justice Department surely

27

needed Longarm, uncouth as he might sometimes act, more than a pretty gal needed a spooky servant who had as likely brought it all on his own fool self. So Lone Star's wire was reposing out of sight in a desk drawer as Longarm arrived, shot a guilty glance at the banjo clock on the wall, and said, "I've looked high and I've looked low, Billy. So far I haven't managed to find me an *innocent* Japanese in Denver. I've talked to all the porters at the Union Depot, and while they feel sure they'd recall even a Chinaman on his way to or getting off a train, they ain't. Most of the transient hotels in town discourage anyone who ain't lily-white from checking in. I tried some rooming houses as take in Chinese, and they ought to be ashamed of themselves for charging so much for so little. Needless to say, all the desk clerks involved speak fair Chinese, and they agree it would be hard for someone to get by 'em talking Japanese. Has it occurred to you yet that the tip we got on Nakamura being in town could have been a ruse?"

Vail nodded and said, "You ain't the only bright one working here. Like you, I was hard put to come up with any Japanese in Denver, let alone enough to wire tips in about others. But as I was gnawing on that and a chicken wing last night, it occurred to my wife that a lady she shops with knows another lady who's married up with a missionary. In his misspent youth he spent some time in the Japans, trying to convert the rascals. He didn't do so good, and that's why they got him preaching here in Denver these days. But while he was over there he had to learn the lingo. So, after supper, I run over to his manse with that fool wire none of us could read."

"Could he read it, Billy?"

"There'd be no point to this story if he hadn't been able to. I have to hand it to that old boy, too. For he not only read it for me but pointed out a serious mistake somebody made. I told him he'd make a fine lawman, did he ever get tired of saving souls, but he says he had enough to worry about."

Longarm sighed. "I sure wish you'd get to the point, Billy."

Vail lit a smoke to prolong the suspense. Then he grinned and said, "The wire was more flimflam, sent by the same rascal as tried to sucker us before, I'll vow. It said Nakamura was holed up in a Denver whorehouse, planning to rob a bank."

Longarm shook his head. "I can't see Emma Gould or even French Rose hiding out a gang of Orientals."

Vail said, "I *said* it was all bullshit, damn it. The wire was sent from Frisco, pretending to come from the consulate out there. The slick missionary said it was signed wrong, no doubt by some half-educated Japanese as doesn't know his onions. It was signed in the name of the Emperor of Japan."

Longarm looked blank.

Vail chortled. "No real high-toned Japanese would do such a thing. It's considered crude. Common folk is allowed to say they got an emperor, since that's what they have. But my minister translator tells me that a two-sword noble, whatever in thunder *that* is, never mentions working for any old emperor. He calls himself a humble servant of the Divine Chrysanthemum. Ain't that strange?"

Longarm fished out a cheroot of his own to light as he said, "I've been told they're long on fancy talk. Reckon it's all right to work for a flower if you want to. No doubt the rascal who sent us that wire was afraid we wouldn't get what he meant unless he said right out he worked for the imperial government."

"I tried her that way with the reverend. He told me it won't wash. He thinks they sent us a false lead, knowing we'd have trouble getting it translated and wanting us to feel slick when we did. He said any Japanese as wanted us to savvy the wire right off would have sent it in English if he knew anything. So he signed it wrong because he *didn't*, see?"

"Not exactly," said Longarm. "It's too complicated for

me. Why don't we get in touch with Jessie Starbuck and ask *her* to figure it out? She's good at puzzles and her sidekick, Ki, thinks even more like a Japanese. I don't, and I'm still confused as hell."

Vail said, "I ain't. I don't need outside help. That loco wire was sent from San Francisco to make us think Nakamura was somewhere else. He went over the hill in San Francisco. So what'll you bet he never left the Bay Area?"

Longarm blew a thoughtful smoke ring before he said, "Makes as much sense as him being here in Denver, where I doubt he *could* be. Folk out yonder are more used to Oriental faces. The Frisco Chinatown is bigger than Dodge and nobody talks to strangers, lest they belong to another tong. But what would a runaway samurai do in Chinatown?"

Vail said, "Got another wire on that, in sensible English, just this morning. Washington embassy says they fear the gang has been sticking up stages. Tried to pass for a Mex gang as they throwed down on Wells Fargo. But it's hard to fool a California shotgun messenger with just a big straw hat, and he allowed they looked like Chinamen in Mex duds. Your turn."

Longarm studied the tip of his cheroot as he drew a mental map in his head. "Billy, the only stages still in business out that way don't run anywhere near the Bay Area," he said at last. "You have to get over to the Sierra before you can catch a stagecoach."

"Don't teach your granny to suck eggs, old son," Vail said. "Assume they hop a train to, say, Folsum, pick up some mounts, and ride up into the hills where the stages still run. After robbing one or more they'd just have to get back aboard another train, and they'd be hiding out in Chinatown while the posse was still looking for 'em. That's how the James–Younger gang got to Northfield, remember?"

"I wasn't there. But, yeah, it works. Are you hinting I have to catch a train as well, or can we leave it to the Frisco marshal's office?"

Vail growled, "Let 'em look for their *own* owlhoots. Henry is typing your travel orders up, out front. We got dibs on the sons of bitches."

"Yeah, but, Billy, the deputies already out there have to know Frisco better than me, and they might not cotton to my horning in."

"Don't tell 'em you're in town, then. Let 'em guess. I thought you said you wanted to get out of town this weekend, anyway."

Longarm grinned sheepishly. "I'd forgotten about that infernal opera. I still think it's a long shot, but I'm on my way."

Vail waited until Longarm had gone home to pack before he strolled out front and asked, "Henry, you finished high school. If you aimed to set up Japanese consulates on the West Coast, where would you start?"

Henry looked as if he thought he was being tested and answered, "I guess Frisco would be most logical, sir."

Vail said, "No cigar. I don't want Longarm pestered in Frisco. He has enough on his plate. Try again."

Henry did. "Let's see, you'd want a deep-water port, and they don't have many out that way. How about Seattle or San Diego, sir? They're both navy towns, and you know how nosy the Japanese are."

Vail grinned and said, "Diego it shall be, then. A certain party I know is slick enough to find out Longarm headed for California even if I don't tell her. Diego is five hundred miles or more south of Frisco, so that ought to do. I got to write me a reply to a telegram, Henry. As soon as I'm done I'll want you to run her over to the Western Union for me, hear?"

Lone Star had not simply waited after sending her urgent wire to Longarm. She could have hardly run her huge Circle Star spread and far-flung Starbuck Enterprises with a couple of good men. So she had her own army of employees and business associates to call on. Though she hesitated to ask even Ki or Longarm to risk their lives for her

31

and few, in truth, would have been much use in a situation as deadly as this.

But as Longarm was gathering his possibles up in Denver, Jessie was sipping tea in Houston with an elderly Japanese jeweler who owed much of his success in Texas to the Starbuck family and, more important, remembered it and was grateful.

At the moment, they knelt across from one another in the back room of an old Spanish 'dobe he had somehow managed to turn into a fair imitation of a Shinto shrine. Having known Jessie's father before she was born, he insisted she call him Uncle Kenji. Having learned much about his culture at her late father's knee, she of course insisted on calling him Kenji-San. In the privacy of his own home, the gentle old man preferred to wear the traditional black kimono polka-dotted with his clan crest in white embroidery. Jessie had changed to a dark blouse and a split leather riding skirt that morning. Her boots and guns had come off before she'd joined her host on the immaculate white tatamis around the tea service.

The tea he served her was flavored with neither sugar nor knockout drops. Kenji-San waited until she had consumed two cups and complimented him on the crackle glazing of a brown pot holding a single spray of yellow rosebuds on a nearby shelf before he hissed and murmured, "*Arigato,* my child. As ever, you are too kind. The vase is nothing; it has only been in my family a few generations. I thought you might find the Texas roses pleasing. I cut them last night, after you first came to me with a worried mind. Would you find it desirable to hear what I have learned about the matter, honorable daughter of a revered old friend?"

Jessie nodded and said, "*Hai!* Forgive my rudeness, Kenji-San, but I am worried sick about poor Ki."

The courtly old man sighed. "I assumed as much. That is why I brought the distressing matter up so abruptly. As I told you last night, I am of course on a bowing acquaintance with more than one official of the local Japanese con-

32

sulate. Like other wives, their wives find jewelry desirable, and my people prefer to do business with their own kind. I have been assured they are holding nobody prisoner on the consulate grounds at the moment. I was told this by an official of two-sword rank."

Jessie frowned and asked, "What makes you think his word is worth warm spit, Kenji-San? Ki would never lie to me, and I showed you the note he left me."

The old man nodded. "Your use of rouge was most inventive, even though in truth the ninja they sent to tear but one leaf off that pad must have been a mere baka or in a great hurry. I am sure a person you trust would not lie to you."

She insisted, *"Someone* has to be lying. Who's left if we agree it couldn't have been Ki? What makes you so sure you can trust this friend of yours at the consulate?"

Kenji-San looked confused. "Oh, I would hardly call such a dreadful person a *friend!* He is very undesirable to do business with and on occasion he can even be *rude!"*

"Yet you take his word against Ki's?"

The old man sighed. "Forgive me, child, I mean you no disrespect, and I know you understand my language and my people amazingly well, for one of you people. But you still have much to learn about the way we think. We are a very complicated people and sometimes we confuse ourselves. As I said, the man I questioned about the matter is a dreadful person. But no Japanese of his rank would tell an outright lie. What would he do if he was found out?"

Jessie felt like Alice at the Mad Hatter's tea party. "You tell me, Kenji-San. How does one of your two-sword men handle it if he's caught in a bare-faced fib?"

Kenji-San said bleakly, "There is only one thing he could do, and ripping one's belly open can be painful even with the sharpest blade."

He saw she was still confused, so he added, "There is no way to excuse a flat lie. So when an honorable Japanese does not find it desirable to tell the truth, he or she *evades* it. A Jesuit missionary I once knew told me some of the

33

ways we have of getting around the truth are as evil as lying, but we don't see it that way. I was very careful to make sure the man I spoke with told me, simply, he knew of no prisoners or even unusual guests at the consulate. If he had not wished to say this he would have changed the subject to perhaps a jade pin for his wife. But he denied it plainly, almost rudely, so I feel sure your Ki is not being held there."

Jessie sipped more tea as she digested his logic. Then she decided, "All right. Let's say some fake consular official lured Ki somewhere else. Whoever he's with has to be holding him against his will, right?"

Kenji-San poured more tea for her before he asked gently, "Is it not true the strange young man called Ki is very large, and skilled in both the eastern and western martial arts?"

She started to ask what he meant. Then she nodded grimly and said, *"Hai,* Ki might have left with a fake diplomat, but he'd never have gone anywhere else but the consulate, at gunpoint. Yet you say he can't be there. So what's left?"

"They are holding him somewhere else, of course. The man I spoke to almost gloated as he assured me your suspicions were foolish and that he would be pleased to show my barbarian friends about the compound as long as they were willing to remove their cowboy boots. On the other hand, when I asked him if the name Ki meant anything to him, he changed the subject."

"Couldn't you have gotten him back on it, Kenji-San?"

"Dear me, how? A Japanese of the merchant class simply has no way to steer the conversation of a two-sword man. I had no need to, in any case. Had he never heard of a man called Ki, he would have simply said so."

Jessie nodded in understanding. "In other words, they lured Ki to the consulate, somehow got the drop on him, then got him *out*, pronto, lest I do just what I've a mind to do as soon as Longarm gets here. But why would the Japa-

34

nese government do such a dangerous favor for those American crooks I told you about?"

The old man shrugged and said, "I find this a great puzzlement, too, my child. Under the shogunate, powerful war lords tended to do any crazy thing they felt like. Perhaps that is why there is no shogunate these days. Despite that silly business about an all-powerful Mikado you might have heard, the present government is a constitutional monarchy, modeled on the British system. He who bears the chrysanthemum has little or nothing to do with running the government. Our present prime minister is not an evil person. Osaka is a big city. So I would have to know more of this textile mill so interested in doing business with you before I could even suggest corruption on a lower level."

"You have corruption in your new government, Kenji-San?"

"Of course. Don't you?"

Jessie smiled ruefully and said, "Touché. I have my Wall Street broker working on that angle. So far all he's discovered is that the credentials Skane offered were false. His credit would have been fine if the trading firm he said he was with had ever heard of him."

"Ah, so, and Skane-San is dead," sighed Kenji-San. "The people who murdered him to still his mouth may contact you again, of course," he went on.

Jessie nodded grimly. "Of course. They'd have no reason to hold Ki if they weren't still out to make me see things their way. But surely you can't expect me to give in to them?"

Kenji-San smiled softly and said, "You forget I knew your late father when we and the world were younger, my child. I often teased him about having Japanese blood he did not desire to talk about, since he was, in truth, a born samurai. But there are times for open defiance and there are times when the willow must consider bending. Perhaps if you were to pretend to go along with their desires long enough to obtain Ki's freedom—"

35

Jessie cut in, "The word of a Texas lady is important to her, too! I guess that makes me a two-sword gal, huh?"

Kenji-San chuckled fondly. "I would be most distressed to watch you commit hara-kiri, as you people persist in calling it. I said the Starbucks were a samurai clan. But it seems to me those wicked cotton traders have you over a washtub, no?"

"No. They have me over a barrel. My best bet would be to take a leaf from your Japanese book and say neither no nor yes until I can get a better grip on this awful mess. A white gang could be holding Ki most anywhere. Texas is a big place. It sure would have been simpler to storm that one consulate. But if they say they're open for inspection ...Oops, could that have been a ruse to get me inside those walls as well?"

Kenji-San shook his head. "Too complicated for even a corrupt Japanese official. It would have been all too easy to satisfy others, there, they had reason to detain Ki. He is, after all, part Japanese, and who knows what his family may have done to displease its government? Holding a blond white woman against her will would make even an Imperial Marine wonder, and young men away from home write letters home. Besides, you could hardly give in to their demands if they held you as well. May I humbly suggest you go back to the Circle Star and await further developments?"

Jessie shook her head and said, "I'm not leaving Houston till I find out where in town they're holding Ki!"

Kenji-San didn't argue. He never did. He only made her drink some more tea before he escorted her to the back door of his rambling business establishment.

Jessie followed that alley and several others back to her hotel. She entered via the lobby this time to see if there were any messages for her. The desk clerk gave her two. One was a plain white envelope addressed to her in Ki's handwriting. The other was a Western Union yellow. She opened Ki's message first with trembling hands. It read,

"Jessie Starbuck-San"—a little formal, considering—and went on, "My hosts have asked me to assure you I am alive and being treated well. Please tell my other friends in the army, the navy, and above all the marines. They tell me to tell you that you have one week to decide whether I live or die. They are very dramatic. I agreed to write this only on condition I be allowed to assure you I am not afraid and don't expect you to do anything against your own best interests. As for me, I never found any gold on the golden mountain, so what the hell."

She read it over again. She understood the part about telling it to the marines. That last part about a golden mountain was rather cryptic, although she sensed it was a code Ki hoped Japanese would not understand either. She tore open the telegram from Longarm's office, thinking it was from him, and read: "SORRY AS DELETED BY WESTERN UNION STOP MEAN OLD BILLY VAIL IS SENDING ME SAN DIEGO AFTER OTHER ORNERY JAPANESE STOP TRY THE RANGERS STOP CUSTIS WITH REGRETS."

Jessie blinked in surprise and murmured half aloud, "That's a hell of a way to talk to an old friend and occasional lover! Whatever could have gotten into the mean old thing?"

Then, as she headed for the stairs, she put the two messages together. Mention of San Diego had reminded her of California and of course the Chinese, not Japanese, called California the *golden mountain!* Since neither she, Ki, nor Longarm qualified as Sons of Han, that had to be what Ki had meant. And dear Custis had been careful about what *he* wired as well, knowing his wire could be intercepted. He was ever-bashful about endearments in public, since their somewhat unusual romantic feelings were private, and he would of course say he was after *other* wicked Japanese to throw the one in Houston off. But how many wicked Japanese could there be? And Ki had as much as said they were taking him to California!

37

Longarm, bless his heart, was already on his way to rescue Ki, and if she didn't get cracking it would all be over before she could get to San Diego.

She dashed upstairs and started packing.

Chapter 4

Since Denver was closer to the West Coast than Houston, Longarm had a good lead on Lone Star, but he would have been mighty surprised to learn they were having a race. Knowing nothing of her troubles, he was at the moment more interested in a petite brunette seated alone at a tiny table in the club car. It was sort of dumb of her to wear maroon satin so close to the open doorway to the observation platform of a train running on soft coal. She was either an inexperienced traveler or a lady who enjoyed being the object of considerable admiration, despite her demure ways.

As Longarm admired her from his vantage point at the bar, he tried to tell himself his hunch was silly. But there was something about the way the sunlight through the dusty glass lit her exotic complexion and the way her sloe eyes were set above her high cheekbones that made a man with wayward Orientals on his mind wonder. And she could be on her way to Frisco if she meant to change at Cheyenne.

He put down his empty beer schooner and took off his pancaked Stetson as he ambled her way. She looked up warily when he paused to look down at her and ask politely, "No offense, ma'am, but by any chance might you be at all of the Oriental persuasion?"

She gasped incredulously. "Is that any way to address a woman of good family from the Tidewater, sir? It's a good thing for you I'm a weak, helpless woman instead of a man, for if you were talking to one of my *brothers* right now you'd be in a whole lot of trouble!"

He had her pegged, now that he'd heard her speak. So he bowed humbly and told her, "I'm from West-By-God-Virginia, where some of us ain't been raised so gentle, ma'am. I'm sorry if I offended you. It's just that you reminded me of a pal of mine who's part Japanese. *Quality* Japanese, of course. I can see, now, what a fool I was to think he might have had some mighty pretty kissing cousins. It must have been a trick of the light from where I was standing. Up close, anyone can see you don't look Oriental, and if you'll forgive me, I'll just crawl out of your sight with my tail between my legs."

She dimpled up at him despite herself and he moved on out to the platform, putting his hat back on and bracing himself against the rail as he cupped his hands around a waterproof match to get a smoke going. It wasn't easy. They were going over fifty miles an hour on a straight and level grade with the Front Range watching, purple, from the western skyline. Had it been up to Longarm, they would have been going faster, for he was anxious to reach the West Coast.

He had the cheroot half smoked when the little brunette joined him back there, looking about as if she really expected to find a chair. She moved closer to inform him, "All right, I know you're the law. I took the liberty of asking the barkeep in there just now. You don't want to have me arrested when we reach Cheyenne, for I'm not that girl you people keep taking me for. My name is Melony Fairfax. I'm a famous actress, and you'll just be making a fool of yourself if you try to run me in again!"

Longarm nodded soberly and said, "I don't recall running you in the first time, Miss Melony, and please don't get upset again if I tell you I don't have anyone answering to your description on my wanted list. You say there's a gal who *looks* like you who may be wanted by the law?"

She wrinkled her pert nose and said, "Her name is Willie Bragg and they say she may be a quadroon. I ask you, do I look like a quadroon to you?"

Longarm figured octaroon would be closer, but he didn't think it would be polite to say so. "Just what has this gal been up to, aside from impersonating you, Miss Melony?" he asked.

She sniffed. "Something they call a badger game, whatever that may be. The silly woman was involved in some sort of shooting affair down in Pueblo a few days ago and the law there wants her as a witness. That's all I know. I wouldn't know *that* much if the Denver police hadn't arrested me and held me for seventy-two hours on suspicion, the mean things."

Longarm nodded. "Now that you mention it, I read about the case in the *Denver Post*. They said the luck of a notorious pair of con artists ran out when a married man they expected to be packing a bankroll produced a .44-40 Colt instead. Pueblo was a dumb place to pull the old badger game, if you ask me. Any gent with enough money to matter, down there, is likely to be a hard-rock miner or cattleman. They had to let you go after seventy-two for lack of evidence, eh?"

"They had to let me out of that awful place because I wasn't that badger gal some say I look a little like."

Longarm smiled thinly and replied, "That's what I just said. No doubt, as the matrons handed back your hatpins and other such lethal weapons, they sort of hinted it would be just as well if the sun didn't set on your pretty little head inside the Denver city limits?"

41

"I wouldn't know about that. I'm on my way to Cheyenne to see about a part in a play. Don't you believe me?"

"Anyone can see you're a born actress, Miss Melony. Would it relieve your mind if I told you I'm federal and that the shooting of a petty con man hardly ever comes under my jurisdiction?"

She shrugged. "Why should *I* care? He sounds like the sort of person I'd never want to associate with."

Longarm agreed she looked too refined and moved back inside.

She followed and, when he took a table near the bar, joined him at it, uninvited. He didn't care. He figured to be stuck in Cheyenne for a spell, and the pretty little thing had just spent three nights alone in jail. One of the waiters came over to take their orders. She said she would like gin and tonic. Longarm repressed a shudder and ordered Maryland rye and branch water.

In the awkward time between ordering and drinking she dimpled at him some more and asked, "Do you really think I look Oriental? Nobody's ever told me *that* before."

"Such things are hard to decide. This other pal of mine, a Texas rider called Ki, don't look exactly anything. He's almost as big as me. But nobody argues when he dresses oddly and says he's a Japanese fighting man in a mighty surly mood, either. It's a lot easier to tell when someone's one breed or another. Folk are a heap like horses, that way. Anyone can tell a thoroughbred from a Morgan or a Spanish barb. But mix 'em up some and you wind up with a plain old mustang. Me and that professor Darwin think the human race likely started out as sort of Indians, and—"

"Good heavens!" she cut in. "Are you saying Adam and Eve were Cherokee or Sioux?"

He chuckled and said, "Even Indians have domesticated to where you can sometimes guess their nation. But before folk bred their fool selves fancy, I suspect they all looked sort of the same."

She told him that sounded silly as the waiter placed their drinks in front of them. He clinked glasses with her before he said, "Breeds of horses, breeds of dogs, and breeds of humankind is all the products of domestication. Mix any of the three up enough and you get a critter who's got to be closer to the one and original whatever. The mongrel horse is a cowpony. The mongrel dog looks like an Indian dog or them dogs running wild in Africa. That's why it's so hard to figure out what a mongrel human might be."

She said, "Pooh, who do you think domesticated us into more than one race, if you're so smart?"

He shrugged. "Us, I reckon. Professor Darwin and me figure that as folk got separated in smaller tribes from wherever they started out as Indians, the personal tastes of each bunch encouraged boys and gals who looked like that to get together more. Lord knows why anyone would favor freckles over, say, a big nose. But some did, some didn't, and we wound up coming in all shapes and sizes."

"Don't you mean *colors?*" she asked, staring past him at the rolling foothills outside.

He shrugged. "That, too. Even amongst one family, some prefers blondes and some brunettes."

Her voice was almost a whisper as she said, "Well, I don't see why anyone would ever want to breed themselves to another race."

He noticed she had already finished her drink and he signaled for a refill. "I dunno. We're not talking about such wide leaps, remember. Breeding a white horse to black could take a spell. Starting with, say, buckskins you could wind up with black and white ponies in half the time. Now that the world's gotten smaller, with everybody bumping into one another, the process may be going the other way and we'll all end up cowponies again some day. Don't know if that'll save us a lot of dumb fights or not. As I'll not be about, by that time, I don't have to worry about it."

He was still working on his first drink. As she drained her second he said, "I don't want you to think I'm cheap,

Miss Melony, but we're a mile or more above sea level, and liquor catches up with folk quicker at high altitude than you might have noticed."

She said, "Don't worry about me. I can handle my liquor and this thin, dry air makes a girl thirsty. Do you really think I look sort of Oriental?"

He finished his first drink and signaled for two more as he said, "Let's just say exotic and get off the subject."

She waited until their drinks arrived before she shot him an arch look and confided, "We always thought one of my grandmothers looked sort of Chinese. Her father was a clipper-ship captain in the China trade, and nobody seemed to recall just who her mother might have been. Do you suppose I *could* have a dip of Oriental in me, way, way back?"

He knew she wanted him to nod. So he did, even though her new family legend wouldn't work. Knowing she might meet less polite mathematicians in the future, he said, "Your great-grandfather would have been in the China trade before the clipper ships got going, Miss Melony. He likely skippered a trading brig. You see, David McKay didn't build the first clipper ships till just before I was born, and I ain't old enough to be your great-grandfather, no offense."

She nodded soberly, considering the way she was putting that gin away, and said, "That's right. It was a brig indeed, now that it's all coming back to me. It took the poor old dear so long to get to China and back, it was only natural he took up with a high-born princess of Far Cathay."

"I'd make her a rich silk merchant's daughter," he cut in. "For even an American skipper would play hell courting a gal in that forbidden city I read about one time. As a matter of fact, I know a gent whose folk *might* have met that way. She was a proud old samurai's daughter and he was a Yankee diplomat, I think. Their son don't talk about it much, and he's a lot closer to the beginning of the tale than you'd be."

"Are you calling me a liar, you mean thing?"

Longarm made a great show of looking at his pocket-watch and said, "Lord, how time flies, talking to a pretty lady. We'll be in Cheyenne in less'n an hour and I got to gather my possibles up forward. It's sure been nice talking to you, Miss Melony."

Far to the south, Lone Star had no one to talk to in her private compartment aboard the Southern Pacific express. Starbuck Enterprises kept many a private car parked on many a railroad siding. But Jessie Starbuck was in a hurry as well as rich, and the small but luxurious first-class compartment was an improvement on many a way she'd had to get someplace in a hurry in the past.

Because it was private, and because the Texas sun was lashing the dusty plains outside to baked clay and bleached straw, Lone Star lay stripped to the buff on her lower berth, her hair down and a book in her hand, though she might as well have been reading upside down. She had too much on her mind to follow the plot about a love-starved English gal and a moody sissy no real woman would have wasted a fan flutter on. San Diego was so far, and Ki had so little time if they'd meant what they'd said about the time they'd given her to think it over. She had pulled some strings in Houston assuring her through connections all the way out to the West Coast. Even so, the telegraph poles whipping past the window to her right read no more than sixty miles an hour, and she knew they would slow down to a crawl past El Paso.

She tossed the novel aside and considered ringing for the porter, then decided not to. It would only mean slipping into her kimono in this prickly heat, and she knew Texas heat too well to think any refreshments on the safe side of chloroform would really help. Getting drunk at a time like this could be suicidal, and lemonade only helped going down.

Suddenly, the compartment door slid open. Jessie was Victorian enough to feel embarrassed when a strange man

45

entered, then shut the door behind him, grinning down at her. But she made no attempt to cover her private parts, for *he* was covering *her* with an S&W Detective Special, and there were times a girl needed all the edge she could manage. Knowing the effect her naked body might be having on the grinning brute, Jessie stared up at him impassively and asked sweetly, "Didn't anyone ever teach you to knock, sir?"

There was a long silence as they sized each other up to the serenade of the clicking wheels below. Lone Star knew what he was looking at. She was looking up at a white man of about thirty-five, dressed cow and needing a bath as well as a shave. He wore no gun rig around his hips. He had obviously boarded the train with the little sneaky gun under his grimy charro jacket. How he had picked the lock on her compartment door without her hearing him above the rumble of the train was less important than what happened next.

Lone Star moved slowly as if in fear of him, her bare back against the windowsill and her long bare legs toward him, raising her knees. He licked his lips as he stared down and marveled, "Oh, yeah, they told me you was pretty, even with your duds on."

"Surely you don't mean to take advantage of me, sir," Lone Star pleaded in as giddy-gal a tone as she could manage. He laughed and said, "I'd sure like to. I can't. My orders was to see just how we stand about that business deal, Lone Star."

She looked innocent. "What business deal did you have in mind?" she asked as she let her thighs part just enough to hurt him more.

He gulped and said, "Don't play games with me, girl. We don't know how you got poor Skane to change the way the play was to go. But since he did, and paid for it, that don't matter. I don't mean to boast, but this time you ain't dealing with a fat kid. I'm the real thing, and trying to put one over on *me* could get you hurt. So let's get down to business."

She said, "I wish we could. Would you mind handing me that kimono on the hook beside you? I feel rather awkward in this costume."

He grinned. "I like you fine the way you is. They warned me you was in the habit of throwing hot lead and cold steel at poor unsuspecting brutes when you was all dressed up for business. Just stay put where I can study on your less dangerous bare ass, whilst we get some cards on the table, hear?"

"Oh, heavens, we both know you have me completely in your power. I'll just get it myself, if you don't know how to act like a gentleman around a naked lady."

She moved as if to rise. He moved closer, warning her not to. She had hoped he might. Striking with the blurring speed of sidewinders, her one bare heel caught him just above the left knee, breaking his thigh bone, as her other foot sent the gunslick's pistol toward the ceiling, breaking his right wrist in the process. She caught the pistol, coming down, as she rose in one fluid motion to stand over him, her left instep firmly but gently braced against the fallen man's Adam's apple as she sweetly said, "I hate noise. So perhaps I'll just crush your windpipe like a beetle."

He moaned, "I sure wish you wouldn't, ma'am. For I'm already in considersome pain!"

She reached for her kimono with her free hand. "You've seen the show for today, you overconfident animal. I still haven't heard why I shouldn't kill you."

"You mean there's a chance I could talk my way back into your good graces, Miss Lone Star?"

She slipped into her kimono with her foot in place against his throat, then sat on the edge of her berth, covering him with his own weapon. "You'd better begin by telling me things I wish to hear. For openers, where's Ki?" she asked.

"The dragons got him," he said. "I don't know where. I ain't felt this bad since the time I got stampeded, and even then my pals had the kindness to set my busted bones right away. I needs a doc, bad, you cruel-kicking little thing!"

47

"Look on the bright side. You're still alive. What do you mean about dragons, for heaven's sake? Is the infernal *Klan* mixed up in this business as well?"

He propped himself up on the elbow of his otherwise useless right arm. "I just work here," he told her. "Skane was the one as said something about dragons. All I seen was some sneaky tooth-sucking Japs. I never seen that Jap of your'n at all. All the gents I've been working with is white. The boss hired him some Jap as rides with Cockroach Sam's gang to kidnap your segundo. You wouldn't have a drink around here, would you, Miss Lone Star?"

She slid sideways to where she could reach into a built-in drawer near the head of her berth and got out a silver flask. She tossed it to the rug between them and said, "Cockroach Sam sounds silly for anyone. Try Koroi Ryu-San."

He reached for the flask with his free hand. "That sounds something like it. Beats me what it might mean."

As he unscrewed the cap with his teeth she mused aloud, half to herself, "The black dragon society is a criminal organization made up of unemployed samurai and just plain crooks. What in the world could they be doing in *Texas?*"

He took a healthy swig, wheezed, and said, "That's good stuff, whatever in thunder it is. Can we talk about getting a doc for me, now? I'm really hurting."

She said, "We'll talk about that at the next stop. Unless you want to get off now, on the fly. I'd feel a lot friendlier toward you if you could manage to remember the name of the *white* polecat behind all this foolishness."

He took another swig and said, "I was hired through Skane and only met him once. We called him Boss. He called the sneaky Jap he was drinking in a back room with Cockroach Sam, like I said. Look, Miss Lone Star, I'm just a good old boy who's learned he can make more money with a gun than a throw-rope. I'm too far down on the totem pole to know much more than you do, now. The boss wanted to cut hisself into Starbuck Enterprises. He had your segundo kidnapped in order for you to see the light. Someone else entire seen you buying tickets for this here train. You wasn't supposed to do that. You was supposed to do like the boss said. I was told to follow you and see if you could be turned around and persuaded to behave yourself. I wasn't told to hurt you. They said they'd have my hide if I did. They neglected to inform me you was some kind of female mule. So here I am with my poor old bones all busted, and you know as much as I can tell you."

"You said you only met this mysterious boss once. Skane was killed before I went anywhere near the Houston depot. What was the name of the man who told you to follow me? And I swear I'll break your other leg if you say it was just a good old boy."

The injured tough gulped and said, "We call him Laredo and you ain't far off, Miss Lone Star. Us gents they hired to do the heavy work are nothing more than glorified cowhands. Laredo woke me up and said the boss wanted me to do as I just tried my best to. I mean to have some harsh words with him about it if I ever live to see him. For he might have told a pard you was dangerous as hell, even naked and unarmed!"

He noted the dangerous glint in Lone Star's eye and quickly added, "Look, I can prove my good faith. I admit I come in here to scare you. But, like I said, I was under orders to do you no real harm."

"How are you going to prove that?" she asked quietly.

He smiled boyishly. "That gun you took from me ain't loaded. You're covering me with an empty wheel. But, as you can see, I'm still acting meek as a lamb."

Lone Star didn't drop her eyes from him as she raised an eyebrow and told him, "That sounds stupid, even coming from you. I think I must have been four years old when my late father warned me never to aim my first .22 at anyone unless I was serious."

He said, "Your dad and mine would have agreed about that. But orders is orders. Hand me that pop gun and I'll break the wheel open and show you."

49

Lone Star felt there had to be a better way. So she pulled the trigger. The S&W went off and so did the top of his head. As he rolled out flat on the rug the grips of a vest pocket ace-in-the-hole were exposed. She stared soberly down at the mess at her feet for a time. Then she muttered, "Everything *else* he said was just as likely a big fib, too."

Had anyone hearing the single shot meant to do anything about it, they'd have made it to the door she was covering by now. So it was time to tidy up. She rose, stepped over the corpse in her bare feet, and made sure said door was locked. Then she put the S&W aside and cranked the one window all the way open.

A lesser woman could not have hauled that much limp and literally dead weight off the floor and across the berth. It was enough of a job for the athletic Lone Star. But she managed and, the next time the train swung gently to the left, she rolled the cadaver over the sill, secure in the knowledge the windows ahead and behind were facing away as he hit the dust outside. She tossed the top cover of her berth out after him. Explaining a missing sheet to the porter would be easier than explaining blood on the same. She moved to the built-in corner washstand and helped herself to more of the Southern Pacific's linen to clean up the rest of the mess she'd made. The hardwood paneling was easy to wipe clean with a damp cloth. The rug took more water and more work. There was no way to remove the stains completely. But what were a few more nondescript stains on an already well-traveled rug?

She got rid of the bloody rags, washed herself clean and proceeded to get dressed. She strapped her .45-framed .38 over her riding skirts and let her Stetson hang down her back on its thong as she gathered her other belongings and packed the two carpetbags she'd boarded with. Then, and only then, she consulted her watch and the railroad timetable she had demanded.

She had been aboard over four hours. The last stop had been San Antonio. It was an express, so it wouldn't stop again until Langtry, and then only to jerk water. They knew she was aboard, but they would hardly expect her to get off at such a godforsaken little border town if they knew she had a through ticket to San Diego. They could have someone waiting at El Paso to see what the gunslick they'd sent to bother her had to say. She nodded to herself and sat back down. Langtry it had to be. How on earth she was to get anywhere important from such an unimportant place was something she could worry about when she got there.

★
Chapter 5

In a hotel room near the Cheyenne depot, Miss Melony Fairfax was toying with the hair on Longarm's naked chest, a shapely naked thigh across his belly, as she crooned, "Oh, that was lovely, darling. But now that I can think straight again I wish you'd tell me how we wound up like this so sudden."

He patted her bare shoulder fondly and enjoyed a luxurious drag on the smoke they were sharing as he told her, "It's no great mystery. I told you my westbound train will be here in about an hour. There's times the froggy has the time to come a-courting and there's times to get right to it, if you mean to get to it at all."

She snuggled closer and giggled. "A poor gal just doesn't have a chance with you, once you get some gin in her, you naughty boy." She ran her hand down his belly as she asked, "How much time do we have, now, darling?"

He reached out to snuff the cheroot, saying, "Just about time enough." She gasped as he rolled her on her back and protested, "Take it easy."

At that moment the hall door opened and a portly gent in a loud checked suit and white planter's hat stepped in to stare down at them with considerable outrage as he loudly demanded, "What are you doing in bed with my wife, sir?"

Longarm had heard the pass key click. He growled, "What in the hell does it *look* like I'm doing to her, you fool? It ain't going to work this time. So why don't you be a sport and leave us alone to finish?"

The badger gaped like a carp coming up for air. "God damn it, Willie, you was supposed to *stall*, not really *screw* the mark!"

The girl with her nails dug into Longarm's bare back moaned, "Oh, Christ, will you get *out* of here, Mr. Nelson? I never gave the damned signal, and I fear I'm in love!"

Nelson, if that was his name, took a step closer. Then he went pale and froze as he found himself staring down the twin muzzles of the derringer Longarm kept handy for such occasions. Longarm said, "You heard the lady. Get out of here. Now. I mean it."

The badger quickly vacated the premises. Longarm moved to brace a bentwood chair under the doorknob before he turned back to the girl and said, "As I was saying before we were so rudely interrupted . . ."

But now she was crying, fit to bust. She went on sobbing as she asked, "Oh, whatever must you think of me now?"

"Hell, you told him you hadn't waved him in for the shakedown, and even a badger girl has a right to *enjoy* life," he soothed.

"You knew all the time?"

"Not for sure. But a gent in my line of work learns to consider every angle. I thought you said another sucker gunned your man in Pueblo, honey."

She protested, "Mr. Nelson is not my man. He's a business partner. He recruited me in Denver by paying my bail."

Longarm stared down soberly at her and muttered, "Jumping bail, interstate, is a lot more serious than being run out of town like you said. But as you may have noticed, I'm too compromised to arrest you now. So we'll say no more about it."

Melony, Willie, or whoever the hell she might be sniffed at him from the bed, "He'll surely beat me, or worse, as soon as you leave town, you know."

"He didn't look tough enough to beat *men*. If I were you I'd consider leaving town as well. I know better than to suggest you find another line of work. Few barmaids can make as much in a week as a pretty gal can shake a married man down for. On the other hand, barmaiding ain't as dangerous an occupation, as you may have noticed down Pueblo way."

She moved closer to put her arms around him again as she insisted, "I meant to reform after seeing my old pard's manly form stretched stark at my feet like that. But what was I to do when Mr. Nelson offered to get me out of that horrid old jail?"

He shrugged her off to don his hickory shirt as he replied, "You could have said no. That might have meant a few more days under lock and key. Now you're a fugitive from justice with a dumb brute free to rough you up all he wants, since you're in a poor position to call the law on him."

He saw she was about to start really bawling. So he smiled reassuringly and told her, "Look, Miss. I ain't supposed to tell you this, but we hardly ever worry about petty crooks once they've put some space between them and a lower court. You're only wanted as a witness and they won't want to delay that trial in Pueblo long. The man as gunned a badger in self-defense will get off unless he's just unpopular as hell in his own neighborhood. Just shake off that Nelson cuss, keep your nose clean for a spell, and we'll say no more about it, hear?"

She still looked undecided. Longarm rose to finish putting himself together, bent to kiss her cheek, and picked up his possibles. He had given her good advice. The rest was up to her.

He went downstairs, keeping his gun hand free, and made it to the nearby depot without meeting Nelson or any other stupid-looking gents. He noticed an Oriental in the waiting room. The stranger wasn't looking his way, and even a lawman on the trail of a wayward Japanese would look silly questioning each and every Oriental west of the Big Muddy. So he went out to the platform and, sure enough, the westbound steamed into the station shortly thereafter.

Seeing the conductor was a gent he had once saved from train robbers, Longarm said, "Howdy, Murph. I'm bound for the Golden Gate and my office expects me to sit up all the way in a damned old coach seat."

Conductor Murphy said, "You don't have to, pard. We're traveling light this trip and I see no reason why a man of your distinction must ride uncomfortable when we have three unbooked compartments forward. Take your gear up to Compartment F and tell anyone who asks about it I said it was all right."

They shook on it and Longarm moved toward the engine, feeling sorry for the coach passengers he passed. A pretty gal in an ugly hat looked like she'd already ridden farther than she'd wanted to, stuck in a dusty plush seat, sucking on an orange. Longarm moved on to his free accommodations and let himself in. He reminded himself to save that conductor's life again sometime as he opened the window and sat down on the made-up berth.

A few minutes later they were on their way. He heard a rap on the door and, thinking it was one of the train crew, rose to open it.

Melony Fairfax, or Willie Bragg, came in, her hair poorly pinned and looking as if she'd been running lately. She dropped her straw bag and hung on to him for support as she gasped, "Oh, I was so afraid I wouldn't make it, darling!"

He sat her down. There was nothing else one could do with a lady aboard a speeding train. "No offense, but I don't recall inviting you to come along, honey," he said. "I told you I'm a peace officer and you're a wanted fugitive. In a few short hours we'll be crossing yet another state line and I've already stretched federal law all out of shape for you. Where's our old playmate, Nelson, by the way?"

"Back there in Cheyenne, of course. I had to get away from him, didn't I? My face must be a mess. There was no time to bathe and dress properly after you deserted me, you mean thing."

He swore softly. "Use that sink in yon corner if you like. You no doubt told the train crew you was traveling with me?" he asked.

"I had to, dear. How else was I to find you?"

He laughed despite himself. "How else indeed? All right, the fat's in the fire, and I didn't have time to pick up anything to read aboard this train, in any case. But how far were you planning on going with me?"

He saw that she was peeling off her duds again and added, "I don't mean that way. When was you figuring on getting off this fool train?"

She shot him an arch look over her bare shoulder. "All the way, both ways. There's a lot of things we've yet to try, and I've always meant to visit San Francisco. I may have some relatives out that way, now that we've figured I could be maybe part Chinese."

He laughed again, but murmured, "Hell, that gal in the ugly hat looked like *she* might be going all the way, too."

Far to the south, aboard another train, Ki was still feeling groggy from the effects of all the drugs they'd given him. But he had now recovered enough to realize he was face down on a carpeted floor and that the vibrations he felt under him could be nothing but railroad wheels. He was chained hand and foot. The chains clanked when Ki rolled over and tried to sit up. A brutal boot kicked him flat again and a brutal voice said in Japanese, "Lie still. I do not find it desirable for you to move, Ki-San. I, too, am trained in both the armed and unarmed martial arts. But why take chances with a man with your reputation?"

Ki lay still as he murmured politely, "You have the advantage of me as to names, my honorable enemy."

The other laughed and told him, "If I desired a half-barbarian to mouth my illustrious name, I would offer it to him. All it is desirable for you to know is that you are a captive of the Black Dragon and that if you are very very well behaved your death may not be a painful one. You have heard of the Black Dragon, of course?"

Ki grimaced. "Some people are never satisfied with their government. I know of our secret society. Now I shall tell you another secret. I am going to vomit all over this rug unless you let me sit up and have some air. I am sick to my stomach from the tea an unpleasant person served me and, while I am certain it could not have been you, someone has recently pissed on this floor."

His captor laughed. "I forbid you to vomit in this hot, stuffy compartment. If I allow you to sit at the far end of this berth near the open window, you must understand you shall die if you make one false move. My orders are to deliver you to the seaport where a Japanese cruiser may pick you up without having to go all the way around Cape Horn. It is not important you arrive there alive. Your head in a jar will do as well, should you decide to be stupid."

Ki said he got the picture. The Black Dragon hauled him roughly up to the berth and shoved him to the far end with his back against the bulkhead. The sharp slap he administered as well was to be expected from one who put on samurai airs but had the accent of a peasant. Now that he could see his tormentor, Ki saw that he was much broader and only a little shorter than himself. The thug's flat moon face betrayed more peasant cunning than intelligence. Even if he hadn't been holding a .45 on Ki, the hand he held it in was that of a crude unceremonial throat-smasher. Ki inhaled a grateful gulp of hot but fresh West Texas air and his guard snapped, "Watch those feet!"

Ki smiled at him and asked, "Do I still frighten you, facing a gun, with my wrists and ankles chained?"

The Black Dragon sneered and said, "Nothing frightens me. I am trained to regard my own life as unimportant, next to our cause."

"One can see that you are a fighting machine. May I ask how my own humble existence affects your great cause? I am not a true son of Japan, let alone involved in Japanese rebellions."

The thug snapped, "Bite your tongue. We are not the rebels. The idiots who overthrew the shogunate in favor of the rightful emperor were the revolutionaries. We only mean to put things back in their proper order."

Anyone else might have found his logic bewildering. Ki was Japanese enough to understand but American enough to smile thinly and say, "Forgive me. I forgot the rightful emperor had no right to rule his empire."

The sarcasm was lost on the Black Dragon, who nodded soberly. "Just so. The royal court had no cause to interfere in the running of the country. Their task was to attend to ceremonial detail while we of the warrior caste attended to such matters. We mean no harm to the Son of Heaven. Once we take over his government again, he shall be free as ever to zuzu at the ladies of his court and ride his snow-white stallion on ceremonial occasions."

"While the great damio clans go back to the dark ages, of course?"

"What was wrong with the dark ages? That was when Japan was great. The government we have now is ridiculous. In the good old days a samurai was free to test a new blade on the first peasant he encountered. Now they can put one in prison for a thing like that. One is not even to rape peasant girls these days, even if they are very desirable!"

Ki said, "I said I understood the desires of the Black

Dragon Society. I still fail to see what these chains have to do with them."

The Black Dragon shrugged and replied, "I don't know, either. I think you are being held hostage in order that some barbarians may do the bidding of other such scum our leaders do some sort of business with. Officially, you have been arrested on some charge or other. Please don't tell me you have never committed any crimes in Japan. I know that. Sometimes it is desirable to try a man for a crime whether he committed it or not."

Ki didn't argue. He knew that even before a Japanese court with no axe to grind the accused was required to prove his or her innocence, and despite dramatic reforms in recent years, evidence obtained under torture was still admissable. "Perhaps I am being dense, but I fail to see why even the Black Dragon Society would go to so much trouble. Why take me so far if in the end all they desire is my death?" he asked.

The thug at the far end of the berth grinned wickedly and waved the gun muzzle. "I feel much the same way."

"And of course until my death I am being detained more or less *legally,* should outsiders be rude enough to ask?"

"You are asking too many questions about matters you have no control over in any case."

Ki shrugged. Then he noticed the train was slowing down and said so. The Black Dragon said, "We must be stopping for water. The barbarian who conducts this train says we must stop at a place called Langtry to take on engine water. Do not behave in a silly manner when we stop there. I can kill silently, if I must."

Ki was sure he could. There wasn't a bit of give to the chains holding his hands behind him. The bound captive stared absently out at the handful of cattle-loading ramps and the dusty little trail town beyond as the train came to a hissing stop. Without the movement of air through the open window, Texas felt even worse. Somewhere out of sight, up ahead, there came a dull clatter of metal. As he stared listlessly he saw a trim-figured woman in a riding outfit and gun rig walking away from the train with her luggage.

It couldn't be. But there was no mistaking that familiar walk and unbound hair. It was Jessie Starbuck! She'd been aboard this same train all the time, and now she was walking away from it!

But why? If she knew he was aboard, this was hardly the way to rescue him. He knew she wouldn't hesitate out of fear. Why was she passing up such a good chance? Surely she knew he'd hardly sit still if she chose to kick in that thin door and, even with one of them chained hand and foot, no one man would stand a chance against the two of them.

The armed thug across from Ki noticed Jessie's trim retreating figure about the same time and observed, "I have never had a cowgirl. That one looks like the kind I would desire to start with."

Ki didn't answer. He was finding it hard enough to breathe. The deadly bastard had the drop on Jessie from behind. It made him feel like a traitor. But to keep the other man from wondering too much he said, "She is no doubt a trail-town whore. It will soon be roundup time and she may want to set up shop before all the cowboys get to town."

The Black Dragon agreed with an evil laugh. Then the train started up with a jerk and, mercifully, they were under way again and Jessie was out of pistol range. Ki could only watch, anguished and bewildered, as her trim figure receded to a distant dot and vanished. "I sure hope you know what you're doing," he muttered in English.

The Black Dragon asked, "What did you say?"

Ki replied, "I was just making an unseemly remark about that whore back there."

Chapter 6

The only person involved who could have felt more bewildered than Ki at the moment was a thin-lipped man in Houston who dressed like an undertaker even though he told people he was an importer of Oriental goods. His name was Posner, and he would have shared his information better with the Japanese he had met in a certain back room by the ship's channel had he known what the two telegrams he had received late that afternoon really meant. He told the Black Dragon, "Jessie Starbuck was not aboard that train when it arrived at El Paso a few minutes ago. My man Slim didn't get off, either, Yanada-San."

Yanada sucked his teeth and said, "But how are we to know the results of Slim-San's interview with the Starbuck girl if he got off somewhere else?"

"Good question. He must have followed her when *she* got off somewhere else," Posner said.

"Do you think that would have been wise, Posner-San? The woman is said to be most dangerous, and why would she have gotten off unless she knew Slim-San was following her?"

"I don't know. If Slim doesn't wire in soon, we'll know it *was* a bad move."

"The captive, Ki, is still aboard, of course?"

"So my people in El Paso say. We thought at first, when she boarded the same train, she had somehow caught on to us. But in that case, why in hell did she get *off?*"

Yanada sighed. "To go somewhere else, I imagine. It was up to *you* to keep track of these crazy cowboys and cowgirls. Is that not so?"

Posner waved the other wire from Cheyenne and said, "It ain't easy. I told you we were keeping an eye on the Starbuck gal's friend and mighty dangerous lawman, Longarm, didn't I?"

"Just so. What is this Longarm up to, that we should feel at all concerned about? I told you certain confederates had arranged to send him after a red herring, to keep her from contacting him in Denver. He should be on his way to San Francisco at the moment, if our little game of Go went as planned."

Posner said, "That's where he's headed, all right. But get this. He's been joined by some gal of Oriental appearance, and mighty sneaky at that. They got on the train separately as it was leaving Cheyenne. Lucky for us, one of the boys you lent us heard her ask the way to his compartment as she was boarding. It would have been all too easy to miss."

Yanada sighed. "I feel most in a confusion. No women on *our* side could be involved."

"I wouldn't worry about her if I thought she was a plant of the Black Dragon. Do you reckon some sneak on the *other* side could be pulling something sneaky?"

Yanada thought, sucking his teeth, and finally opined, "That hardly seems possible. The ruse we used on Longarm was ever so clever. There really *is* a Japanese criminal called Nakamura, and the consulate in Washington really thinks the State Department is assisting my misguided government." He grimaced and added, "It is a fool's errand, of course. No mere barbarian could hope to track down a samurai and trained bushi. In any case, what good would it do to send a Japanese woman to join Longarm?"

"He might have asked for a translator. Longarm's smart enough to know he don't know everything. Cheyenne says she don't look pure Jap, no offense. She could be Eurasian, like old Ki. Hell, for all we know, she could be his sister or something."

Yanada shook his head. "A Go master studies his worthy opponent before beginning the game. Ki has no sister. Is not El Paso more or less south of Salt Lake City?"

"South-southeast. Why do you ask?"

"Forgiving me, you do not play games as complex as Go, I fear. You say Jessie Starbuck detrained somewhere near El Paso. Her good friend, Longarm, is heading for Salt Lake City with another woman who may speak Japanese."

Posner frowned. "Sure, but we have Longarm headed for Frisco and Ki headed for Diego, and... Oh, Jesus, what if Lone Star figured it all out and, feeling somewhat outgunned, headed north to join forces with Longarm?"

Yanada smiled coldly. "Despite all our planning, Lone Star and Longarm have been in contact all the time! She knows where we are sending Ki. We had better take even greater precautions. For if Lone Star and Longarm are working together, as secretly as it now seems, we could be in trouble!"

Posner sighed and said, "*Could* be ain't the way I'd put it. *Either* of them two spells more trouble than *I* like to get in. If they join forces, we'd best call the whole thing off, Yanada-San."

The Black Dragon's eyes went Apache-cold as he hissed and said, "Let us understand one another, Posner-San. *You* called on *us* for help and, as you people say, a deal is a dealing."

"Yeah, but with Lone Star backed by Longarm——"

"A deal is still a dealing," the Oriental cut in. In a more

reassuring tone he went on, "Our people in the field hold diplomatic immunity and, if that fails, it is only twice as hard to shoot two people as one. We still hold all the advantage. If the stubborn girl prefers a war against hopeless odds to cooperating with our trading venture, let them try, if they wish."

Posner sighed. "Oh, they'll likely wish. And when they come it'll be with hell's bells on and the devil take the hindmost! I sure hope you know just what you're doing, Yanada-San!"

"Oh, I am always knowing what I am doing. Remember that, should you choose to be backing out this late in a game I am just starting to find interesting!"

Since neither Lone Star nor Longarm knew they were supposed to be playing Go with the sinister Yanada, neither had made the moves the Black Dragon had predicted.

Jessie Starbuck's move had been elegant in its simplicity. Marching from the railroad platform to the only general store in Langtry, she had purchased a calico print mother hubbard, the sort of straw hat with artificial cherries a farm girl might have thought the latest fashion, and a pair of horn-rimmed reading glasses. The Mexican girl in charge of the store let Jessie change in the back and fed her some frijoles before the next local train arrived. Looking like a shapeless, older nester gal, Jessie had simply boarded and paid the conductor for a coach seat. Neither he nor anyone else paid much attention to the poor drab as she settled down for a slower and less comfortable westbound ride. For, while Jessie was a natural beauty, her regular features made it easy to alter her appearance with a few simple tricks and a little skillfully applied makeup. With her distinctive hair pinned severely up under her atrocious new hat, her lush lips and healthy tan covered by cheap rice powder, and the padding under her shapeless dress concealing her gun rig as well as her shapely figure, she'd have been hard to recognize even without the owlish glasses. Since nobody expected her to be on that particular train, nobody even tried.

At El Paso she purchased some oranges and a ham sandwich on rye from an Oriental candy butcher who barely noticed her.

Meanwhile, far to the north, Longarm's train hadn't stopped at Salt Lake City. It had stopped at Ogden to change engines before proceeding west across the desert. It was too dark out now to admire the most boring scenery in the West, and Longarm and Melony could barely see what they were doing to one another.

He suggested it was time to rest up and share another smoke, adding, "We got plenty of time before this train gets to Reno, old pard."

Melony rolled off to plaster her nude body to his side as he lit up. As he took the first drag she asked him, "What was that about Reno, dear?"

"That's where you'd best get off. You'll find it's only a short ride from Reno down to the silver country around Virginia City," he told her.

She protested, "I don't want to go to Virginia City! I'm on my way to Frisco with *you!*"

He patted her bare rump fondly. "No, you ain't. That could add up to trouble for both of us. City police with time on their hands watch for wanted fugitives at big-city depots. Lawmen like me have no business getting off cross-country trains in the company of wanted fugitives unless we got 'em handcuffed. Nobody with a lick of sense ever gets off at Reno, so nobody will be expecting you to. I would have made you get off back at Ogden if I wasn't such an understanding cuss. I didn't think an adventurous little thing like you would enjoy starting over in a Mormon town where you can't even order black coffee to wake up with. You'll make out a heap better in the silver country ahead."

She refused the offer of a drag on his cheroot and sniffed, "I can't believe you'd treat me so, after all the

67

wicked things I've been letting you do to me, you brute!"

"Hell, honey, slap and tickle is just natural. Being stupid is what I call wicked. As a man who packs a badge, I know all too well how much trouble screwing *seems* to cause. But it ain't exactly the screwing. It's the screwing of the wrong person at the wrong time or place that really does the damage. A smart man or woman has to control all his or her natural cravings when they get in the way of smart. Try to remember that when you get off at Reno."

"I told you I was considering going straight. What if I was to reform after we got to Frisco?"

"Anything's possible. The notion's still dumb. Even if they didn't pick you up there we'd still be parting friendly only a few hours later than Reno, honey. I told you I was on a mission, solo. I got a lot of places to be and a lot of folk to see. No offense, but even pretty moss can slow a rolling stone down, and I don't get paid to slow down."

She asked, hopefully, "If things was different, if I was an innocent gal and you was ready to settle down, would you still be as anxious to get rid of me?"

"Things *ain't* different, Melony, so why make life more wistful by pondering such pretty bubbles filled with nothing but dream-stuff? If it's any comfort to you—I know it ain't to me—I've had this same dumb conversation before and the answer has always had to be the same. A man who packs a badge and keeps the hours I have to would be a pure skunk to settle down with one poor gal, even if he was bullet-proof. I've been to enough funerals to know how few lawmen are, and it hurts to see that look in a widow's eyes, even when she ain't your own widow. Maybe someday, after I hang up my guns for keeps, I'll settle down with some poor fool gal who can manage to keep house on my pension. But that's a long ways off and, meanwhile, I ain't being cruel to you, I'm just being sensible."

She sniffed. "Haven't you ever met a girl who meant anything at all to you, Custis?"

He didn't answer for a time. Then he said, "It happens. Sometimes, yeah, it does make a man wonder if he ain't a fool to fight his feelings for the sake of his duty."

"Then you have been in love, really in love, Custis?"

"I got the same feelings most men has. I just has to control 'em better."

She said, "Tell me about love. I'd really like to know. I've often wondered what it would feel like to be really in love."

He grimaced and told her, "Awful. Wonderful and awful. Might feel different if it could work forever-after, like in fairy tales. But forever is a lie, no matter what that Prince told Snow White."

His cheroot suddenly tasted stale and he snubbed it out as he told her, or perhaps the desert stars outside, "Met a gal called Roping Sally, once. Only gal I ever met as could rope better than me, and she could cuss considerable as well. Yet at night, in bed, she was so soft and sweet and . . . Hell, in the end she was bushwhacked by a bastard who was after me, and I don't like to think about Roping Sally no more."

Melony asked, "Was she the only one, ever?"

He felt even worse, but he had to either talk to her or screw her some more. "I'm human. A widow-gal called Kim may have burned some holes in my heart. But she was smart as me and we had to agree we weren't headed the same way through life. Met up with her in Chicago, again, not long ago. We damn near ruined that hotel bed, talking about old times. But it still made no sense in the cold gray dawn, and she asked me not to look her up the next time I passed her spread up near Bitter Creek."

"I can see why she'd feel bitter. What did she look like?"

"Oh, pretty, blonde, sat a horse well, and knew more about cows than many a top hand," said Longarm. Then he frowned thoughtfully and mused aloud, half to himself, "Now that I study on it, Roping Sally was much the same, albeit tougher. I must have me a weak spot for blondes as can ride and rope. But poor Roping Sally's dead, Kim never wants to see me again, and the other one's too rich and complicated to consider settling down with for keeps. So I reckon I'm safe."

Melony pouted and sniffed, "Oh? And who might this *other* gal be?"

Longarm chuckled. "Her name don't matter to you. If ever we meet again I have no call to tell her about a pretty brunette called Melony, right?"

"I should hope so. When are you planning on meeting this cowgirl you fancy so much?"

He shrugged and answered, "Never, if I'm lucky. Like I said, sometimes it can hurt. She's just a good old gal I know down Texas way. As I'm bound for California, let's talk about something else."

Melony reached for his privates again and said, "All right, you bastard. As long as I have to get off at Reno I mean to make sure you never forget *me*, either!"

But she did get off at Reno, crying fit to bust, when the train stopped there to change engines for the climb over the Sierra Nevada, and by breakfast time he'd recovered enough to ask the pretty blond gal in the ugly hat if she'd like to share some ham and eggs with him.

She demurely allowed she would. Her name was Helen and she seemed considerably frazzled and no-doubt bored by her long coach journey, sitting up, she said, all the way from Chicago. She told him she lived on Telegraph Hill, if ever this awful train got to Oakland.

It did, by the time they'd gotten to know one another well enough to matter. They got even friendlier on the ferry from Oakland to Frisco, though she fussed at him for not calling it San Francisco. He said he was sorry and in return she allowed it would be all right for him to escort her home. So he hailed a cab in front of the ferry building, loaded all their possibles in the boot with the driver, and almost got her there.

They trotted along Columbus Avenue with no trouble and even made it partway up the slopes of Telegraph Hill. But then they came to a slope no horse born of mortal mare could have managed, and Helen said she was used to walking the rest of the way.

What she'd really meant was climbing, Longarm saw, as he followed with their luggage. Half the streets up Telegraph Hill were really stairs. Longarm had once been up the far slope after someone less pretty. Helen had to be even more used to mountain climbing home. But they were both panting for air by the time they got to her doorway. The house was a small frame structure clinging to the slope. Helen invited him in for a cup of coffee. She turned out to be a dressmaker living alone. She had told him on the ferry she was an ambitious gal who felt she could do better in the far West than in her native Chicago.

After two cups of coffee at her tiny kitchen table, Helen commenced to look as if she felt awkward. Longarm said, "Well, I have to pay a visit to the Japanese consulate across town. So I'd best be on my way, Miss Helen."

He couldn't tell whether this made her feel better or worse, so he added, "If you wouldn't mind, I sure would like to leave my possibles here, at least until I can figure where I'll be staying in town."

She dimpled knowingly and said she'd be proud to watch his gear for him. As she walked him to the door, she softly murmured, "I was wondering whether we'd be seeing one another again. It's so nice to meet a gent who isn't either shy or too pushy."

He stared down at her innocently and said, "I sure hope you don't think I asked to leave my stuff here as an excuse to come calling on you some more, Miss Helen."

She smiled knowingly and asked, "Didn't you?"

He grinned sheepishly and said, "Yeah. Ain't I the old sneak?"

She laughed. "Make sure you come after dark, then. I have nosy neighbors, and we wouldn't want them talking about me even worse than they already do."

He said that sounded fair and wondered if she expected him to kiss or shake goodbye. He decided a handshake was

71

safer as well as more seemly. He left her with the distinct impression he was a smooth gent who could bide his time.

As Longarm was working his way back down Telegraph Hill, feeling unusually innocent, a man who considered himself a Go master was scowling down at another urgent wire Posner had just received in Houston. The Black Dragon said, "I was right. If Longarm was just seen arriving in San Francisco with a most attractive blond woman, Lone Star must have joined him, as I said she meant to. Why are you telling me I am wrong?"

"Because your notion won't work," insisted the worried white man. "There just ain't no way Jessie Starbuck could have got so far so fast without wings, damn it! Besides, Longarm got on the U.P. at Cheyenne with a Jap gal, remember?"

"But he got off with a woman answering to Lone Star's description. How do you know she does *not* have wings? Your man in San Francisco says he lost them when they got out of a cab in the Italian section and maybe sprouted *more* wings. Longarm is not Italian. Lone Star is not Italian. They must have known they were being followed. Oh, the cleverness of those two! This is really getting interesting."

Posner shook his head and said, "Dumb, you mean. Look, Longarm arrived on the West Coast right on schedule. Lone Star never arrived at all."

Yanada cut in, "She got off before El Paso to join him."

Posner snapped, "I ain't finished. Anyone can see she got off. There was no way in hell she could have then run seven hundred miles within minutes to catch Longarm's train on the infernal fly! It just won't work. Even had he got off to wait for her along the U.P. line, which we know he never did, she couldn't have got there *yet*. We're talking a whole lot of high desert, cut all to hell with canyons, and the Grand Canyon's only one of 'em. You can't make that trip by rail because there ain't no rails. It's at least a two-week ride by horseflesh too fast to dream of."

The Black Dragon scanned the telegram again and said, "Nevertheless, she *did* it. Longarm arrived in San Francisco with a woman who looks like Lone Star and, more important, *acts* like Lone Star! Had she been merely some woman he was meeting on train there would have been no reason for them to throwing off your tailing ones so cleverly."

"It's still pure impossible. And what about that gal he was with afore it got so confusing?"

Yanada shrugged. "She got on with him separately. So why could she not find it desirable to get off separately? The Oriental woman working with them is surely up to some other odd business with that odd couple. I fail to see why you are sweating so, Posner-San."

"That's because you don't know this country the way I do. The Japans entire is no bigger than California alone. So you gents ain't used to considering real distances. I've heard they're trying to invent flying machines back East. If Lone Star's with Longarm right now she must have *bought* one! She's rich enough, and the two of them are crazy enough, to do anything. I want to get up from the table, Yanada-San. This game has got too rich for my blood!"

Yanada smiled thinly. "Do not make such remarks if you do not find the sight of blood desirable. We need that trading agreement for more reasons than the money you may make from it. Certain promises have been made back in my country, and I am not ready to commit my belly to the blade for shaming my cause!"

Posner tried again. "Yanada-San, them two or now more are *dangerous*, even when they ain't somehow acting *impossible!*"

Yanada said, "Hai, it is time, perhaps, to even the odds? The one called Ki is out of action. The one called Lone Star must be left alive in order that she cooperate with us after we are teaching her the error of her ways. But I see no reason why the continued existing of Longarm would be at all desirable, do you?"

"I never have liked the son of a bitch. But taking him out won't be easy. For many a man has tried and many a man has died trying!"

"Just so. But is it not true he must approach our Japanese consulate in San Francisco, sooner or later, no matter how many clever moves he may make?" Yanada insisted.

Posner still looked worried, but said, "That's the first sensible suggestion you've come up with in quite a spell. With Longarm out of the way, we'd be right back where we started with Lone Star. Who's going to lay for him? One of your boys out there?"

Yanada shook his head. "No. One of *your* men. Did you think our consulate there was in Chinatown? Orientals loitering in the surrounding streets could attract attention. A well-dressed American with his gun out of sight would not. We shall allow you the honor of assassinating Longarm. You had better see to it at once, before he can arrange a meeting there."

Posner gasped. "Look here, you're asking us to take all the risk, and it's not fair! You can always go back to the Japans if things go wrong. I can't. And I sure don't want to be stuck here to face the music if things go wrong."

"I was led to believe you were a man of courage, Posner-San," Yanada sneered.

"Courage is easier to talk than do, damn it! You Black Dragons talk like you can eat cucumbers and do wonders, but so far, all I've seen is . . . Jesus Christ!"

Yanada slipped his blade out of sight before Posner had even seen it, to leave the white man staring down at his own bare flesh through the neatly sliced X through his vest, shirt, and undershirt. Yanada hadn't drawn a drop of blood. He hadn't wanted to. He hissed politely, bowed, and said, "I shall leave you now to contemplate the manner in which you find it most desirable to arrange the demise of Longarm. I sincerely hope, when next we are meeting, you shall be able to inform me he died well?"

Posner shuddered. "Well, seeing as you put it that way. I can only do my best," he said weakly.

The Japanese left. Posner moved to a far door and rapped sharply. A now less raggedly dressed hand came in, stared soberly down at the sliced-open duds of his boss, and asked, "How'd you manage to tear your frontside open like that, boss?"

"I had help," Posner said. "Never mind about that. Who's the best hired gun we know in Frisco, Jim?"

Jim thought and answered, "Best man on our payroll would be Kellog. Best gunfighter in Frisco would be Ivory Ashcroft. He works freelance and they say he'd murder his own mother, cheap. Why do you ask, boss?"

"We need the best to go up against the best, even from the back. Let's contact Ashcroft pronto, afore my wardrobe gets ruint entire!"

★

Chapter 7

Not knowing he was supposed to be getting assassinated near the Japanese consulate, Longarm was in Chinatown. He had learned in his Indian scouting days to circle the target for sign before moving in. It could feel tedious. But on more than one occasion he had saved green troopers from the sort of situation the hasty George Armstrong Custer had gotten himself into on the Little Bighorn.

It wasn't his first trip to Frisco or even to Chinatown. But he still had to poke along Grant Avenue until he located a certain discreet doorway between a novelty shop and a Chinese restaurant. He couldn't read the Chinese lettering above the door, of course, but the lettering was in raised silver on a black background instead of the usual gold and red. He didn't try to enter by the front way. Talking to a smart Oriental playing dumb could get tedious. He retraced his steps along the avenue, counting the cracks between brick fronts, till he came to a gap and slipped into it.

The narrow alleyway was dark, even by broad daylight.

He moved up a short flight of greasy brick steps to the slightly wider service alley running in line with the storefronts facing Grant Avenue. He unbuttoned the front of his frock coat. It hardly mattered if his cross-draw rig showed in this dim light. He counted brick backs until he came to a sloping cellar door, glanced both ways, and opened it. As he moved down greasy steps into the dank darkness he heard a nightingale whistle behind him. He smiled thinly. There were no such birds in Frisco, even in broad day.

He struck a match to see where he was going now. They knew he was coming. At the end of a narrow passage stood an imposing oak door with lettering on it which no doubt said "Keep Out." He didn't try it. He knew it was a fake, set against a solid stone wall to offer outsiders a tempting target to ram. The real entrance looked more like a broom closet, and was locked, of course. So he got out his pocketknife, opened a special blade, and made short work of the bolt.

As he put his burglar tool away he got out his wallet, unpinned his federal badge, and stuck it to his left lapel. For hatchet men tended to offer money to a nosy lawman before they killed him if that didn't work.

He took a deep breath and opened the door. A short, dark passage led to a dimly lit open space. It was lined with bunk beds all around and the air was blue with smoke. Men and some women, a few of them American, reclined listlessly on the bunks, paying him no attention. But the old woman in the blue denim pajamas who came in the far side with a fresh supply of opium gaped at him as if she'd seen a ghost and spun around to run out, yelling, in sing-song Cantonese.

Longarm followed her until he came to a flight of steps going up. He slid open the panel at the top. It was only a secret panel from the front, and stepped out into a brighter room filled with Chinese of all ages and descriptions playing all sorts of games at various tables. The place grew quiet as a tomb as the tall man boldly passed by, saying,

"Don't mind me, gents. I play cards for money now and again myself."

He made it unmolested through the gambling parlor, but his luck ran out in the hallway beyond. A young but larger than usual Chinese wearing a Western-style business suit stood blocking the way as if he'd been expecting company. He smiled politely as he held the meat cleaver in his right hand and said, "Forgive me, Officer. You must have the date confused. It was yesterday we were supposed to pay off your captain and, as we did, I can't help wondering what you are doing here."

"You read this badge wrong, friend. I'm here on more serious business. I came to see Fong Lu."

"I fear you have the address wrong, then. There is no such person on these premises."

Longarm kept smiling. "I know better, and make sure your pard with the felt-soled slippers, behind me, stays right where he is. You really ought to have these floors fixed."

The hatchet man repressed a chuckle and said, "Thank you. We shall. And now, if you would allow me to lead you out by the front way, it should save you a lot of steps."

Longarm said, "I don't want to go anywhere but up to Fong Lu's office. You can go on up and tell him I'm here, first, if you've a mind to. I'm U. S. Deputy Custis Long. He may remember me best as Longarm."

The hatchet man stopped smiling. He stared soberly at the lawman for a time, then he said, "So you say. What is it you really want from us? You like dream pipe, nice girl?"

"I want Fong Lu, and I ain't got time for games."

The other man studied Longarm some more. They both knew he could be making a fatal mistake no matter what he decided.

"You wait here, right here, if you don't want us to feed the crabs in the bay your flesh, a slice at a time," he said at last.

He turned and moved silently away. His high-button shoes must have cost some, coming with soft gum heels and soles like that. Longarm reached under his coat, got out two cheroots, and turned to ask, pleasantly, "Care for a smoke?"

The husky, scar-faced Chinese standing there with a lumberman's double-bladed felling axe didn't answer. So Longarm put one smoke away and lit the other.

He had almost finished it when the other hatchet man came back alone, to say something to his pard and say, "This way, please," to Longarm.

The lawman followed the professional criminal up yet another flight of stairs. They weren't the same ones he recalled from his last visit. "You boys sure are handy with tools. I bet the Yankee architect who designed these buildings in the beginning would never recognize their innards now. Tell me, is it true there's seven stories of secret tunnels under this part of town?" he asked.

The hatchet man laughed boyishly. "Only one or two. We keep the white girls we kidnap all the time up in the attics, so we don't have to listen to them screaming about the sewer rats."

They moved along a paneled hallway toward a jade-green door. Longarm wasn't surprised when his guide slid a wall panel open instead. He had visited Fong Lu's secret digs before.

The windowless but luxurious apartment was scented with sandalwood joss sticks and papered with blue silk brocade. A gilt dragon writhing across the blue of one wall stared at him with an empty eye socket for a moment. Then its bloodshot eye popped back in place and Fong Lu popped out of yet another sliding panel. Longarm said, "Howdy, Fong Lu. I like your new dress. You sure are a cautious little thing."

The tiny Chinese woman said, "I have to be. Why on earth did you tell my men you thought I was a man, Custis?"

"You told me the last time I was here you used a man's

name because a tong leader with a gal's name might sound sissy. I figured you'd want to be called a *he,* to go with your name."

She dismissed Longarm's guide with a look and led her guest to a divan. "You confused my boys. That can be dangerous, dear," she told Longarm.

He sat down with her, noticing how one of her shapely little legs popped out the slit of her blue brocade dress and remembering she never did anything by accident. "They was trying to confuse *me,* and I'm dangerous, too," he told her. As she raised her small hands to clap them, he quickly added, "I don't want tea and a full-course meal, no offense."

She lowered her long clawed hands, leaned back invitingly, and murmured, "Oh? What *do* you want, then?"

"I'm in town on business. Not *your* business, of course. Like I told you the last time, none of the naughty things you deal in are federal offenses, though some come close."

"Aren't you uncomfortable in that stuffy coat and hat, Custis? Why don't you take them off!" she purred.

He did, wondering if he was being wise. The little tong leader was pretty. He'd about recovered from his train ride with Melony, who, now that he studied on the real thing, didn't really look Chinese at all. But the consulate had to close some time today and he'd been sent out here to catch more dangerous criminals, not to play slap and tickle.

He removed his gun rig as well, seeing as he seemed to be among friends now, and told her about the renegade samurai he was after. Fong Lu laughed incredulously. "He'd hardly be hiding out in this part of town. We don't like *honest* Japanese. We find them very hard to get along with, even harder than you people. Some of you, at least, *try* to understand our ways. Those damned Japanese think their ways are the *only* ways. They even get Lord Buddha wrong. They act as if he was a sword fighter."

"Let's not argue about religion. My point is that all Orientals tend to stand out among my people, and we often can't tell a Japanese from a Chinese, no offense. There's

81

hardly no Chinese up in the Mother Lode, where Nakamura held up that stage a few days ago. So him and his considerable gang have to be hiding out somewhere a dozen of them could sort of blend in. A railroad worker's camp don't seem likely as Chinatown."

She said, "I'd have heard about a new Oriental gang, or even thirteen honest new faces in Chinatown. I make it a point to know about such matters."

"I figured as much. That's why I come to talk to you before I asked the Japanese consulate where the rascals might be right now. Ain't it at all possible a handful of mighty quiet strangers could be holed up in an area this big, one or two at a time slipping out for food and drink now and again, late at night?"

She dimpled. "Late at night would be the wrong time indeed. My boys can't be everywhere at once. The main streets are crowded during the daylight hours. So, yes, it's barely possible some very foolish landlord may have rented quarters to strangers without reporting the matter to my hatchet men. I don't think I want to tell a lawman what will happen when and if I find out a son of Han has behaved so foolishly. Why don't you take off your vest as well, Custis?"

"It ain't that hot in here," he said.

"Do you want to bet?" she asked. "I'll spread the word among my people for you. If this Nakamura is anywhere in Chinatown or, for that matter, anywhere in the city, I'll know within twenty-four hours. How would you like him and his cutthroats delivered, dear?"

"Not with their throats cut. I'd have a time explaining that in my report. I'll be staying at the Palace. I have to. There's a Western Union nearby, and my home office likes to keep tabs on me. Do you find out anything, I'd sure be obliged if you got word to me. That's all I want your boys to do. I can do my own arresting."

She frowned and said, "One man against thirteen?"

"We got federal troops out to the Presidio if Nakamura

82

aims to make a war of it," he said. "I just want you to tell me where I might find the rascals. I mean that, Fong Lu."

She sighed. "Spoilsport. If you don't feel up to calling me something nicer, my private name is Mei-Ling. For some reason I feel more feminine when I'm around you, dear. Do you feel masculine around me?"

He didn't answer.

She looked hurt and murmured, "I know. You don't like Chinese women."

That wasn't what was stopping him. He thought they'd settled it, last time, that a lawman who made love to a professional criminal he might someday have to arrest was a fool, even when he wasn't on duty. She'd been mighty mad about it, now that he thought back, and this time he really needed her help. So he grinned and said, "Well, the Japanese consulate ought to stay open till five, at least."

He didn't have to say another word before she was out of her one-piece dress, standing before him for inspection in her felt-soled black-silk slippers. She cupped her small but well formed breasts in her hands and thrust her pelvis boldly toward him as she asked demurely, "You like?"

He laughed and said he did indeed as he proceeded to shuck his own duds. Her slender but seemingly boneless body was even nicer than he'd suspected.

He reached for her tiny waist and discovered he could almost span it with his big hands.

She moaned with desire as he bent to kiss one of her nipples. She hissed, "Why, Custis, what a nice idea."

Not even a dragon lady could last forever. So it was mid-afternoon when Longarm finally got to the Japanese consulate in the business district. The Imperial Marines posted to either side of the front entrance neither looked at him nor spoke when spoken to, so he figured they were just for show and went on in. In the marble-floored foyer he found an information desk manned by a skinny little gent. Longarm had to tell him what he wanted more than once before the Oriental wrote something on paper and hissed at him to go there.

It would have been easier had the letters looked more American, but as the numbers were the same, Longarm finally found the right door after a couple of wrong turns and a stroll through a garden with a mighty real-looking waterfall and a pond filled with some mighty queer-looking fish.

Maruyama, the military attaché, was a queer fish in his own right, but he seemed to be a friendly cuss. He never stopped grinning. He offered Longarm a seat in his American-style office and made him drink some tea before he would tell Longarm they had no idea where the Nakamura gang could be right now.

The attaché said, "Is true wicked men recently robbing staging coach on Mother Lode. But since then nobody is robbing by Nakamura. Nobody is seeing by Nakamura. My word, how shall we be carrying such a confusion?"

Longarm asked politely, "Would you say all that again?" and the young officer grinned wider, red-faced, and rang a bell on his desk. An older gent in a business suit came in. They spoke to one another a spell and the translator took over as the military man dashed out.

The older Japanese sat down in his place. "Please don't laugh at Major Maruyama. That clerk sent you to the wrong office and Maruyama-San is really very intelligent, despite his English."

Longarm nodded. "His English is better than my Japanese, and he never laughed at me for calling him Mr. San. That's sort of like 'mister' in your lingo, right?"

The older man said, "It is translated as sir, madam, or honorable. None are exactly right. You may call me Mr. Futaba, if you wish. What Major Maruyama was trying to tell you was that we have lost the tangled trail of the renegade and his band."

"You have your own agents out looking for him, sir?"

"Of course. It is most desirable that he be stopped before he can bring more disgrace to his class and his country. Whatever must you Americans think of a Japanese officer behaving so badly in a guest country!"

Longarm smiled sincerely and said, "Oh, it ain't all that bad, sir. We got lots of army and navy deserters raising hell all over. If only you'd allow us to place Nakamura and his boys on our wanted list and maybe post a modest reward on 'em, we'd no doubt have 'em rounded up for you all in no time."

Futaba blanched. "Never! That would make us look like barbarians!"

"Well, hell, they *are* barbarians, no offense. It ain't as if we mean to hang the rascals ourselves, you know. The State Department says they're to be handed over to Japanese authority for trial. We just want to *catch* the sons of bitches before they hurt too many people, and it sure would be a lot easier if we didn't have to move so delicate."

Futaba sighed. "I know. We have suggested as much to Tokyo. They insist no word of the matter appear in your American newspapers. You see, the *San Francisco Examiner* is delivered to the divine palace regularly. The Divine Chrysanthemum has a subscription."

"Somebody sends newspapers to a *flower?*" marveled Longarm.

Futaba looked around sort of sneaky and, in the tone of voice he might have used to tell a dirty joke, he murmured, "All right, to *you* we are talking about . . . the emperor!"

Longarm tried not to grin as he nodded and said, "I get it. Mum's the word. But ain't the mum supposed to know what his own diplomatic corps is up to?"

Futaba sighed some more. "If it were up to me, he'd at least be told as much as the Queen of England is told. But, like her, he is not disturbed by the petty details of the government that serves in his name. For, if he *did* learn he was losing face because of this distressing matter, he would be most distressed, and someone would have to do some-

85

thing to atone for his displeasure, at once."

Longarm whistled. "You mean members of the Japanese government might have to commit hara-kiri if the emperor read in the Frisco papers that one of his samurai was acting wild?"

Futaba shrugged and replied, "Since the Restoration such a drastic act is no longer required by law. Although some gentlemen of the old school may still feel honor-bound to do so as a last resort. The point is not that Naka-mura and his men have been acting wild, as you put it, but that the government of the Divine Son of Heaven has lost *control* of the situation. We, of course, mean to inform the palace of the whole matter after we have restored our face. Crime is not unheard-of in Japan. It is simply that one does not appear in the newspapers until justice has been done and honor has been satisfied!"

Longarm shrugged and said, "It's just as well the James–Younger gang robs trains over here, then. For, last I heard, old Jesse was still running loose, and I'd surely hate to cut my gizzard open with a bread knife because I don't know where in thunder the son of a bitch might *be* right now."

"You people simply don't understand our ways, I fear."

"I just said that. I fear we'll play pure hell catching outlaws Japanese-style in the American West, too. From the little you all are willing to tell us, Nakamura and his gang figure as trained fighting men, with more odds on their side than they deserve!"

Futaba said, "I assure you we are cooperating with you as much as we can. If we had any idea where he and his bushi were right now we would tell you. Our field agents feel certain they must have moved inland, across the Sierra Nevada, after their last robbery."

"Dressed Mex, in the Nevada desert, and none of *our* boys has spotted 'em? I doubt it. For one thing, they went to some trouble to convince us they was in or about Denver with that false tip. A man don't tip false about where he's *heading*. So they can't be heading east. I figure they're still out here on the coast, where there's more Orientals to hide among."

"You could be right. If any of them are here in the Bay Area, we have no idea where."

Longarm hesitated before he said, "Try not to take this wrong. You look like an honest gent and I know *I* ain't in league with no bandits of any kind. But have you ever heard of an inside job?"

"Of course. But surely you can't even be dreaming that the fugitives are hiding here among us?" the official asked.

Longarm shook his head. "Not out back with them funny big fish. More like in the carriage house of some diplomatic gent who lives off the post. You all do go home at night to other parts of this city, don't you?"

"Of course. I, for one, live with my family in the Mission District. But that would mean outright treason on the part of one of our own!" Futaba protested.

"Nakamura *was* one of your own, before he went over the hill, as I recall," Longarm said. "He was posted here as a security officer. The soldiers he took with him were posted here as guards. All of 'em had time to make friends before they started acting so mean. They only need *one*, with diplomatic immunity, and there you go."

Futaba gasped like one of the funny fish in the garden and said, "Your suggestion is monstrous! I would trust Major Maruyama with my life!"

"I feel sure you could, if he got Nakamura's job, after. I doubt we have to worry about higher officials, sir. A smaller frog in your puddle would do just as well, did he have separate quarters and a diplomatic pass. For he could take in all the supplies that many men would need, between jobs, and if I saw him doing it I wouldn't be able to get a damned old search warrant from any judge in Frisco."

Futaba looked grim. *"We* don't need search warrants! I thank you for the clever suggestion and I assure you we'll get right to it!" he said.

Longarm rose, saying, "I'll be at the Palace Hotel for now. I sure hope you boys will let me know if you catch 'em that way. Or at least let me know it's all right with you if I head back to Denver. I'm good at taking hints, and that's all I'd need."

Futaba thanked him for being so understanding and rose to escort him out. When the diplomat followed him through the garden as well, Longarm said he could find his own way. But Futaba insisted it wasn't done that way where he came from, and he took his guest all the way out to the front steps. They shook hands there, between the impassive Japanese Marines, and parted friendly.

Longarm headed across the avenue to hail a cab going his way to the Palace. He saw none, so he shrugged and started walking. He had only gone a few paces when he heard someone screaming in Japanese and turned around to see what was up.

What was up was a monstrous Lemat revolver in the two-handed grip of a total stranger who obviously knew him. Longarm didn't have time to swear as he crabbed sideways, slapping leather, even as he realized, sickly, that he wasn't going to make it. Then the skinny assassin with the big gun snapped sideways, too, as a military rifle squibbed from the far side of the street and put a .30-30 round through his rib cage from side to side. He bounced off a cast-iron storefront, still on his feet and still aiming at Longarm, as the latter cleared his own revolver to plant a .44-40 slug just above his heart. That did it, but the Lemat went off with a horrendous roar as he went down. As the still shaken Longarm moved gingerly closer, the young Japanese Marine who had fired ran across the street. Longarm bent to pick up the killer's big ivory-gripped weapon. The other Marine and Mister Futaba ran up just then.

By this time a Frisco beat man was rounding the far corner, his own gun out as he waved his nightstick and told everyone to stand still. Longarm called out, "It's all over. Me and this young man here are peace officers, like you. The only crook in range is that one on the walk, there."

The copper badge moved closer and looked down.

"He was trying to kill me with this," Longarm went on.

The copper badge stared soberly at the baby cannon Longarm was holding up as he put his own Colt away. Then he told Longarm, "He must have been wanting you dead indeed! That thing looks like it throws twelve-gauge!"

"It does. Lucky for me, these Japanese gents spotted him throwing down on me from behind," Longarm said.

The copper badge said, "Did they now? Well, it just goes to show there's good and bad in all of us." He turned to Futaba to ask who the dead killer might be.

The Japanese protested, "I didn't even see it. I ran out when I heard Hirata, here, shout a warning and fire. Don't ask him anything. Hirata does not speak English."

From the way both young Marines were grinning, Longarm felt sure that was true. He told his fellow American lawman, "They saved my hide. That rascal couldn't have had any connection with the consulate across the street."

"Sure, how do you know, if you don't know who he was?"

"I never said I didn't know who he was. He's on a mess of wanted fliers. In life he was known as Ivory Ashcroft. I don't know why Ashcroft went with Ivory. He was a hired gun. A former bounty hunter who took to hunting most anyone for money. I can't say whether he was hunting me for someone or just because I'm so sweet and he was so mean."

By this time a considerable crowd had gathered. When someone asked what had happened another explained, "The Japs just killed that white man, there."

Someone else had to yell, "Hot damn! Let's string 'em up!"

Nobody was about to rush two rifles, but Futaba looked scared.

Longarm told him, "You all had best get back across the street, now. Tell both your boys I know I owe 'em, and . . . How do you say thanks in your lingo, sir?"

Futaba told him, and Longarm said, *"Arigato."* They

grinned back at him like kids and replied that he was welcome, he figured. Then they left.

Longarm and the copper badge kept anyone from stealing the dead man's boots until the morgue wagon came to collect him. Longarm tried to get out of the paperwork by telling the coppers he wasn't allowed to file for rewards, even though the late Ivory Ashcroft had considerable paper posted on him. But this time it didn't work, and he had to go to the station house with them to put it all down on paper, in triplicate.

Chapter 8

Like many a flirtatious fellow traveler, Helen Rossi seemed more willing to bat her pretty lashes than to get down to cases on her sofa-couch. She was more than willing to kiss, only she said he was awfully fresh when he felt her up through her duds. And she crossed her legs firmly when he got his free hand to the soft thigh flesh above her frilly garter. "Oh, Custis, not *here!* What will the neighbors think?" she insisted.

He glanced at the heavy drapes she had drawn across her window before offering him coffee and cake. He said, "We could always go to my place. I told you I was booked into a mighty nice room at the Palace Hotel."

She gasped. "Oh, I could never go to a man's room in even a fancy hotel! What would people think?"

"Nothing. The hotel's so big a body could get lost in it and there's a lock on every door. They got them new-fangled telephones in every room, and you can send downstairs for food, drink, and even ice water. So once you're holed up above the big old lobby and fancy inside courtyard you're holed up more private than in a private home."

By this time he'd slipped his hand halfway out of her skirts, and she snuggled closer and said, "That's easy for a man of the world like you to say. I find the idea a little sordid."

He shrugged. "Sordid ain't the word for the Palace Hotel. Sordid is the *way* one enjoys life, not the enjoyments. I read that over in France some sort of underground mushroom called a truffle grows on oak roots in the woods."

"What's that got to do with the way your hand is creeping up my thigh again?" she cut in.

"I'm coming to that. I read they train old hogs to root in the dirt for the truffles and, when they find one, a dumb old peon with dirty hands digs it out, washes it off, and sends it to the big city. Then high-toned ladies and gents get to eat 'em, refined, off fancy plates in fancy places," he explained.

She grabbed his wrist in the nick of time, and asked if there was any point to his travelogue.

"Sure. I'm saying it ain't what one enjoys, discreet and refined, as much as it is the way one goes about it. Anyone can see a rooting hog is a mere pig about truffles. Yet they must taste about the same to the ladies and gents as eat 'em less disgusting. Don't it seem more refined for a couple of good pals to do things right, on clean linen far from nosy neighbors, than to wrestle on a sofa-couch and worry about getting caught?"

She said, "We wouldn't *be* wrestling, damn it, if you'd behave like a proper gentleman."

That sounded fair, so he disengaged from the tedious battle. "Well, one way or another, we both need some sleep tonight if we ever mean to get up in the cold gray dawn. So I thank you for guarding my possibles for me all this time and I thank you for the coffee and cake as well. It's getting late and I'd best be on my way."

She protested, "It's not ten yet, Custis," as he rose from her side and bent to pick up his bag from the floor at one end of the battle ground.

"That's late enough, if your neighbors are really watching your house with such interest," he said. "I'd sure hate for us to have the name without the game, and we're apt to, if I creep out your door any later."

"Let me pour you another cup of coffee, at least," she tried.

He smiled wistfully down at her. "I'm already sort of overstimulated for sleeping solo, honey. I'm sorry if I overstimulated you as well. Both men and women deserve something a mite better than one another, I fear. But that's the way life is, and I'll let my fool self out."

She rose to follow him to her door, pleading, "Wait, you have me all confused."

But he took the knob in hand and twisted as he told her gently, "There's nothing to be confused about, Helen. I'm a grown man and you ain't no kid neither, no offense. So I see no call for kid games. You don't want to draw gossip in your own neighborhood. I can't argue with a lady about that. You know my name, and do you ask for me by the same at my hotel they'll be proud to call me on the house phone and, if I'm in or out, your nosy old neighbor gals will never know about it."

He had the door open by now, so he couldn't kiss her goodbye whether she wanted him to or not. He ducked out and closed the door behind him. As he strode away in the dark, something smacked into the far side of the door and busted all to hell. It sounded like a coffee cup, from the tinkle.

Longarm chuckled and found some steps down the steep slopes of Telegraph Hill. There were no streetlamps, but there was a rail, and down had to be the right direction. So it only took him a few minutes to find his way back to Columbus Avenue. He turned left to follow it downtown to his own quarters for the night. The avenue itself could have used more gas lamps. He knew he was still in a tough part of Frisco, so he wasn't surprised to note some of the streetlamps were busted and all were widely spaced. But he only had a mile or less to go, and it figured to get more seemly once he got to a big old Catholic church he recalled from earlier visits.

Columbus Avenue didn't pass through Chinatown, but skirted it. He wasn't surprised when a couple of Chinese kids stopped him on a corner to ask if he would like to buy a ticket for the Chinese lottery. He started to say no. Then he remembered something Mei-Ling Fong Lu had suggested as they were getting dressed and said he'd take one.

It cost two bits. He put it in his pocket without trying to read any sneaky messages that might be written on it. The light was too poor to make out the printed numbers. Two blocks on he found his way blocked by a pair of bigger strangers. He let his coat swing open, thoughtfully. But one said, "Hold your fire, Longarm. We'd be working for Boss Buckley."

Longarm stopped but held on to his bag, lest he have to chase it somewhere, sudden. "I didn't suspicion any of Buckley's Lambs could be selling lottery tickets. What can I do for you boys, if it don't hurt?"

The leader of the two-man pack said, "We heard you was back in town. The boss wants to know if this is anything he ought to be after worrying about."

Longarm chuckled. "You can tell Blind Boss Buckley I may pay a call on him before I leave town, if only as a last resort. I'll be surprised as hell if the *white* twilight world can help me, this time. But I'm paid to grasp at straws. Is it safe to assume I'll be able to find him forted up in the same place as before?"

"You can start there. One of the boys will take you from there if the boss wants to see you. Sure and won't you be after giving us just a hint of what you'd be after?"

Longarm considered and said, "I'm trying to cut the trail of an Oriental gang. Ain't ready to say any names in vain in such a public place. But we're talking a dozen or so bandits, not hatchet men, disconnected from any Frisco tongs. They robbed a stage, over to the Mother Lode, a few days ago. Don't know if they've been robbing closer to the Bay. Are we getting warm?"

The tough nodded. "Sure. We heard about them crazy Japs. Boss Buckley ain't as blind as he looks. He keeps an eye on everything. That Jap gang ain't in town."

"Do we know for sure or are we guessing?" Longarm asked.

"We know for sure. The boss has contacts with the tongs as well as the courthouse gang and the copper badges. It's hard to win an election and impossible to pirate oysters without a nod from the head of Himself, as well you know."

Longarm produced cheroots for the three of them as he mused aloud, "I'd have heard by now, as well, if a cable car had been held up inside the city linits. Of course, between jobs, a big city would make a dandy hideout."

The informative tough struck a match for the three of them. "The Jap agents who were discussing the matter with us had the same grand notion. They offered money for the whereabouts of the rascals. So we've been looking high and low all over Frisco for the sons of bitches. I'm sorry indeed to have to say it, Longarm, but the Lambs can't help you this time."

Longarm gripped his cheroot with his teeth and his bag more firmly with his fist. "You already have. Your words of cheer may have saved me a trip to a mighty surly neighborhood. Would you tell Boss Buckley I can be reached at the Palace Hotel if his Lambs stumble over any sign at all?"

They said they would and drifted off in the dark to frighten other folk as Longarm continued on his weary way. He was stopped twice more by Chinese waifs selling lottery tickets. This put him out six bits. But if even one of them had a message from the tong scribbled on it, the price was cheap.

None of them did, he saw, when he got to his hotel, sat at a table in the well-lit palm court, and spread all three tickets flat to examine. He'd simply bought three damned old tickets to the Chinese lottery. He started to tear them up. Then he folded them neatly and put them away in a fob pocket he wasn't using for anything better. The Chinese lottery, while illegal, was run honestly enough.

As he rose from the table Longarm noticed a statuesque redhead peeking at him from under her boater and veil. He didn't peek back. He knew by midnight he'd be mad as hell at himself, but he'd had a rough day and he faced another that figured to be either exciting or tedious as hell. So he decided to sleep alone, unless, of course, old Helen showed up. A man had to consider his duty first, but there was no sense overdoing anything.

Helen Rossi never showed up, so Longarm awoke well rested and, worse yet, didn't see the redhead when he went down to breakfast.

Far to the south, Lone Star was alighting from her train stiff and tired. But when she checked into the General Grant the big brass bedstead didn't tempt her at all. She changed out of her farm-girl disguise to a more comfortable dark riding outfit, cut citified enough to avoid attracting much attention, and went back downstairs. She'd eaten aboard the train that morning. It had been one of the few comforts the Southern Pacific had to offer coach passengers. So she wasn't hungry as she walked to the nearest livery and hired a mount and sidesaddle.

The stable horse was a chestnut mare which had seen better days and apparently didn't want to see another outside her stall. But riding astride or sidesaddle, a Starbuck could handle anything on four legs. The next thing the stubborn mare knew, she was proceeding up the coast road at a brisk trot.

A mile outside the city limits, a narrower trail branched off the wagon trace, leading to a lonesome wind-pruned oak on a high point overlooking the Pacific. The rider waiting for her there looked Mexican till one got close enough to see the sallow face under the broad-brimmed hat. As Jessie reined in she said, "I was afraid you might not have gotten the wire I sent from Langtry, Yoko-San."

The half-Mexican, half-Japanese girl in masculine *vaquero* attire replied, "As you see, we did, Jessie. My father could not tell me why you said I was to meet you dressed as a man. Do you find it desirable for me to know?"

Lone Star explained, "Anyone passing by ought to take us for a naughty white girl meeting her Mexican beau, someplace her father or husband might not pass by often. People only snoop into those matters they can't size up as dirty, easily."

"Unless they are very interested indeed," said the pretty girl.

Lone Star shrugged. "We're both packing guns, and your father suggested this meeting place the last time we had such business, because it's guarded on three sides by sheer cliffs and we have a clear field of fire between here and the road. May I assume he looked into the matter of our mutual friend, Ki, since he got my wire?"

The pretty daughter of a Japanese silk importer and a Mexican beauty from nearby Tijuana nodded and said, "Hai. Ki may be held in the consulate here, as you suggested. We cannot be sure. As you correctly guessed, my father has some friendly contacts with members of the diplomatic corps. Alas, others are not so friendly. My father's clan, as you must know, are loyal to the Chrysanthemum. Some few but highly placed officials at the consulate, though they would never admit it, seem to be Kuroi Ruy!"

Lone Star nodded. "Tell me more about this Black Dragon Society. It sounds more Chinese than Japanese, to me."

Yoko shook her head. "Many traditions of the older Chinese civilization entered Japan to suffer a sea-change only your people seem confused about, Jessie-San. To the Chinese, the dragon is a happy beast. Japanese regard him much as your people do. So the conservatives who seek to restore the old war lords of Japan chose a ferocious black dragon as their emblem."

"I assumed as much. Could there be any connection between your black dragons and the Chinese Triad?"

Yoko grimaced. "Impossible. While both outlawed organizations finance themselves with criminal activities, they have opposite goals, Jessie-San. The Triad and the tongs seek rough justice for working-class Chinese and hope, in time, to establish a more democratic government in China. The Black Dragon seeks to take over a reasonably democratic Japanese government in order that the little people may be ground under as before. They are very dangerous as well as mad. My father fears that should the old war lords ever gain control of the Chrysanthemum throne again it could lead to war with this, his adopted country, so needless to say he stands ready to fight them with you to the death!"

Lone Star smiled a bit wryly at the thought of her late father's elderly business associate even raising his voice over the price of silk. But she said politely, "I'm not here to argue Japanese politics. Our own are enough to lose sleep over at times. I'm simply here to rescue Ki. I can't do that until I know for sure where they're holding him."

Yoko sighed. "You would not stand a chance if you *could* be sure, Jessie-San. That consulate was first built when the shogunate still held power, and even the most liberal Japanese official is most distrustful, by your standards. The walls are thick as well as high and well guarded, day and night, by trained warriors."

"By ninjas, Yoko-San?"

"Imperial Marines, led by sergeants of the ronan class. The security officer is Count Togo, of the old war lord class. We don't know whether he is Black Dragon or simply very severe. He makes his men train constantly, as if he expected to go to war with the American fleet stationed here in San Diego any minute. They are trained to fight as dirty as ninjas, as well as with their new repeating rifles, Jessie-San. They get no leave from their post. Count Togo has issued standing orders to shoot anyone atop the walls on sight. So we have no contact at all with lesser ranks who may or may not be guarding prisoners inside."

98

Lone Star's mount was fighting the bit in order to graze. So she let it, asking just how much open ground around the consulate walls they were talking about.

"There was a fisherman's shack between the rear wall and the mud flats of the harbor," Yoko told her. "Count Togo bought it, at a handsome price, and ordered it torn down. There is no way to get near the walls on three sides without crossing open ground, lit up at night by lanterns."

"What about the fourth side, then?"

"That fronts on the road out front, of course. There is one gate. The only break in the walls. The traditional monban who allows people in or out is backed up by Marines at his side and covering the street from above. As I said, they seem to be set up for a siege."

Lone Star smiled grimly. "That sounds fair. They *are* under siege, by *me*. I asked your father to try to figure out why on earth they kidnapped Ki in the first place. Did he say anything about that?"

The other girl nodded and said, "He agrees the import deal they offered you would be but a foot in the door, and that you did well to refuse them, even if it means Ki's life in the end."

Lone Star sighed. "If I thought there was no hope I'd have to give in to them before I'd let them kill Ki!"

Yoko shook her head. "One does not give into the Kuroi Ruy, Jessie-San. One avoids it, fights it, or allows it to swallow one whole. My father says they are not out for the modest profit they mentioned to you. They are out to control Starbuck Enterprises lock, stock, and barrel. Just as they now control many of the banks and businesses in Japan. Nobody *says* a bank has been devoured by a dragon, of course. One still sees the same tellers at the cages, one morning, but when one asks to see the former branch manager, nobody seems to know where he is these days."

Lone Star nodded. "A cartel tried that on Starbuck Industries before my father's body had had time to cool. I showed them a thing or two about messing with anyone who bore his name. It looks as if I'll have to straighten out these Japanese brutes as well."

"My father says, whenever you are ready, he can provide you with a dozen good men. Not trained ninjas, alas, but brave and willing to fight in a common cause."

Lone Star was touched, and said so, but added, "I can't ask a friend with no military training to go up against Marines. I *have* some backup, I hope. I expected to find him at the hotel. He tends to stay at the best, when he's using his special expense account. I guess the next thing I have to do is canvas all the other good hotels in San Diego, letting them take me for just what I'll look like, most likely. It sure is a neat way to sneak into town discreetly. But maybe if I tint my hair and wear a nice heavy veil I won't get us both killed."

Her mind made up, she smiled and said, "We can't go on meeting like this, *caballero*. My husband may be getting suspicious. So let's just kiss goodbye and I'll head back to town first."

Yoko blinked, blushed, and asked, "Are you serious? Do you really find it desirable to kiss another woman, Jessie-San?"

Lone Star laughed. "Not as a rule, and only in a sisterly way, if ever. This was supposed to look like a lovers' tryst, not a secret meeting, remember?"

Yoko gulped, reined her own mount closer, and leaned out to go through the motions. Their lips only brushed for a moment, and then only because of the way their mounts moved under them.

Yoko laughed nervously and said, "You're right. We're sure to be caught by your husband unless we come to our senses. Could I ask another favor, Jessie-San?"

"As long as I get to keep my clothes on, *caballero*."

Yoko blushed furiously. "I'm not that way, either. I was wondering if we could drop this Japanese stuff. You must have heard my mother was Mexican."

"I did indeed. But weren't you raised Japanese, after she died, Yoko-San?"

"I was, but some of my kin and a lot of my friends are just plain Mexican-American. I'm as comfortable speaking English as Japanese, and Spanish is even easier. So since *you're* not really Japanese . . ."

Lone Star nodded, switched to Spanish, and said, "Only in front of your father, then, *amiga mia?*"

"*Sí sí, amiga,*" laughed Yoko. As Lone Star left, she added, "Go with God," in Spanish as well.

Lone Star knew she and the other girl had established a trust as she rode back to town alone. Some men might not have understood. But there was nothing like sharing a harmless secret to forge a bond between two women. She understood Yoko now, better than she might have otherwise. Like Ki, Yoko was perhaps a bit confused about identity. As the product of two widely diverse worlds, she understood both while feeling not truly a part of either. As a Starbuck of pure Anglo-Saxon background, Lone Star understood the world of Ki and Yoko, but never doubted who and what she was, a Texan, ready to back Texas against all comers. She wondered what it would feel like to be, say, half Comanche, like dear old Quanna Parker. How would someone half Comanche and half Anglo-Saxon feel about the Adobe Walls fight? Which set of ancestors would a kid wind up rooting for, hearing that as a bedtime story?

On the other hand, since Japan had never fought America, perhaps Ki and poor little Yoko didn't have that much to worry about. Perhaps it was more like having a family skeleton one was forced to carry about in public. Ki had hinted more than once that no Japanese approved of his parents' marriage and of course California statute law refused to recognize interracial marriages as well. That was no doubt the reason Ki had kicked that man in Dodge through the front window of the Long Branch, just for calling him a bastard.

She rode back to the livery and parted company with the

101

mare, who didn't seem to admire her either. Back at the General Grant she checked at the desk for messages. There were none. Surely Custis would guess she had to be at *some* infernal hotel if she hadn't checked into his by now?

She went to a drug store and purchased some hair rinse meant to add life to the tresses of a light brunette or make a blonde look a lot darker. She had a veil in her luggage, upstairs, of course. As she crossed back to go up and get to work she saw that the hotel newsstand carried out-of-town papers. She stopped to look for a Houston paper when her eye was caught by the heading on the front page of the *San Francisco Examiner*.

It read, "SHOOTOUT NEAR JAPANESE CONSULATE!"

She said, "That sounds like my kind of fun," as she paid for the paper and took it with her to read privately.

She spread it on her bed as she got out her rinse. But she saw she wasn't going to be checking hotel registers in disguise, after all, as she read on. She swore and asked the silent front page, "Custis, what on earth are you doing in San Francisco when I need you here in San Diego?"

There was more on a back page. She sat down on the bed and read it through twice, searching for any possible explanation, but the *Examiner* offered none. It merely said a wanted killer had thrown down on a well-known deputy U. S. marshal by the name of Custis Long, across the street from the San Francisco consulate, with results anyone who knew Longarm at all well could have predicted. No charges had been filed, since the late Ivory Ashcroft was in no condition to be booked and the survivor of the shootout was only to be congratulated for ridding the city of a dangerous pest. There was nothing at all about what Longarm might be doing so far north or even where he was staying in town.

Lone Star started packing, muttering aloud, "You'd just better be at a hotel near the depot, Custis Long. For if you're shacked up with some Frisco frump I'll feed *both* your hearts to the hawks!"

★

Chapter 9

The long train ride up the Pacific coast would ever be distinguished more by scenery than speed. Longarm was moving about even slower, by shank's mare or cable car, in his vain attempt to cut the trail of the Nakamura gang. So, of the three friends, Ki was having the most interesting day.

It began when he was led from his basement cell to a steam-filled chamber by a brace of Marine guards who left him in the charge of two petite servant girls in short white kimonos. One of them unlocked his chains as the other seated him on a low wooden bench and proceeded to remove his rumpled clothing. Ki didn't argue. The big hot tub causing all that steam looked inviting, and while Ki was perhaps not as fanatic about the subject as most Japanese, he felt really grimy after his long, sooty trip from Texas. Ki *was* Oriental enough to feel no Victorian shame about his naked body as the two girls began to lather and sponge him before allowing him to enter the tub. He asked them if they had names. They both giggled, covering their teeth with their free hands, modestly. In the end all three of them wound up in the hot tub, laughing fit to bust.

An American might have taken less time to consider this an open invitation to an orgy. Ki knew the Japanese side of his family compartmentalized nudity and sex and, for all Ki knew, this was some kind of test. So he tried to behave, even though he was getting excited, for one girl was slender as a willow, the other was pleasantly plump, and both had breasts that bobbed pleasantly in the clear hot water.

The custom called for fellow bathers of both sexes to soak sedately side by side. So Ki assumed the plump one was trying to break the ice, if ice was the word, when she continued to rub him literally down. A few swirling moments later they were having an even better time.

Then the thinner one told her friend it was her turn, so Ki obliged her. Soon the three of them were on the wet tile floor in a writhing pile of delightful confusion. Ki was gentleman enough, in the end, to lie on his back on the tiles as the two of them took turns. It seemed unlikely they got to do anything like this often. He knew it was the custom for high-ranking Japanese to ignore their servants as fellow humans. But when he asked about that, neither girl answered. He was sure they'd been told just to give him a bath and not talk to him. Whoever had given the order, bless him, had neglected to say they should not enjoy themselves in the process.

Despite their enthusiasm, they must have been keeping track of the time. For suddenly they both got off him, slipped into their skimpy kimonos, and produced a larger white cotton kimono for him to wear.

As one dried him off the other fastened a white obi around his waist. Ki didn't comment on the subtle insult. Perhaps they didn't know the white sash was the mark of a rankless servant or student. As the thin one knelt to slip split-toed tabi socks on his bare feet, Ki glanced wistfully at his boots and business suit on another bench. It was a subtle way to search a prisoner as well, and now that he had his chains off, Ki had been looking forward to removing the lining from his jacket.

The giggling girls shoved him out into the corridor for the Marines to take charge of again. They led him to yet another basement room. It was windowless, dimly lit by paper lanterns, but fitted out in a mixture of Oriental and occidental styles no doubt intended to impress.

The severe-looking young man seated at a western desk was wearing what looked like a British navy officer's white summer kit. A regular officer's sword lay atop his blotter, lest Ki fail to see it. But a traditional Katana and Ko-Dachi were on proud display on a teakwood sword rack on a nearby shelf. There was no chair or even cushion on Ki's side of the desk. He knew he was supposed to either kneel or remain standing for the interview. Ki felt American enough to remain standing. The hard-looking officer sat down. In perfect English, he said, "I am Count Heihachiro Togo. Ki is, of course, a nickname?"

Ki said, "Hai, Togo-San!"

The officer looked pained. He said, "You shall address me in English, outcast. I need the practice, and you are not a true Japanese in any case."

Ki didn't answer. He knew the officer was trying to anger him, and there were at least two military rifles covering Ki's back.

Togo took a pleated length of rice paper from a desk drawer and held it out to Ki, saying, "I want you to sign this for us. It is a mere formality. Don't bother yourself if you can't read it."

Ki moved to take the paper, unfolded it, and proceeded to read the formal katakana script. As he had expected, it was a confession. The charge was rather misty, but then, Japanese was a rather misty language, even when it wasn't phrased in legalese.

Ki bowed slightly and placed the unsigned confession on the desk between them. "If I understood those charges, I would no doubt respectfully deny them. I have never met those people I am supposed to be connected to. I have never held secret evil thoughts about the Chrysanthemum Throne because, with all due respect, I hardly ever think of it."

Togo frowned. "I told you it was just a formality. We could hardly expect *you* to understand such matters."

Ki smiled thinly. "I do. A samurai may commit the rite of Seppuko if he has disgraced himself. He *never* signs a *confession!*"

The Japanese noble growled deep in his throat and muttered, "You evoke the code of Bushido? You dare? I have read your dossier. I know some consider you a samurai, but, man to man, we both know this is impossible. By what right could you be a samurai? Who is your Daimyo, if you are a samurai?"

"Jessica Starbuck, daughter of the late Alex Starbuck, who made me segundo of the Circle Star some time ago."

"Don't be ridiculous. That is cowboy talk. Who ever heard of a Texas Daimyo clan?"

Ki answered proudly, "Me. The Circle Star is much larger, and much richer, than the holdings of any war lord in my late mother's homeland. You said we were talking man to man. I put it to you, man to man, that Bushido, for all its flowery formality, comes down in the end to raw power. The Starbuck clan is more powerful than any Japanese clan has been since the Restoration. I rest my case."

Togo smiled despite himself. "Your argument sounds more Jesuit than Japanese. Who might have trained you in the way of a samurai, half-caste?"

Ki smiled back. "A master. Would you like to test my skills? I see we have two swords handy at the moment."

The Marines behind him sucked in their breaths and the count's eyes blazed dangerously. Then he recovered and said curtly, "I do not engage in blood sports while on duty. Otherwise it might be interesting."

He reached in the drawer again, took out one of the shuriken stars his own people had removed from Ki's coat lining, and skillfully spun it across the room to thud into a post before he asked wryly, "What was this ninja toy doing in the possession of a noble samurai, ninja?"

Ki's tone was as sardonic when he replied, "If I am a ninja, what are you? You throw a shuriken well for a noble too proud to fight with anything but proper weapons. Tell me, since you seem to be a lieutenant commander as well, does your Imperial Navy go into battle armed only with cold steel?"

Togo smiled, almost boyishly, and said, "Very well, we live in changing times. If I accept you may be some sort of samurai, will you sign this paper for me?"

Ki shook his head. "That would be a contradiction in terms. A samurai does not admit dishonor, even when he may be guilty."

"We have *ways* of making people do as they are told, you know."

"I know. You could just as easily forge my name to that document. I don't think you will. I think you, too, are a man of the Bushido code. To present a confession obtained under duress would be the same as lying, and though I don't think I like you at all, I do not think you are a liar."

The officer tried not to look pleased as he said, "Very well. A confession would only simplify your trial a bit, in any case. You shall be taken back to your holding cell for now. In a day or so a swift steamer will be arriving to take you to Tokyo, where perhaps less noble police officials will no doubt make you wish you *had* kept things simple."

He nodded to Ki's guards. "May I respectfully ask a few more questions, sir?" Ki asked.

Togo shook his head. "*I* ask the questions here."

"Damn it, I don't have any idea what this is all about! Why are you really holding me? When I do get my boots back?"

Togo smiled softly. "You are being held because men of authority above me find it desirable. You shall never see your original cowboy costume again because, you see, we *found* the saw blade hidden under that boot heel. You and I shall both be comfortable enough if you wear what you have on, for now."

As the Marines took Ki by each arm he swore and said, "The least you can do is issue me a decent obi, damn it!"

Togo thought, nodded, and said, "Very well. Would a black belt make you feel more comfortable?"

Longarm failed to spot that flirtatious redhead in the crowded hotel dining room that evening. It had been like that all day. His pals at the Japanese consulate, if they *were* his pals, had told him they'd checked out his suggestion the Nakamura gang could have pals there and, so far, come up with nothing. Futabi had been slick enough to check grocery accounts as well. He said no consular folk living off the post had suddenly taken to ordering the kind of supplies it would take to feed thirteen extra head.

Longarm had bought so many Chinese lottery tickets his home office was going to have a fit about his expense account. But if his tong pals had found any leads, Mei-Ling Fong Lu must have forgotten her own suggestion. He wasn't sure he was up to going back to ask her personally. He was sort of tired after all the legwork he'd been doing and, while a statuesque redhead seemed just the thing for dessert, he wasn't up to bedroom acrobatics this evening.

Neither Buckley's Lambs nor the police had anything to offer. This wasn't surprising. He would have been more surprised had wild-eyed owlhoots sought protection and, since they hadn't, it was safe to assume the coppers were telling the truth when they said they had nothing on their blotters about Japanese sticking up stagecoaches on Market Street. The furor about the death of Ivory Ashcroft had already drifted to the back pages of the *Examiner* with nothing new added. Billy Vail had scolded Longarm by wire about that, suggesting he pay attention to the infernal case he'd been sent out on.

After supper Longarm strolled to the Western Union to wire Vail he was trying and had nothing new to offer. As he left the telegraph office a pair of hardcased-looking gents in townee duds over riding boots and gun rigs fell in on either side of him. "Hold your fire, Denver. We're federal, too, and our boss is mad as hell at you," one of them said.

He regarded the badge one flashed at him. "I've been meaning to pay a courtesy call on the marshal's office out here, gents. But to tell the truth I've been sort of busy."

The deputy on his left growled, "So we noticed, in the damned *Examiner*. Ivory Ashcroft was *ours*, Longarm. You might have had some decency about that."

Longarm said, "I would have, had not he acted so indecent. It was a Japanese Marine as shot him, to begin with."

The one on his right said, "We can read, Denver. What's all this about, anyways? That's what our own marshal really wanted us to ask about."

Longarm said, "I'm under special orders from State. I reckon it's safe to tell you I'm after a renegade Oriental called Nakamura, seeing as he's been robbing folk on your beat."

The first one said, "You're wrong. That robbery up in the Mother Lode woods was outside our jurisdiction. Them loco Japanese ain't here in Frisco."

"How do you know? Have you looked?"

"Some. There's no call to look for gents as ain't done nothing on one's beat, you know."

Longarm knew now why the case had been shoved on Billy Vail's desk instead of the one out here. He was too polite to say so. He said, "Well, don't get your bowels in an uproar. I ain't been able to cut their trail out here, neither. So as soon as I get the word from home I'll likely be leaving your fair city to your undivided industrious attention."

"We'll be holding you to that, Longarm," said the one on his left, more grimly than polite. Longarm was tempted, but pistol-whipping a fellow peace officer on Market Street wouldn't prove anything. So he let it go and they let him go near the entrance of his hotel.

He hadn't planned on going upstairs this early, but now that he studied on it, there were worse places to be. Someone could still be laying for him in the gathering darkness, and neither the flirt on Telegraph Hill nor the flirt he'd seen earlier in the palm court seemed really to want him. Another night alone in bed wouldn't kill him and his feet were starting to hurt. So he bought some reading material and smokes at the lobby newsstand and went on up to his hired digs.

He tossed the papers and magazines aside, undressed, and took a long hot soak. Then he dried and stretched out naked on the bedstead to read himself to sleep.

It was easier than he'd hoped. He'd really been around that day, so when he found himself reading the same lines more than once he snubbed out his cheroot, trimmed the lamp, and rolled over in the dark for some shuteye.

He had no idea how long he'd been asleep, or indeed just where he was and why his alarm clock was ringing so funny when he woke up all the way and reached for the newfangled invention on the bed table next to him.

The desk clerk at the other end of the telephone line told him, "Marshal Long, there's a strawberry blonde headed your way with an uncertain gleam in her eye, and I thought you should be the first to know."

Longarm said, "You thought right. Would her name by any chance be Miss Helen Rossi?"

"She didn't say. She asked if you might be here and when I allowed you were in Room 307 she headed for the stairs before we could stop her. Knowing you were the law, I figured you could deal with the matter as well or better than our house detective, so . . ."

"I know the lady in question," Longarm assured him. "We'll try not to make too much noise."

He started to relight his lamp. Then he wondered why anyone would want to do a dumb thing like that. Wrapping a towel around his middle was polite enough, considering. So when he heard a discreet tapping on his chamber door he just opened it, hauled her in for a good old kiss, and picked her up to carry her over to the bed. As he put her down and proceeded to undress her she giggled and whispered, "You're tickling me." He wasn't in the mood for dumb conversations about truffles and such, this evening. So he kissed her some more to shut her up as he got enough of her undressed to start tickling her right.

She moaned in pleased surprise as he lowered his lips to an exposed breast to warm her a mite more before he made his first serious move. It was odd, but it felt like they were old chums who'd done this sort of thing before. She'd sure recovered nicely from her shy ways up on Telegraph Hill. Maybe she *had* been worried about her neighbors and not just teasing, after all. But as he spread her trembling thighs, she rose to meet his entering thrust in a manner too familiar, and too marvelous, to be anyone else but the one woman on earth who could do it just so.

He gulped and stammered, "Jessie?" as she wrapped her strong horsewoman's legs around his waist.

She replied, conversationally, "Who on earth were you expecting, Queen Victoria?"

He laughed, said not exactly, and then they went deliciously mad for a while. For each had gone without for a spell when they found themselves in bed with the perfect partner.

Longarm tried to hold back. He could, with many a conquest. But Lone Star was more than a conquest. She was the real thing and, even if she hadn't been, a woman to match his passion. Despite her smaller feminine body she was strong as many a man and he didn't have to worry about hurting her strong young body. As they came up for air, she said, "Wait, sweetheart. We have to talk."

He withdrew from her reluctantly and got a cheroot going for them to share as he told her to shoot.

Lone Star said, "It is Ki I came to see you about." She chuckled. "I wasn't expecting to come before we could talk about him. But, honestly, we really need your help this time, darling."

She went on, "I'd forgotten how handsome you were till you lit that match just now. I don't feel like smoking tonight. I've picked up enough bad habits from you since first we met just after Dad was murdered."

111

"We solved that case, Jessie. What sort of a mess are you and that fool Ki in this time?" he asked.

She told him, from the beginning, as they lay snuggled together in the dark. She felt comforted for the first time since Ki had vanished, by the calm strength of a true friend who was as good a fighter as a lover. When she'd finished telling him the little she really knew, Longarm sighed and said, "Jessie, you know that did you tell me you wanted the moon I'd sure throw my rope as high as it would go. You know I've risked my badge for you in the past as well. But we'd best study on this situation."

He felt her stiffen and patted her bare shoulder soothingly as he insisted, "Simmer down. I ain't saying I ain't willing. I'll just be switched with snakes if I can figure *how!*"

"I feel sure they're holding Ki in the San Diego consulate, dear, and with your help . . ."

"Feeling and knowing are two different things entire," he said. "We don't know Ki's anywhere near Diego and, even if he could be, I was sent to *Frisco,* after other Japanese entire."

"Oh, that's something I forgot to ask in all this excitement! Why on earth did you say you were on your way to San Diego if you were coming here? Were you trying to avoid me?"

He grimaced. "No. Billy Vail might have been. He gave me a direct order not to contact you or Ki about the case I'm supposed to be paying more attention to than any Texas kidnapping, no offense."

She sighed. "That sounds like Uncle Billy, bless his heart. I never would have thought to look for Ki in San Diego if he hadn't been so helpful."

Longarm said, "I ain't sure he'd like to hear that. The first thing I have to do is convince him the rascals he sent me here to get ain't here. He's under pressure from Washington, so he'd have to fire me for real if I went off on my own just now."

"We might be able to dream up an excuse, if we put both our naughty little heads together," she said.

He stubbed out the smoke and took her in both arms again. "I ain't supposed to tell you about my problem, and I already know about yours. So what say we fool around some more, you sweet loving little thing?"

She said, "Not yet. We've plenty of time for that, and I'll feel more in the mood once my mind's more at rest. Tell me about the case you're on up here. You say Japanese are involved?"

"Yeah. We seem to be having a run on the critters, between us. You'd sure make a good spy, Jessie. But it's Billy Vail's own fault for acting so sneaky." Then he added, "Look, it's a long, tedious tale." But he proceeded to bring her up to date on the Nakamura gang.

She considered, thoughtfully, "It would explain a lot if the Black Dragon Society had a hand in all this mysterious business. I was reading all the local California papers on that slowpoke train and I may have something to show you. Do you want to read the papers now, dear?"

He chuckled, kissed her, and said, "Might as well."

She sat up. He lit the lamp, glanced her way, and said, "You sure are one hell of a woman, Jessie Starbuck!"

She was if anything more lovely in the lamplight by her absence of maidenly modesty. She said, "Thanks. You're pretty, too. Where did I put those damned papers? Oh, I left them on my train seat. But never mind. One was from Pueblo de Los Angeles and it said a band of about a dozen Mexicans had held up the stage between there and San Fernando."

He leaned his bare back against the headboard, shrugged, and said, "Mexicans make more sense, that close to the border. But, come to study on it, that's a little far north for border raiders. The vigilantes down that way put the last home-grown Mexican bandit, Vasquez, out of business four or five years ago."

She moved up beside him, draping a bare leg over one

113

of his. "Anyone can buy a big sombrero, and you said Nakamura had one on when he stopped that stage up *this* way, remember?"

He put an arm around her shoulders as he told her, "We're still guessing instead of knowing, pard. Tell me some more about that dragon stuff. I know a . . . tong leader, a lot closer, who admires dragons beyond what I'd call common sense."

She snuggled closer. "The Japanese Black Dragon doesn't seem to have any Chinese connections. It's a secret society dedicated to infiltrating the modern Japanese government so as to sort of turn the clock back."

She went on to elaborate in full. When she had, Longarm told her, "I don't see how Nakamura could fit in with such odd notions, odd as his own notions seem to be."

"Didn't you say you suspected at least some consular officials could be covering up for him?" she asked.

"Yeah. For one thing, they keep calling him a samurai, when even *I* know better."

She started to ask a dumb question, then brightened and said, "That's right! There's no such thing as a renegade samurai, to their way of thinking. A samurai without any master is called a *ronin!* Our old housekeeper used to tell me bedtime stories about wandering half-bandit ronin, not samurai! My God, you have a retentive memory, Custis!"

He shrugged modestly. "I'm supposed to. It's been trained. I forget things, same as anyone else. The best thing about my memory is that it's either-or."

"Either or what, dear?"

"Either I remember or I don't. I forget names, even faces, but when I remember I remember entire. The whole scene comes back to me like I'm sort of, well, watching it happen right now. What I *don't* do is fill in the blank spaces with made-up details. A lot of folk do, you know. It sure complicates my job. For a lawman never knows for sure, when a suspect remembers wrong, whether the cuss is lying or just filling the cracks with guessing-putty. Mayhaps, to a Japanese talking fast in another lingo, renegade samurai seems easier to say than ronin. Not too many of us would know what a ronin was to begin with."

"I catch slips like that all the time," she said. "Why do you say your Nakamura can't be tied in with the Black Dragons?"

He explained, "I never said he couldn't be. I said it don't seem likely, now that I know what them dragons *want*. Nakamura *had* a government position, a key position as a security officer at an important post. How much infiltrating could he do by deserting the government them dragons is trying to take over?"

She nodded soberly. "Damn, I wish you weren't that smart. In other words, even if you thought the Nakamura gang was working its way south along the coast ranges, you'd still have no reason to crash into that consulate with me, right?"

"Justice would have my hide for even trying, if I knew for certain Nakamura was sitting in Ki's lap, inside a damned old fort with diplomatic immunity. Where in hell do you think you could be going at this hour, girl?"

Lone Star continued to rise. "For openers, I feel sure my clothes must be around here somewhere. I understand your position, Custis. I can't ask you to risk your badge and your pension along with your life, just for my sake."

He reached swiftly to haul her back down, her reddish-gold hair flying wildly, as he growled, "I sure wish women listened better than they flounced. God damn it, Jessie, I thought we was friends. Maybe more than friends."

Her voice was resigned and perhaps a little bitter as she lay unresisting in his arms. "You know how I feel about you, damn it. We wouldn't be so good in bed together if our minds didn't mesh so well. I know you'd help me if you could. I know how it makes you feel to have to refuse me, and I feel enough for you to understand and respect your reasons. But let me up, dear. For I can't rescue Ki alone and I have to look for help *somewhere*."

Longarm rolled his eyes up at the ceiling. "Ain't the critters you made from Adam's rib a pain in the ass, Lord?

115

All a poor man has to do is kiss one of 'em good, and the next thing he knows they're telling him they *understand* him."

She protested, "I *do* understand, and I said I wasn't mad. I'm just not in the mood for that sort of stuff right now!"

"Hush up and listen, damn it," he said. "I never said I wouldn't help you. I only said it was foolish as hell of me. Before we head south, I only have to wire Denver that I've reason to suspect the Nakamura gang could be headed for the border. That ought to cover my fool ass till I can think up the next move. Lord knows I don't have any right *now* as make a lick of sense!"

She laughed, pasted her nude body to his naked chest, and told him, "You're dead wrong, darling. I distinctly recall you wanted to make love to me some more and I'll be switched if I don't think that's one hell of a good idea!"

He reached out to trim the lamp again, but Lone Star stopped him. "Leave it on. I told you we were both pretty and now I would like some light on the subject. So just lie still."

★
Chapter 10

Longarm wasn't too upset by the fact that the train ride down to San Diego would take them a whole day. He still had no idea what in thunder they could do about Ki once they got there and, after the night they had had, he could sure use a whole day's rest.

The beautiful woman beside him seemed subdued for some reason, and by the time they passed Salinas she was sound asleep with her head on his shoulder. He stared out at the passing brown hills as he murmured, "That'll learn you to show off, I hope."

He knew she had other lovers. He knew he, of all men, had no right to feel jealous. But there were times, when she was surrendering to him so completely, when he had to wish she was all his and his alone. He hoped she felt the same way, although he wasn't sure why.

For Jessie Starbuck was his dream come true. Many a time he'd wished for a woman just like Jessie. For there were times a man wished for a true friend one could level with, between the good times. He liked being with her even when he didn't feel like making love to her.

He was honest enough with himself to consider they could actually be in love, but pragmatic enough to see why they were not meant by fate ever to be more than what they were to each other. They made a great team whenever they were together, but more often they were pulling different wagons. She was fixing to someday wind up a great lady. She already had wealth and social position that made him feel useless when he couldn't fight for her. He was fixing, at best, to wind up in Billy Vail's chair, or at worst in an early grave. Either way, he would never wind up with the wherewithal to hold up his end when things were calmer and she was sitting down for supper in a velvet gown, having her fancy French wine poured by a snooty rascal paid to do nothing better.

He knew, for women talk more than men, that a man in his position with her could maybe pin her down for keeps, assuming he was a shameless no-good who'd pull such a dirty trick on a pal. But he had never asked, she had never asked, and here they were, two old pals on their way to get in even bigger trouble.

The tracks curved around to avoid a smooth, grassy hill dotted with oak and blanketed with golden grass, rippled by the wind. Lone Star opened her eyes and murmured, "Oh, how lovely." Then she observed, "It must be cheat grass, standing so ungrazed this late after the rains out here."

She seemed confused when he bent to kiss her gently. "Damn it, cowgirl, I really think you're swell," he said softly.

She stretched like a kitten, snuggled down against him again, and murmured, "You're swell, too, but I feel like I've just been dragged through a keyhole backwards. Do you mind if I go back to sleep, dearest?"

He stared out the window. "You can sleep all you like, honey. For you're about my dearest, too."

He meant it. It made him feel a mite guilty about the

widow woman on Sherman Avenue and Miss Morgana Floyd of the Arvada Orphan Asylum. For they were dear to him, too, each in her own way. But he couldn't talk to them the way he could to Lone Star and, come to think of it, he doubted either would be much use to him in a gunfight. But since none of his gals ever heard of one another from him, he saw no harm in liking Lone Star best.

Meanwhile, back in Denver, old Billy Vail would have been tearing his hair out if he had any to spare. For the latest news on Nakamura was mighty upsetting.

It had come to Vail in the form of a higher-ranking federal agent, who wanted to know why on earth Vail's top deputy was wasting time in San Francisco at this late date. He said, "Damn it, Marshal, the Mex-dressed gang that just held up a post office while discussing the matter in Japanese did so south of Orange County, Southern California, and the post office wants us to do something about it, fast!"

"Consider it done," Vail snapped, "as soon as I can get a wire off to Longarm in Frisco!"

Vail yelled for his clerk, Henry, loud. As the terrified-looking Henry came in from the outer office Vail told him, "Take a message to Longarm, day rates."

Henry gulped and said, "He's not there now, sir."

Vail scowled and the other agent smirked, until Henry waved a sheet of yellow paper and continued, "I was just about to bring this wire from Longarm in to you, sir. I just signed for it out front. As per your standing instructions I read it first to see if it was important enough to bother you about."

Vail groaned. "Don't explain why you read it! Tell me what it says!"

"Longarm says he's on his way south to San Diego," Henry told him. "He says he has reason to believe the Nakamura gang might be heading that way."

Vail's chubby face went happy as he made Henry repeat

the message so the other man could get to look even more confounded. Then Vail smiled up at him sweetly and said, "There you go. Did I send a deputy or did I send a deputy?"

The bearer of less good news stammered, "I don't understand. We only got word about that post office robbery in Southern California a few minutes ago. Those crazy Japanese just left."

Henry brightened and told them, "Oh, I forgot that part. Longarm says he has reason to suspect they may be headed for the border, south of San Diego."

Vail was almost ready to leap up and hug Henry. But he just beamed and said, "You see, we call him Longarm partly because his name is Long and mostly because he's one long arm of this here law!"

"He'd have to be, to start heading for Southern California before anyone else knew the gang was there!" his erstwhile tormentor said. "I know those coast trains. If he says he just left that means he boarded over an hour ago, *before* they held up that post office!"

Vail looked superior, buffing his nails on his vest, as he answered smugly, "I told you boys I was sending the best. Don't worry about how my boys find out things. They has *orders* to find out things, and then go *git* the sons of bitches!"

Ki was not the sort of man who would have waited passively even had he known help was on the way. He had gotten himself into and out of many a scrape before going to work for Jessie's father shortly before Alex Starbuck was killed. He still had no idea how he'd wound up in this fix, but he knew he wanted out, so he was working on it.

It wasn't easy. Thanks to his otherwise enjoyable bath and change of costume he had nothing to work with but split-toed socks, kimono, sash, and his own powerful flesh. They had neglected to chain him again. No doubt they thought they didn't have to. He was confined to a tiny

120

basement cell, locked behind a door of riveted armor plate. Togo had said he was a navy man of the new school. That door figured to stand up to a navy four-pounder.

The walls, like the floor, were solid concrete. The ceiling above was wood, but over twelve feet high. The only furnishings Ki had to work with consisted of a sleeping mat and a wooden slop bucket. When they fed him he got the use of a wooden bowl and chopsticks for a few minutes. Then they took them back.

Ki had paced his cell for quite some time and thought he knew it better than he had ever wanted to before he noticed something about the wood joists above him. Unless a Japanese carpenter had been sloppy, an unlikely possibility, the walls of this cell were not quite plumb. That seemed more possible. The consulate could well have been erected over earlier foundations, and old San Diego, Ki recalled, had been built by Mission Indians who might not have enjoyed their work.

Ki moved three times around the cell, eyes closed, judging the corner angles with his bare hands until he was sure the corner to the left of the door was the one built at less than right angles. It didn't amount to much. But the rough walls, slanting just a little bit more toward one another than usual, offered him a little hope.

Ki glanced at the solid glass block offering some light from outside when the sun was up. It was too light outside to get serious yet. But since nobody could see what he might be up to, it was time to test his idea.

Knowing cloth would slip, Ki kicked off the socks and removed the cotton kimono. Stark naked, he wedged his back as far as he could get it into the corner. Then he pressed his bare arms against the rough cement to either side, palms flat, and raised a bare heel to wedge into the corner under his bare behind. He threw more weight on his cocked leg. His heel did not slip. He raised the other bare foot from the floor. It hurt like hell, but now he had both feet off the floor and jammed in the corner. Slowly, em-

121

ploying muscular control as well as strength few men could have approached, Ki found he could inch himself higher if he really put his mind to it.

He did, grunting aloud, "Next time I'll scrub my *own* back, damn it!"

The rough surfaces scrubbed Ki's back indeed as he worked his way higher, inch by inch. He was astonishingly high when he heard a key turning in the heavy steel door and dropped lightly to his bare feet.

The two Marines who'd come for him again stared impassively at the stark naked prisoner. One said, "They find it desirable to talk to you some more."

"I'd better get dressed," Ki said.

"We were not ordered to dress you. We were ordered to bring you. Now!" the Marine snapped.

Ki shrugged and stepped from his cell, naked as a babe. If they were trying to humiliate him, so be it. A real man could only be humiliated if he *felt* humiliated, and Ki was not ashamed of his body.

They took him back to Count Togo's security office. Togo showed no sign of surprise. A heavier-set individual in a black kimono and samurai topknot, seated near the officer's desk, sucked in his breath and demanded, "Is that any way to report to one's superiors, you bastard?"

Count Togo smiled thinly. "I told you he was a rather unusual young man, Fujiwara-San."

Ki said nothing. He felt neither a fool or a bastard.

Fujiwara shrugged. "Count Togo says you refused to sign the confession I prepared for you to sign. Do you think that was wise?" he asked Ki.

Ki kept a straight face as he asked politely, "Are we talking about your fanciful document or me, Fujiwara?"

The obvious aristocrat of the old school gasped and roared, "You call me by name, without adding the proper term of respect? What are you, a suicidal maniac?"

Ki smiled down at him. "What are you going to do about it, have me arrested? I am always happy to show

122

respect to those who respect me. Nobody who calls me a bastard rates a 'San' from *this* samurai!"

Fujiwara turned to Togo to complain, "By every spirit of Shinto, I do believe this fool is challenging me!"

Togo nodded pleasantly. "I do believe you may be right. I told you he was an unusual young man, Fujiwara-San."

The outraged official turned back to Ki to growl, "First you refuse to sign the paper I dictated and now you put on the airs of a man with two-sword rank? Don't you realize I could have you tortured?"

Ki nodded. "Hai, that would certainly take less courage than acting like a *man* who feels insulted. I see you wear both the katana and ko-dashi in your black belt. Tell me, do you use the long blade or the short blade on your fingernails, mighty threatener of naked prisoners?"

"He is only trying to provoke you," Togo said.

Fujiwara rose ominously from his seat, gripping his swords. "He has," he purred. "Would you be greatly offended if I taught him proper manners here and now, Togo-San?"

The younger officer sighed and said, "I do wish the two of you could have it out out in the corridor. These walls have just been painted."

Fujiwara grinned at Ki. "It's not too late to grovel, half-breed. I am not an unreasonable man. Cutting you in two would neither please me nor displease me."

Ki suppressed a laugh. "It certainly would displease me to be cut in half. But I'll die before I'll grovel," he replied.

Fujiwara marched toward the door. "Very well," he snapped. "Let us get it over with. Would someone give this idiot something to defend himself with? I prefer to do these things properly."

Togo rose behind his desk. "I wish you wouldn't do this, Fujiwara-San. The man has yet to stand trial," he warned.

"How can he stand trial if he refuses to admit he is guilty? Besides, he won't *have* to stand trial if we settle things the old-fashioned way. Come on, all of you, this shouldn't take long, but you may enjoy my swordplay. I do not mean to boast, but I am brilliant with the katana."

They all followed him out to the corridor. Ki had no choice. Ki and no doubt Fujiwara expected one of the Marines to offer him at least a bayonet to defend himself with. Ki and no doubt Fujiwara were surprised as hell when Count Togo, last to leave the office, presented Ki with the traditional katana that had been on display inside. As their eyes met, Ki politely said, "You do me great honor, Togo-San."

The tough young officer replied, "I know. It's the least I can do if you are really a samurai. It won't do you any good if you are not."

Ki hissed, drew the long curved blade, and returned the scabbard to its owner. He was about to turn, facing what he knew would be a long, tedious series of feints until one of the other of them made that one slash that counted in a katana duel. But his back was still to Fujiwara when the nearest Marine flinched. Ki heard someone screaming, "Kiaiiii!" and dropped to the cement as naked steel sang through the space where his naked back had just been.

Someone was shouting, "No! That's not the way!" Ki rolled on his back, blade raised defensively, to see his opponent right above him, sword raised to chop straight down. The katana was designed for slashing, not stabbing. But it had a point, the shortest distance between two points was still a straight line. So Ki thrust straight, driving the curved blade up into treacherous guts.

Fujiwara let go of his own blade and tried to leap off Ki's without much luck. Ki withdrew it from his writhing flesh as he rose to his own feet. Fujiwara sobbed, "Don't just stand there! Get this over with! I'm in agony!"

As Ki stood bemused Togo held out a hand and demanded, "Allow me. He was my superior official here."

Ki handed Togo the blood-slicked blade. Togo raised it in two hands, slashed down, and decapitated Fujiwara to put him out of his misery. Somehow, Ki felt this would be the wrong time to ask if he could have that sword back.

Togo stared thoughtfully at him, blade in hand, for the long silence that followed. Then the count nodded curtly and told Ki, "You had better return to your cell now. A tea clipper just entered the harbor with reports of a typhoon well out in the Pacific. The steamer coming for you does not take green water over her bows well, so it may be delayed. In the meantime, we shall try to make you as comfortable as possible."

Ki stared soberly past him at the mess on the floor. "You could have stopped that, you know," he said.

Togo smiled thinly. "Of course. But it would have been difficult. He wanted to fight you. He was my superior. So what was I to do?"

Ki raised an eyebrow. "I assumed that was how you were going to word it in your report. I suppose it pains you a lot now that you'll be moving up one notch here, right?"

Togo smiled, almost sincerely, and said, "One does what one can to get ahead in this hard world. Try to keep that in mind. As we just saw, my late superior was a fool as well as a braggart, and in the end he was a coward. I assure you I am none of those things."

"That's fair," Ki said, "neither am I."

Jessie had first checked into the General Grant looking a lot different and signing a false name, so nobody found it too strange when she and Longarm checked in that evening as Mr. and Mrs. Crawford from Tucson.

She stepped into the bath adjacent to their room as Longarm got their luggage out of the way and stepped out onto a balcony that came with the small but fancy corner suite. There wasn't much out there to look at. The sun was down and a mist was blowing in off the sea.

He ducked back in, shucking his hat, coat, and gun rig, which he hung, of course, from a bedpost on his side. Traveling with an old pal, a man didn't have to ask which side of the bed was his. It was a nice big old bed and, when he tested it with his rump, it didn't inform the whole world with its bedsprings that someone might be moving about on it.

Jessie came out of the bath, naked as a jay, running a comb through her golden hair. Longarm said, "That was sure fast," and she said, "I didn't take time to tub. I just sponged that train trip off a mite. It's dark out now, so what are we waiting for?"

Longarm started to unbutton his clothing. Jessie laughed and said, "Not that, you sweet fool. We have to go save Ki. Let me get dressed."

Longarm pulled her down on the bed beside him and as she began to struggle he said, "Hold it! We can't go running off into the night like headless chickens, honey. We have to *study* on the infernal matter first."

She relaxed in his arms, but insisted, "I've *been* studying on it for a good twelve hours on that creeping old train. The only thing I can come up with is the rear wall facing the water. It may not be as well guarded. We'll need some way to approach from the harbor side, of course. Those mud flats should be covered by enough water to float a skiff, at least, at high tide."

He kissed her. "You slept more than me aboard that train," he reminded her. "Getting in ain't the main worry. I've stood guard, myself, as a young recruit. I don't doubt, now, any halfway smart Indian could have slipped in past me late at night when I was half asleep and wondering where in hell that corporal was with my relief. But, dumb as I was, getting past me on the way *out* would have been a horse of a different color. For I'm sure I'd have woke up entire once I heard bugles, guns, and officers sounding off."

His free hand had wandered on its own to a firm breast and Lone Star as absently placed her hand on his wrist to encourage his devotion. "Pooh, if we take the wall sentries out and move on from there sort of Apache—"

"To *where?*" he cut in. "That compound takes up a

126

whole city block and they could have Ki locked up anywhere, if he's there at all, which we don't know for certain. Can't you just see me going from door to door in the dark calling out, 'Hey, Ki, are you *in* there?'"

She laughed at the picture, but said, "I don't think you're scared. I think you just want to lay me again."

He laughed. "Wrong, both ways, no offense. I ain't scared and I may need my strength for wall climbing. But let's take this apple a bite at a time, Jessie. First off, tell me some more about them Orientals here in Diego who might be able to help us."

"I did. Little Yoko's just a girl and her old father couldn't fight his way out of a paper bag," she replied.

He said, "The first time I said *you* were just a girl you damn near punched my head off. But let's not worry about how tough this other gal and her dad might be. You were right to turn down their offer of a brave but untrained crew. I'm not sure we've got all the juice out of that bunch, though. What are the odds on a silk merchant or two doing a little advance scout work for us?"

She shook her head. "I told you on the train. Tradesfolk from outside, even Orientals, are only allowed as far into the compound as the offices and maybe the living quarters. Our old friends here know nothing more than we do about the sneaky parts of the layout. They couldn't even tell me where the guard room or the armory was."

Longarm grimaced. "I wish you wouldn't talk about arms and Japanese at the same time. Said armory would no doubt be filled with all sorts of cruel toys like throwing stars and such, right?"

"Wrong. Japanese aristocrats and military men use swords and guns like everyone else. It's the less aristocratic folk, forbidden by law to own proper weapons, who invented all those ninja gadgets."

He shrugged and said, "Whatever. Having watched Ki take gents out with them mighty quiet weapons, I've come to admire 'em for quiet killing. Do you reckon that Yoko gal could get some for us, honey?"

"Perhaps. Her father left Japan before the full Restoration, when a man forbidden to carry regular weapons had to know how to protect himself. But it takes training to handle ninja weapons, and . . . Custis, where do you think you're going with that hand?"

"Nowhere it ain't been before. But you're right. I said we had to save our strength. Does Ki know them silk merchants here in San Diego?"

"Of course. I told you we do business with them. But why do you ask?"

"If Ki knows friendlier Japanese here, he'd be smart enough to beeline for 'em if he got the chance."

"Of course Ki would seek shelter with our friends here, if he could get out. But he hasn't. So they must have him locked up tight."

"If he ain't in Seattle," Longarm grunted. "My point is that we don't have to pick Ki up and carry him out like he was a maiden in distress. All we have to do is get him *loose*. Together in a bunch, or separated, the three of us just have to wind up at the same address, sooner or later. What's the name of that silk warehouse again, Jessie?"

"Yamaha Imports Incorporated. Yamaha's really a suburb of Tokyo, but—"

"Never mind why. Just so none of us don't go somewhere *else*," he cut in. "All right. I can't come up with a better escape route and breathing-space hidey-hole. I got a throw rope among the possibles I brought along, and you're right about me being a mite old to take up star throwing. Ropes are better for getting over walls, anyway. I know you talk some Japanese, for I've heard you doing it. I can talk some Cheyenne, but not well enough to pass for a dog soldier in the dark. So 'fess up. Can you sound good enough to fool a real one?"

"I think so. I told you the old housekeeper who raised me had me speaking more Japanese than English before my father warned her that was no way to raise a Texas kid. I might have a slight accent. My Japanese friends would be too polite to mention a thing like that, of course."

128

"Oh, swell," he said. "The only way to know is to find out. The boat we'll need don't worry me as much."

She said, "I'm sure our friends here can get us a skiff, and— Damn it, there goes that hand again!"

He slid his fingers up to the soft flesh below her navel and told her, *"I'd* best beg, borrow, or steal the boat. Every time we contact anyone we know here we're taking a chance on being spotted. That gal Yoko would know if she's been tailed a lot of late, wouldn't she?"

Lone Star said, "I told you we took every precaution. If the Black Dragons were that interested in her and her kin they'd have simply picked them up by this time. If they even guessed they were business associates of mine they'd have grabbed them as well as Ki, don't you think?"

"I don't know what to think. Anyone who calls his fool self after a lizard is likely to think anything. We have to bank on that warehouse for now, because we have no other choice. But the more we stay away from it the better we can bank on it. So let me worry about the boat."

He started to sit up, then thought better of it. "I wired my office I'd let 'em know when I got where I was going. But by now the office is closed, and what old Billy Vail don't know won't hurt him."

"Then you don't mean to wire him tonight?"

"I just said that. He's sure to wire orders back and, as of the moment, I'm already disobeying orders beyond all common sense. If we get away with your fool notion there'll be no need to wire what I done. If we get caught on diplomatic property, I won't need to wire Billy. He'll hear about it direct, from Washington."

She reached a languid arm up to fondle his hair as she sighed and asked, "Would it really cost you your badge, after all you've done for your department in the past?"

He shrugged. "That would be the nice part, just for openers. I could wind up doing time on a mighty serious federal charge. But, what the hell, we'll probably get killed, anyway."

"I know. It's not too late to back out, darling. You know

I think too much of you to hold you to it."

"Sure, I know. I wouldn't be such a damn fool for a lot of other gals I know. I'd like to back out. What you're asking is dumb as hell. But if I did, you'd just go on and try it on your own, wouldn't you?"

"You know me so well it scares me at times, darling. What time do you think would be best to try, tonight?"

"Two-thirty. Four would be better for breaking and entering, but the almanac says two-thirty is the next high tide, and the one after that comes in after daybreak."

"My God, you've already bought and read a local tide table?"

"On the train. Had to. I figured the mud flats were the only hope, too. Why are you fooling with my trousers now, sweetheart?"

Lone Star dimpled and said, "That's a mighty dumb question."

He laughed. "Are you sure we ought to, Jessie? You know how hot and bothered we tend to get and, if we really aim to row boats and scale walls later tonight, a cold shower together might make more sense."

"You know damned well how much rest we'd get under a shower together, hot or cold. But you have a good point. We'd better not tire one another out. Take off your clothes. I'll show you a neat way to come without doing hardly any work."

Chapter 11

By two-thirty San Diego Harbor lay under a thick pea-soup fog and the mud flats behind the Japanese consulate lay under eighteen inches of filthy salt water. Longarm swore he would never complain about the coal smoke of Denver again as he rowed them quietly through the foggy stink. For a man got used to the dry, thin air of the High Plains, and he'd been feeling sort of soggy ever since arriving on the coast. San Diego Harbor at night *really* took some getting used to. Thanks to the Pacific Fleet moored between Diego and Coronado Island, the water was tainted with raw sewage and dead fish. He wondered what that old waterfront cuss he'd hired this skiff from was wondering about him and Jessie right now. For they'd paid too steep for rental and just about right for stealing when they'd said they meant to row over to Coronado. Had the old man been at all honest he'd have told them a ferry left for there on the hour, but he hadn't. So Longarm didn't feel guilty about stealing his leaky old boat.

He got a lot more worried about getting lost by the time his pretty lookout in the bow whispered, "I think I see a whitewashed wall ahead. A little to your left, dear."

He muttered, "That's portside, you sweet little landlubber. At least, I think it's portside. How far in does this stinky water reach, honey?"

"Don't ask me. Keep rowing. I can barely make out the wall above. Wouldn't it be funny if we were heading for some fool breakwater, Custis?"

He muttered, "You sure have a dismal sense of humor, girl. Oh, hell, I just hit bottom with an oar. But perhaps we can work a mite closer."

They could. By the time the bow under Jessie was grounded too firmly in muck to move farther they were only a yard or so from the loose riprap guarding the base of the stucco wall from there on up. As Lone Star rose to leap ashore he flinched, murmured, "Oh, it was just a rat," and jumped.

She landed gracefully and silently on a granite boulder. Longarm followed, throw rope coiled in his free left hand. He had his .44-40, of course, in the other.

Jessie whispered, "Let's go."

But he held her still. "Hold it. You said the only hole through this wall is on the far side. If only I could see the damned top, I'd know where to throw. But I can't. So I don't."

"Oh, Custis, what are we to do, then? We're so close and yet still so far away!"

"Stand clear and give me elbow room. I've been watching this fog go lighter and darker for a spell. I suspect a lighthouse must be sweeping her beam in vain, considering, but . . . yeah, look how that stucco's getting whiter now, and if that ain't a cannon muzzle jutting out across the harbor up there, it'll have to do."

He shook out a calf-loop and commenced to swing it as Lone Star protested, "Wait, the light's fading again."

But he said, "Hell, ain't you ever worked a roundup

after dark?" and threw. He was almost as surprised as Jessie when his blind throw worked. He jerked the well broken-in manila line to set the noose securely. "That should do her, unless you're heavier than a cannon," he said.

She managed not to laugh out loud. "'Fess up, Custis. That was pure luck, wasn't it?"

He shrugged modestly. "Some. I learned working overtime in my misspent youth that a throw at a glimpse could beat not throwing at all, even if you missed. I'll go first. If I don't get my head blowed off right away, I'll haul you up after me."

As he holstered his revolver and started up hand over hand with his boots against the rough stucco he heard her hiss something about Japanese. He didn't speak Japanese so he didn't see how it could matter. He found out a few seconds later.

He got to the top and slipped through the cannon port to the eight-foot-wide walk atop the wall. There was no railing on the inner side. It just looked dark as well as far to fall. As he turned to haul Lone Star up he heard the scrape of leather on stone and stiffened as someone called out quietly, *"Donata desu ka?"*

He didn't answer. He couldn't think of anything sensible to say as the sentry came into view, sort of, in the fog.

Longarm could just make out the Marine's head and shoulders, outlined against the foggy night sky. Hoping the feeling was mutual, Longarm dropped into a crouch to conceal his own outline as he crawfished away, drawing his .44-40. He knew if push came to shove he could simply shoot his way back to that cannon and slide back down the rope to Jessie, but he didn't want to. So he held his fire as the sentry kept edging forward, repeating whatever in hell he was jawing about. Longarm knew that if the kid had a lick of sense he would be yelling for the corporal of the guard by now. But perhaps he wasn't sure he had really seen anything against the swirling fog.

Now his tone was more urgent and now he wasn't carrying his gun at port arms. Longarm knew human nature well enough to sense that the sentry was fixing to fire if he didn't get some sensible answers. Longarm didn't want to kill a man he didn't have to. So he stood up and sighed, "You got me, pard. I seem to be lost."

The sentry gasped. He might have done most anything, but then Lone Star chopped the back of his neck, hard, with the edge of her palm. As he fell between them Longarm moved in fast to grab the rifle before it could hit, saying, "I said I'd haul you up. But I'm glad you couldn't wait, you sweet little willful child."

Lone Star stooped to feel the pulse of the man. "He should be out for at least an hour, if he's lucky. Let's go!"

Longarm said, "Hold on. We can't just leave him here like a sleeping ugly. I'd best roll him over the side."

"That could kill him sure, dear," she protested. "It's a long way down to those jagged rocks. I've a better idea."

She reached into the capacious right pocket of her split skirt to produce a little silver flask. "I brought some medicinal bourbon along in case we found Ki feeling poorly," she explained. "I feel sure we can spare a few drops."

"Damn it, Jessie, I don't want him woke up. I want him out of action entire!"

Lone Star said, "Pooh, I'm not putting it *in* him. I'm putting it *on* him. He never saw me. He may not be sure he saw you. So when they wake him up, muttering about spooks in the dark, and stinking like a messy drunk..."

"My way might have been kinder in the end," Longarm said, "but go ahead. The corporal of the guard might have suspected something worse if he was off his post entire."

To add to Lone Star's artistry, Longarm propped the unconscious sentry up with his back to the cannon mount and his rifle athwart his thighs. Lone Star put his cap back on him and told him to sleep tight. "Can we move on, now, dear?" she asked.

Longarm said, "Not on. In. For if they post guards at all like we did in my old army, most of 'em should be walking

134

perimeter. Stairwells have a disgusting way of leading down into guard posts. We'd best get off this fool wall."

She stared soberly down into the pitch darkness. "That's a mighty spooky drop, dear. We just agreed it was too far to drop any friends."

"It can't be as far down on the landward side unless they admire flooded cellars at high tide. I ain't asking you to jump. I'll lower you on this rope."

She brightened and said, "Oh, good. Then you can slide down it yourself, right?"

"Not hardly. We might need this rope some more. When you get to the bottom, give a couple of jerks on the line if you want to be hauled back up. Unless it's real dreadful down there, I'll join you the easy way."

She shuddered but took the rope end he offered and wrapped it around her hips, holding on higher as she stepped to the edge and beyond. As he braced his own weight against hers Longarm grinned and said, "Had I known we'd be doing this I'd have never let you eat so much dinner at the hotel earlier."

Then he paid out the line until at last he felt it go slack and was able to judge the distance to the ground inside the wall. It was farther than he'd hoped. But when she didn't signal she wanted to come back up he let go of his end, lowered himself over the edge as far as his arms could stretch, and, wishing he had longer arms, let go.

He hit bottom with a jolt that drove his knees up into his chest, but when he landed on his rump and rolled he could tell he was sprawled in a flowerbed. Lone Star whispered, "Are you hurt?"

He sat up. "Not enough to matter. Where's my throw rope?"

"Here," she said, as he made her out against the sky glow and saw she was standing over him with the rope already coiled. He rose to join her, patting his left side to make sure his old .44-40 had come down the same way with him. He peered about and muttered, "It's black as

135

pitch as far as the eye can see."

"What were you expecting close to three in the morning, a torchlight parade?" she asked. "Come on. We have to find Ki before the sun comes up."

He let her take the lead, having no better ideas on which way to go. They worked their way around a few corners and then they saw a large but dim square of light ahead. "That looks like someone's up late after all," Jessie said.

"Yeah, must be a candle behind one of them sliding paper screens."

"They call it a shoji. Let's see what's on the other side."

It was easy to move in silently across the grass surrounding the small building. Lone Star used her own penknife to poke a tiny hole silently in the shoji's oiled paper as her lover covered her with drawn revolver and bated breath.

She peeked, stifled a giggle, and backed him around the nearest corner before she told him, "Strike one. Private quarters."

He asked what was so funny and she said, "It sure looks silly when someone else is doing it. They seemed to like one another almost as much as we do. She was very young and pretty."

Longarm chuckled. "I'd best just have a peek myself."

She didn't know he was funning. "Don't you dare. He was old and ugly and I don't want you looking at other women, that way, when you're with me," she whispered.

He said, "Neither description fits old Ki. Doubt they'd be holding him in these private quarters in any case. What we ought to be looking for is a more imposing building."

"I'm not sure. Our friends here say the main ones closer to the front gate are more or less open to the public and that nobody seemed to be held there against his or her will."

Longarm shrugged and said, "They put cellars under big buildings, not cottages like these. The federal building back in Denver is open to the public, too. At least most of it is. But I know for a fact all sorts of sneaky stuff goes on in the parts where the public ain't invited."

He glanced at the sky to get his bearings and took the lead as Lone Star followed, asking him what sort of sneaky things went on in the Denver federal building. That was the trouble with talking to women. A man had to consider every word he said or, next thing he knew, he'd be confessing about secretary gals on leather sofas behind locked office doors. He didn't like to lie to anyone. He knew Jessie didn't want to hear about other ladies. So he muttered, "Keep your voice down. I see another light ahead. Looks like it's coming through an archway. They hardly ever put such imposing archways on cottages, so we must be aimed right."

As they worked their way closer they could see that there was indeed an archway—more an arched passageway—leading into what seemed to be a courtyard beyond. Longarm stopped to consider and told Lone Star, "That has to be the main complex. They must use that sort of tunnel to get in and out the back way."

"What are we waiting for, then?" she asked.

He shook his head. "A set of architect's plans would sure come in handy about now. Folk don't light up places they don't aim to notice after dark. Guards get to stay up this late as often as dirty old men. So what'll you bet the guard room opens on that lit-up courtyard?"

"No bet. But wouldn't they be holding Ki somewhere close to their guard room?" she asked.

"Honey, if I knew where they were holding your segundo, or even for sure if he was *on* this infernal post, I wouldn't be sneaking about so much. I can only make out a few square yards of what lies beyond that spooky tunnel. I can't even tell how large it might be, let alone how many doorways might open into it."

Then he stiffened as he heard someone barking orders through the entry. "Take cover!" he whispered, even though, in truth, he grabbed her arm and shoved her down in the shrubbery along the foundation line before flattening out on top of her.

They lay still, all too aware that they were only half

hidden, as the corporal of the guard marched a line of eight Marines out the passageway and into the darkness beyond, barking at them all the way.

When they dared to breathe again Lone Star whispered, "You must weigh a ton. It's funny, but I never seem to notice that when you don't have your pants on. Get off me, silly. You know I couldn't get this split skirt out of the way if I wanted to. It's really built more like a loose pair of pants."

He kissed her, told her he admired the way *she* was built as well, and rolled off to help her to her feet. "I was right about the guard room. Wrong about the time. It must be three if they're changing the guard. So we've been floundering about for half an hour or more and we still ain't nowhere important."

She said, "You're wrong. We know where their guards hole up when they're not out on picket, and Ki's sure to be locked up somewhere close. Now might be the best time to move in, with the corporal of the guard away, right?"

He shook his head. "Wrong. You're forgetting the other officers. They only leave the guard room when it's important. They usually keep at least a squad of supernumeraries as only turn out when the regular pickets commence to cry for help."

He took her by one arm and led her along the back of the complex, out of sight of the rear entrance, as he added, "That should be any minute now. As soon as they find that rascal drunk on duty."

As if on cue, they heard a distant outraged bellow. Lone Star translated, "Post number nine seems to have some kind of an emergency, dear."

They couldn't see the sergeant of the guard tearing out of the complex, but they could hear him and, from the way gravel was crunching, he was not alone. Lone Star smiled and said, "There should be even fewer guards to worry about for the next few minutes at least."

"*One* can be too many to mess with, if he's covering

138

that passageway with a lamp and gun," Longarm warned. "Did that cuss up on the wall yell just what the fuss was?"

"No. He just called for the sergeant of the guard. Is it important?"

"It could be. If I was pulling supernumerary and my sergeant tore out to deal with an emergency, I'd be on the prod till somebody told me what was going on. I don't think as much of that way in, now, and to tell you the truth I never admired it in the first place. There has to be a better way."

They moved on, seeing even less as they got into deeper darkness. "I'll just never understand the way Orientals build things. They seem to either make whole walls of paper or leave no openings at all. Ain't they never heard of windows?" he complained.

"That's the point of shoji screening, dear. If you want to look out you simply slide the whole wall out of the way. If you don't want to, you don't have to," she explained.

He spotted a dim patch of light ahead. "Keep it down and follow me close. I think I see an open cellar door ahead."

They circled a clump of foundation greenery and paused. A sloping cellar door stood open on its hinges. A flight of stone steps led down, dimly illuminated by lanternlight from below. He whispered, "If that ain't a trap, someone wanted to air their cellar. I sure wish I knew which."

She nudged him closer. "They'd hardly set a trap if they weren't expecting visitors, would they?" she observed.

"Right. If they even suspected we were creeping about their grounds they'd have said grounds lit up by torchlight by now. Be careful, though. This would be one hell of a time to roll down a flight of steps, and they're sort of fog-slicked."

He kept the lead and began to ease down the steps, taking them slowly and planting each heel firmly on the wet stone before risking another. The stairway was deep as well as steep. He reached the bottom and turned to see how Lone Star was doing. At that moment the light went out. He heard his lover gasp as something or somebody thudded against her soft flesh. He just had time to say, "Oh, shit, *suckered!*" before a ton of bricks landed on him in the dark and the darkness exploded into a galaxy of tiny pinwheeling stars.

Then he didn't even get to curse for quite a spell. Lone Star couldn't have heard him if he had. They had both been knocked out.

Longarm got to disenjoy some awful dreams before he decided his eyes were really open, even if he couldn't see anything. He realized he lay stark naked, face down, on damp stone or cement. He propped himself up on one bare elbow and groped about in the dark with his free hand until his questing fingers touched a firm, smooth, naked rump and he heard Lone Star asking in a groggy voice, "Don't you ever think of anything else, bless you?"

"Wake up," he muttered. "We ain't in bed."

After a time she answered, "You're right. So where in God's name could we be, darling?"

"Damp cellar, from the smell of it. Are you hurt, Jessie?" he asked.

She sat up, as naked as he in the darkness. "My neck will never be the same. Somebody must have been trying to break it. Where did they hit *you*, Custis?"

"All over, and I'm mad at me, too. I'm sure sorry, Jessie. I should have known that guiding light was too good to be true. I led you smack into an ambush like a raw recruit!"

She moved closer to take him in her arms, soothing, "There, there, I've scouted Comanche and Yaqui in my time and I fell for it, too. Don't you think we'd better get out of here, darling?"

He kissed her and rose to his bare feet, helping her to her own, as he growled, "I don't know how to tell you this, Jessie, but I suspect anyone mean enough to steal our duds as well as our guns might well have thought to lock the

140

door after him as he was leaving."

They explored the stucco walls and the riveted steel door with their fingers. "When you're right you're right," she said at last. "I make it a nine-by-twelve cell. This soggy lump I have one foot on must be a mat. At least they don't mean us to sit bare-bottomed on solid cement."

As she hauled him down beside her he saw she was shivering from the clammy atmosphere, or perhaps from fear. So he took her in his arms again to comfort her. "Well, if they meant to kill us they'd have done so by now, I hope. You know more than me about the way these jaspers think, honey. Do you reckon they'll settle for just turning us over to Uncle Sam, bare-assed and silly-looking as we'll look to him?"

She snuggled closer. "I'm more Texas than they are. I speak the lingo and sometimes I think I understand them, but sometimes even Ki surprises me. I guess you have to be Japanese all the way even to guess their thoughts. Ki says sometimes we surprise him, and he's half American. Do you really think you should be petting me like that, darling? It feels wonderful, but what if that door should open just as we're getting down to some serious loving?"

He sighed. "Yeah. They might not think they've made us feel dumb enough by tossing us in here naked. They could have left us this handy mattress with just what I'm thinking of in mind."

She said, "Don't think about it, then."

"We could always sort of do it standing up, in the corner on the hinge side of that door, you know," he suggested.

She laughed weakly. "Don't tempt me, you cruel thing. We'd still have to stop, sudden, and there are times that could really hurt."

He leaned his bare back against the damp wall. "Yeah. I'd have a time stopping, too. I sure wish they'd left us some matches and at least one damned cheroot. I don't know how long we've been out, but this is already getting tedious as hell."

They sat in silence for a time. Then she murmured, "Do

141

you think they might be planning to shoot us at dawn, Custis?"

He had no idea, but to comfort her he said, "If they aimed to act so formal they'd likely court-martial us first. Since the Japans ain't at war with these United States, executing us as spies wouldn't be right."

"What if they don't care if they're in the right? They had no right to kidnap Ki, did they?" she asked.

He grimaced. "We don't know for sure they ever did. If it was them Black Dragons, and old Ki is Lord knows where, the gents here who captured us on their grounds may just be feeling righteous indignation. Either way, the odds are they'll hand us over to American jurisdiction after they've had some fun with us."

"Not if we've fallen into the hands of the Black Dragon!"

He patted her shoulder. "Even more likely, if that's who suckered us. Had they wanted *you*, they'd have never kidnapped *Ki*. They did that to make you see things their way. I don't see how Starbuck Enterprises could cut a deal with even a pink dragon with you dead or even locked up."

She started to point out the one awful thing he'd left out, but she knew he knew the villains who were trying to horn into her empire would have small use for a lawman who could and no doubt would testify against them in any court of law, Japanese or American. "Oh, darling, I'm so sorry I got you into this," she sobbed. "You told me to begin with it would be foolish as well as dangerous. But I had nobody else to turn to, and . . ."

"Hush," he whispered, kissing her cheek in the dark. "I'm old enough to vote and you ain't allowed to vote at all. So we'll say no more about it."

She said, "We have to. We don't know how much time we have or even whether we'll ever see one another again. Oh, Custis, if only there was some way I could make it up to you!"

"Well, if I stood you in yon corner and sort of spread

my own legs even wider . . ." he began.

He was teasing, of course, but she said, "To hell with convention. If this should be the last time we'll ever get to make love, we'd best do it right, and if they see us, they see us!"

Just then the door opened a crack and they could see by the slit of cellar light that someone was tossing their boots and duds in to them.

As the door clanged shut again, he said, "I suspicion that was a hint for us to get dressed. I sure hope that means we're going someplace."

"I don't know why people always seem to know the worst time to visit, but they do," Jessie muttered.

They both got dressed. Longarm would have been surprised to find his gun rig on the floor, but as he patted himself down he cursed and said, "The bastards even stole my pocketknife."

Then he brightened and added, "At least they left us my smokes and matches." He thumbed a waterproof match alive and, as he saw she was only half dressed, he said, "I keep forgetting how pretty you are, Jessie. Do we ever get out of this fix, remind me to leave the lamp lit the next time."

She dimpled. "You usually do," she said as she buttoned her shirt. He lit a cheroot before the match went out. Their eyes were now so adjusted to the darkness that the walls seemed to light up cherry red every time they shared a drag, seated together on the mat again.

They didn't get to finish the cheroot before the door opened a second time and a brace of Marines ordered them up and out.

Their guards covered them warily as they were escorted along the dimly lit corridor and into Count Togo's spartan office.

The navy man had changed to a black kimono dotted with his clan crest in gold thread. "I hope we didn't get you out of bed," Longarm said.

"As a matter of fact, we've been expecting you all evening," Togo replied, pleasantly.

The two prisoners took the bentwood seats he offered them before he sat down again behind his desk. "I reckon I may as well clear one of your guards of a drunk-on-duty charge, as long as it don't matter, now," Longarm said.

Count Togo smiled thinly. "That seems most considerate of you, Deputy Long," he said. "But did you really think we'd expect a Japanese Marine to get drunk on *bourbon?* My men, as you know, are not allowed into town."

Lone Star said, "Then you know who we are." It was not a question.

Togo nodded. "You are Miss Jessica Starbuck, owner of the Circle Star ranch and much else besides. We have been expecting you ever since your Eurasian foreman was given into my keeping. As great minds run in the same channels, and it is my duty to consider how one might or might not invade imperial property, I have had my eye on the waterfront. So, as soon as my agents told me of a young couple renting a rowboat for a romantic moonlight boat ride in thick fog, with the tide coming in—"

Longarm cut him off. "I figured you had to be smart as hell, about the time we stepped in that trap you set for us. Can we talk about Ki, now? I'm sure glad to hear he's here, after all, for I'd be feeling even dumber if he wasn't."

Count Togo nodded. "That is one of the things I would like to discuss with Miss Starbuck. The Eurasian refuses to confess to the crimes he is charged with, and I confess I find them somewhat vague as well. Do you think, Miss Starbuck, your young friend would be more cooperative if you told him you found this desirable?"

Lone Star glared at Togo and snapped, *"I* don't want to cooperate with you, either! You're not fooling me with this cat-and-mouse game, sir. I told the last rascal fronting for the Black Dragon that it was no dice."

Longarm nudged her booted foot with his own and, knowing she spoke Spanish and hoping Togo didn't, warned her in Spanish not to let the *cabrone* pump her. "It's better to play dumb when you don't have any idea what may be going on," he added.

She nodded. So did Count Togo. He purred, "Let us talk about *El Dragon Negro*, then. I am surprised to learn you Americans have heard of it. We Japanese like to keep our family arguments within the family."

Longarm started to ask a dumb question. Then he nodded and growled, half to himself, "Right, a security officer posted this close to the Mexican border would have to. You're still a *cabrone*, though. I never take nothing back."

"I have a dossier on you as well," Togo said. "This is not the first time you've flouted international law. Miss Starbuck, here, seems to prefer rough gentlemen for some reason. It's a pity. My manners are so much more civilized and, as you see, I am trying to be a friend as well."

Lone Star snapped, "If you're even a decent stranger, suppose you just turn Ki loose, now!"

Togo said, "That may not be as impossible as it seems, since the official I had to answer to for such unusual behavior is no longer with us. But we were talking about the Koroi Ryu, or perhaps I should call it the Black Dragon, too. Your language is so unsubtle. What do you really know about such matters, Miss Starbuck?"

She looked disgusted. "Good Lord, am I supposed to paint you in oils? You have to know details no American could ever grasp. What does it matter? You have Ki. You have us. So let's get down to price!"

Count Togo stared off into space. "What would you consider a fair price, Miss Starbuck?" he murmured thoughtfully.

"Don't be silly. There's no such thing as a *fair* ransom! I can't give you all you want. I have too many business associates with too great a say to let you horn into Starbuck Enterprises, as you demand. But I can give you money, lots of money. So let's talk about that."

Togo almost purred as he said, "Ah, such important American business connections would be far more important to the Black Dragon than mere money, no?"

"Money is all I can give you, damn it!" she said. "You can kill me, and even my friends, but my late father set up his empire so that nobody can horn in."

Longarm said, "You'd better believe her. I was there when some other sneaky foreigners tried. They murdered Alex Starbuck and almost murdered Jessie, Ki, and even me, more than once. But they never got control of the Starbuck empire, which is bigger than the Japans, no offense, and in the end they wound up hurt just awful."

Togo nodded. "I told you we know all about the two of you. I don't think you two know as much about Japanese politics and business methods, which are much the same things. Did you two lost lambs really think you could take on the Koroi Ryu alone?"

"Don't rub it in. I'm sure this is fun, but can any number of mice join this fool game?" Longarm asked.

Togo raised a questioning eyebrow. Longarm said, "You got Jessie, Ki, and me right where you want us. The gal is worried about old Ki. What say you let him sit in?"

Count Togo hesitated. "What's the matter, cat?" Longarm asked. "Don't you reckon you can handle three mice at a time?"

Togo clapped his hands. When a Marine clicked boot heels back at him, Togo snapped some curt orders. Longarm didn't need to have a translation. He didn't look at Lone Star. He was trying not to look smug as it was.

In the time they had to wait, Togo leaned back in his chair and said, "They are bringing him. Perhaps I should warn you both, I am all too aware of what a deadly trio you are, armed or not. I am deadly, too. My men are covering you, and shall be covering you, with orders to shoot to kill, should one of you even tense his or her limbs. Do we understand each other?"

"Sure," Longarm said. "I've visited Indian camps before. Makes more sense to cut a deal than to get all sweated up, anyways."

Togo nodded curtly and turned back to Lone Star. "Let us discuss this matter of Japanese business partners, Miss Starbuck."

"Let's not and say we did," she said. "Money is all you're going to get from me and mine. I can always raise more money. My dad's honor is something else again!"

There was no further argument. Just then the Marines came back, running and yelling fit to bust. Togo leaped to his feet and dashed out after them, doing some mighty serious screaming of his own.

Longarm and Lone Star found themselves alone. She clapped her hands with delight. "Did you hear that, darling?" she asked.

"I heard it. Didn't understand one word. What in thunder was that all about?" he asked.

She said, "Ki's escaped. They don't know how. When they unlocked his cell just now they found him gone, with Ki's duds lying empty on the floor like the goblins got him! Count Togo was saying mean things about their mothers and ordering the grounds lit up and searched inch by inch if they know what's good for them!"

Longarm grinned. "I always said Ki had to be part goblin. But why do you reckon he left his duds behind? Getting out of here figures to be chore enough, without running around bare-ass!"

"Never mind about that. Ki never acts strangely without a good reason. I only hope there's enough darkness left for him to work with."

Longarm shrugged. "With so little territory to move in and so many torches to light it up all around, that hardly matters, Jessie. If he didn't make it over the walls before they noticed he was missing, I don't see how in hell he'll *ever* get out." He looked around cautiously. "Speaking of getting out of here, nobody seems to be guarding us now. Look yonder. That count rascal even left a set of swords behind on that rack!"

She nodded and said, "My dad had a set like that in his

147

den. It was given to him by a Japanese noble he'd done a lot for when the Japans were first opened up to the outside world. That long blade over there is the katana, meant for cutting up other folk. The shorter ko-dashi in the matching sheath is what a disgraced Japanese gent is supposed to use on himself."

"That must smart," Longarm said. "How come they rip their bellies open like that? Wouldn't it feel less painful if they mayhaps cut their own throats?"

"It's supposed to be painful. It proves their manhood, or even womanhood, for that matter. Of course, once they've wiped their shame away by exposing their guts to the air it's all right if a friend finishes them off with the longer katana, as long as it's a matching set, like that one."

He got to his feet, saw no one seemed to be looking, and said, "Well, they taught me how to use a cavalry saber pretty good in my army days, and there's that cute little one for you, so—"

"Don't you *dare!*" she warned, pulling him back down. "Those blades are *family,* Custis. Under the Bushido code Count Togo has to follow, he can *give* you his katana, his house, or even his woman. But should another man even touch his weapons without *permission,* he's honor bound to cut his own guts open if he can't get at those of the one who just disgraced him so!"

Longarm settled back in his seat. "Hell, I'd look like a sissy waving a thing like that in any case. I wonder where our guns are. Do you reckon anyone would get upset if we sort of looked about for 'em, Jessie?"

"Well, nobody seems to be thinking about us at all in all this confusion. Why don't we just see how far we can stroll, holding hands and looking innocent?" Jessie suggested.

"May as well. We're sure not likely to get a better chance, whether they catch Ki again or not!"

★

Chapter 12

Ki was Japanese enough to guess at how his captors might
think and act, but enough of a Texas Indian fighter to know
some other tricks as well. So, while he had indeed scaled
the sharply angled walls of his cell like a human fly, backwards, and found it simple enough to grunt open the floor-
boards above, laid Oriental-style across the rafters without
nailing, Ki had seen as soon as he was in the storeroom
above his cell that he could be leaping from the frying pan
into the fire.

For one thing, the storeroom door was barred from the
outside. For another, the light from the one ventilating grid
warned him the night was nearly gone. Even after breaking
out, he would find himself still on the consulate grounds,
stark naked and unarmed, by the dawn's early light!

So Ki had played an old Kiowa–Apache trick on his
captors. He had simply waited, watching through a crack
in the floorboard, until they had run around in circles
below, even looking for him under the mat, and then left,

not bothering, of course, to lock the door of an empty cell.

By the time they were searching the floors above, Ki was back down in the cell dressing, as he heard them rummaging among the bales and boxes of the storeroom above.

Crouching out of view beside the now open cell door, impassive as an Indian hunter staked out along a game trail, Ki waited an hour or more until it got very quiet and the dawn light through the glass block was shedding enough light in the supposedly empty cell to make him reconsider his options. Rising again, Ki stepped out into the always-gloomy corridor. Wearing the humble plain kimono of a prisoner, slave, or servant, Ki padded along, head humbly down, until he heard boot heels coming his way and ducked into the first doorway he came to.

He found himself in a basement laundry room, unfortunately illuminated all too well by a disgustingly large basement window. He moved to the row of tubs set along the far wall. The washtubs were traditional. The water taps above them were not. He turned on the hot tap, hoping the boilers would be tended at this hour, somewhere in the bowels of this big building. They were, and, as the Japanese find scalding water too cold to bathe in, Ki soon had a fine cloud of steam rising in the cold morning air of the washroom. He didn't turn around as a voice from the doorway called out rather rudely, "Hey, what are you doing, *meshitsukai?*"

That wasn't anyone's name. It was Japanese for servant. Ki felt it safe to answer in the same language. "What does it look like I'm doing? Grab a mop if you want to help. It's not fair for them to expect me to get things ready all by myself."

The Marine in the doorway laughed. "Let the girls get their beauty rest. That bastard Togo never lets us get at the barbarian girls in town. Did you hear about that Ki escaping?"

Ki turned on another hot tap. "Who are you talking about? They never tell us anything."

The Marine said, "They had a Eurasian locked up just down the corridor. I don't know why. But the old man's going mad looking for him right now."

Ki asked, "Why are you looking for him down here, of all places? Do you find it desirable to anger Count Togo?"

The Marine laughed. "Fuck him. Maybe he'll have to commit seppuku, and I'll get to town more often."

Ki went on pretending to busy himself with the washtubs. He wondered why the Marine was still hanging around. He heard the other man lean his rifle against the wall inside the door. Ki figured it was safe to risk a casual peek over his shoulder. The Marine was bigger than he'd expected, with Okinawan features. He smiled at Ki through the steam as he moved closer. "Say, you're not bad-looking at all. I don't suppose you'd know where a lonely man could buy some salve around here, would you?"

Ki tried to keep it light as he replied, "Not really. As you see, I'm merely a laundry boy."

The other sneered. "Don't play coy with me. Don't you think I know what that short kimono means?"

"My kimono shrinks in hot water?" Ki asked.

"Very funny. Don't play games with me, laundry boy. I go back on duty in less than an hour. So that just gives us time."

Ki suppressed a laugh. The Marine took Ki's smile the wrong way. "Come on," he insisted, "don't act like a frightened virgin with me."

Ki protested, "In here? There's not even a shoji between us and the corridor!"

"I know a better place. A tool shed out behind the sand garden. Nobody's using it these days."

Ki started to explain, in a nice way, of course, why the idea didn't really appeal to him at all. Then he had a better idea. "Let's hurry, then, before I'm missed. I don't want to get in trouble."

The Marine took his arm and led him to the door, pick-

ing up the rifle on the way. But out in the corridor the
Marine said, "Listen, we'd better not go out the back way
arm in arm like the good friends we are."

"I agree we have a need to be discreet." Ki smiled
thinly.

The Marine took the lead. "Follow me as if I'm putting
you to work somewhere, then."

Ki tensed slightly as his would-be lover led him up the
back cellar steps and across an expanse of open grass. A
couple of other Marines were coming their way, rifles
slung. As the distance closed, one asked the Marine with
Ki, "Who's your new sweetheart, Yoshio? I haven't seen
her around here before."

The Okinawan laughed lightly. "New laundry boy. I'm
trying to show him how to get ahead on this post."

They all laughed, save for Ki, who would have felt even
more embarrassed if he hadn't been standing on a parade
ground with three armed Imperial Marines who were supposed to be searching high and low for him.

As his newfound would-be friend led Ki on, he said,
"Don't mind them. None of us are really this way. The
duty here just calls for a little help from one's friends."

They passed through a gap between lower buildings and
skirted the edges of a sand garden to avoid messing it.
Beyond, a small, nondescript shed stood half screened by
tall timber-bamboo.

Yoshio proudly displayed the key and said, "Hold my
rifle. I'll unlock the door, and then we'll be in heaven for
almost an hour!"

That wasn't exactly the way things worked out. Once
they were alone in the privacy of the windowless shed, Ki
smiled fondly at his guide. "This is very nice. Are you sure
nobody ever comes here? What about that escaped prisoner
you told me about? What if they decide to search for him
here?"

Yoshio leaned his rifle in a corner. "They already have.
Every inch of the grounds has been searched. They think

he must have leaped into the sea from the rear wall."

"Could he do that?"

"No. The mud flats run out for quite a way. But they did find an abandoned boat down there at daybreak. Why are we talking about this? Take off your clothes. I never brought you here to enjoy a long *conversation.*"

Ki slipped casually out of his kimono, hiding his distaste. The Okinawan grinned and began to drop to his knees before Ki. Ki said, "I'd feel more like it if you took your clothes off as well."

The Okinawan unbuckled his belt and dropped his pants.

Ki had tried to get him out of his uniform because no matter how one killed a man he tended to soil his pants. Ki killed the Marine with one explosive *te* chop.

It only took Ki a few seconds to strip the dead Marine completely. It took him longer getting into the too-tight uniform. Some of the buttons just didn't want to button, while the cap was too large for Ki's head until he stuffed a scrap of his kimono cloth under it.

Ki explored the pockets of his new outfit. He now had a comb, a wallet filled with one American dollar bill and some less fortunate money, along with a large pocketknife and some pocket change, all American, sixty-seven cents' worth.

He shrugged, glanced down at the dead man, and muttered, "All right. They won't be looking for you for about an hour. That might give me time enough to turn into somebody else."

Neither Longarm nor Lone Star had gotten a tenth as far as Ki. For when they had tried to wander out of Count Togo's office, the Marines posted just outside had wandered them right back, and they got to admire the count's carving set some more. It couldn't have been as long as it felt like to them, but it was still some time before Togo came back in, now gussied up in an officer's white tropical kit, to resume his seat behind the desk. "As I was saying before we were

153

so rudely interrupted, I feel your unwarranted trespassing on diplomatic property most undiplomatic, and I think your interest in Japanese internal politics is liable to get a lot of people killed, including you two," he told them.

Lone Star said, "Never mind all that. Where's Ki, now?"

Togo grimaced. "If I knew I would have brought him back here with me. I said before, I have no objection to your speaking with that disturbing young man."

"You mean he's escaped?" demanded Lone Star.

Togo only shot her a look of pure disgust.

Longarm had to laugh. "Hot damn. One gone and two to go. I told you we'd get Ki out one damn way or the other, Jessie!"

Togo snorted. "Such modesty becomes you. That other fool seems to have managed to escape without help from anyone. We're still working on how he did it. Nothing anyone can come up with works."

"How many of your boys did he take out on his way out?" asked Longarm, out of professional curiosity and at least some jealousy. He and Jessie still seemed to be stuck here.

Togo said, "Your friend didn't hurt anybody. In fact, he seems to have done no damage at all. One minute he was locked up alone behind a solid steel door. The next time anyone looked, he wasn't. The door lock had not been tampered with. There was no other way in or out. Only a glass block for daylight, too high to reach from the floor without a ladder. Just in case he had somehow managed to smuggle a ladder in under a short kimono, we investigated that, too. Solid as a rock. While we were about it, I had another distressing thought about ladders, so we searched the storeroom above. Needless to say, we found the door locked on the outside and nobody at all inside."

Longarm chuckled. "That sounds like Ki, sure enough. Now that you've told us how he got away, would you mind telling us what we're in for, next?"

Togo looked embarrassed. "Oh, you really must forgive my manners. In all this excitement I forgot to order your breakfast. You both must be famished. Can you forgive me?"

Longarm said, "Sure. We'll have ham and eggs. What happens after that?"

Togo shrugged. "The tide is out. So your little rowboat will be stranded on the mud flats for some time. Would you accept a ride back to your hotel by carriage?"

His two captives exchanged glances. Lone Star said, "You're right, dear. I'll just bet we don't get ham and eggs, either!"

Longarm yawned. "Some cats just don't know when to quit. I met a mean Lakota, once, with similar views on teasing captives. Come to study on it, though, the Indian had a lot more imagination."

Togo looked confused. "I'm not really sure we can manage ham and eggs, but I assure you we'll make every effort to feed you well."

Longarm said, "Sure, and then we get the buggy ride. Nice try."

"If you mean to let us go, I'd as soon skip breakfast," Jessie said. "Let's get to the price you put on all this sudden courtesy."

The officer scowled, cheeks flushed, and snapped, "Price? You assume a Japanese officer and gentleman would demand *payment* for releasing you? I was told you understood our language and customs, Jessica-San!"

"I surely thought I did. Why are you willing to turn us loose, assuming you mean to turn us loose?" she asked.

Togo rose, clapping his hands, and when a Marine stuck his head in the officer screamed at him, mad as hell, apparently.

Then he sat back down, growling deep in his throat until he got control of himself again, and told them, "I have sent for the things we found desirable to put away for your own safety as well as perhaps our own. I shudder to think what that annoying Ki could do with a *gun* on his way out!"

"We get out guns back?" Longarm asked cautiously.

Togo nodded curtly. "They are your property. Why do you ask so many foolish questions? Don't *you* return people's personal belongings when you have to let them go, Deputy?"

"Yeah, but I'm still trying to figure out why you have to let us go. By any chance would a crusty old cuss called Vail be somewhere near, waving a warrant he told me they'd never give us?"

Togo said, "I don't know what you're talking about. You must be trying to confuse me. Does it amuse you to confuse funny little yellow men from the Far Japans, Yankee?"

"If it did, it would still be fair," Longarm said, "for you're sure confusing us. Lord knows I've no objections. But how come you're letting us go if you don't want nothing in return and nobody seems to be forcing you?"

"That is simple. I no longer find it desirable for you to stay here. You have told me all the things I wished to know. The confusion about your associate, Ki, seems to have taken care of itself. Since he is not here, you have no way to rescue him. Since you are not here to do anything else, I hope, charging you with mere trespassing, as if you were wicked children, would make me look like a silly little man indeed."

He sat up straighter in his chair and almost roared, "We are *not* silly little men! The world may laugh at us now all it likes. But someday we shall show you what we really are!"

Longarm said, "I hope so. No offense, but I'm having a hell of a time figuring you gents out."

Lone Star rose, nudging Longarm to shush him. "I think I'm beginning to follow the count's drift, Custis. There are times when you're sort of amusing, but this isn't one of them. I do believe this gentleman means every word he says."

156

Togo was so angry his English was starting to fizz in his head. He rose, almost sobbing. "Of course I am meaning what I am saying!"

The Marine came back in with two servant girls, one thin and the other sort of fat, both carrying gifts on silk pillows. As Longarm and Lone Star proceeded to strap on their gun rigs and refill their pockets, Longarm told Togo, "Well, all right. I'm sorry I called you a *cabrone*. Do we get some sort of forms to fill out, or what? I don't get run out of consulates often."

Count Togo sighed and said, "Just *go*, please. Nothing about all this will ever appear on paper. Should anyone ever ask, you two stayed overnight as my personal guests. If you say otherwise to anyone, ever, I shall be only too pleased to call you a pair of silly big pink people. My men will escort you out front to the carriage. Please don't hurt any of them. They are only following my orders."

Longarm started to ask whose orders Togo might be following. But Lone Star grabbed his arm. "Will you just let us get *out* of here, damn it?" she hissed.

A few minutes later they were riding out the front gate and getting rifle salutes while they were about it. As the carriage headed for their hotel, Longarm relaxed. "Well," he said, "I've heard about inscrutable Orientals, but that Togo takes the cake, Jessie."

"Why do you suppose he let us off so easy, darling?"

Longarm shrugged. "Saved him some paperwork, for one thing. He had no way of knowing how many others we might have told about our plans. Old Billy Vail *would* raise hell if he thought I was locked up somewhere, and he'd no doubt bust a gut getting me out, if only so he could fire me right. Speaking of Billy, sooner or later I'd best get in touch with him. I ain't sure he believed my reasons for heading down this way with you, Jessie. I know for sure he wouldn't buy it if he knew I was anywhere near *you*."

She had only been half listening. She said, "I think I have it. It works two ways. The Black Dragons can't blackmail me if I'm locked up out of touch with my business associates."

"You mean Togo ain't just an old lovable housecat? What's the second angle, Jessie?"

"He knew we'd come over his garden wall to rescue Ki. So he knew we had some plans for *afterwards*."

"Right. He figures sooner or later Ki will contact us, or we'll go looking for Ki, having a better grasp on where Ki might be." He sat up straighter and looked back for a time before he slumped back down beside her. "Don't see nobody trailing us, though," he muttered.

"Who do you think's driving this carriage, Santa Claus?" she murmured.

"Now that you mention it, them matched chestnuts don't resemble reindeer. I'm sure glad I have no idea where old Ki could be right now, ain't you?"

The driver was too far forward to hear every word they said. But by tacit agreement neither said another word about Ki until they'd been let off in front of the General Grant and were up in their suite again. Then Lone Star, who had been bottled up longer than even a strong woman could stand, blurted, "Oh, Custis, whatever are we to do? If we go anywhere near that silk warehouse we could get poor Ki killed!"

He took her in his arms to soothe her. "Us, too, if they're running scared. They ought to be by now. I know *I'd* be considering cashing my chips and rising from the table about now if I was holding their cards."

"I thought we'd agreed we were playing a strong hand, with all those Marines and officials backing up even meaner sneaks we don't even know about!"

He kissed her lightly. "Half the officials and likely none of the Marines know any more about your troubles with that dragon bunch than you do, Jessie. You're dead right about them being mean and sneaky. They got to stay sneaky even more than they got to stay mean. For if I was the emperor and I found out a mess of lizards was out to

158

steal my government out from under me, I'd sure start showing them what *mean* is!"

She smiled uncertainly. "Well, they were having a time getting me to knuckle under even when they still held Ki."

"And you and me," he added.

She brightened and decided, "I think you're right, darling. When a smart player sees the game is going badly for him he tries to cut his losses, not raise the ante. They should have guessed an attempt to horn in on Starbuck Enterprises was a risky move even before they made it. Now that we've shown them how mean *we* can act, as well, they must see it makes more sense for them to try and horn in on some more sissy outfit."

Longarm considered. "You ain't the only American with interests in the import-export trade, and almost any other outfit has to be more sissy," he agreed. "But the game won't be over until I see you and Ki back to the Circle Star and, even then, you'd best stay forted up a spell. Some gambling men tend to be poor losers. When they see they can't win, chips wind up all over the floor."

She shook her head. "Men like Count Togo never tell anyone they've lost. That's why he let us go, to save his face. A wilder man might have killed us after Ki escaped to ruin his hand. Togo thought it more important to cover up by pretending it was all some sort of misunderstanding and that he was being generous."

"I hope it's that simple. We'd best stay on the prod until we know for sure. How come you're unbuttoning yourself like that, Jessie? It's early, and I'm already in enough trouble."

"After such a rough night, I mean to enjoy a long hot soak and a few minutes in bed before I do anything else. Care to join me?"

He smiled down at her wistfully and said, "You know I would. But I'd sure feel awkward if my boss busted in on us, demanding to know what else I come down to San Diego to do. I don't think old Billy is worldly enough for

159

three in a tub, and unless I calm him down some other way he's likely to fire me for insubordination."

He kissed her. "That would be fair. I ain't been following a single order he gave me since we got on that fool train up in Frisco." Then he left, warning her to lock the door after him and leave it that way.

Lone Star did. Then she ran a hot tub, stripped to the buff, and lathered her tired body from head to toes before getting in.

The fatigue and strain of the long, sleepless night hit her as she lay back to luxuriate in the comforting hot tub. She hooked the nape of her neck over the rounded rear rim and closed her eyes as she sensuously ran her hands over her submerged curves to get rid of any clinging soap film. Then she was sitting bolt upright, covering her wet breasts with her forearms. The door to the bath had just swung open and a deep masculine voice had just said, *"Perdone, Señorita*. Have I the honor of speaking with a friend of U. S. Deputy Custis Long?"

He was a tall, dark, handsome stranger clad in what would have been a typical black charro outfit if the usual silver conchos had not been replaced with big black buttons. He was holding his big black sombrero politely down in his left hand. His gun hand was closer to an ebony-gripped Colt '74, worn low and side-draw.

Lone Star's own .38 was on the lid of the commode, a long reach with a soap-slicked hand. She said, "I fear you have the advantage of me, Señor . . . ?"

"My real name is of no importance, since I seldom use it. I am called El Gato. Longarm has perhaps mentioned me to you at some time?"

She started to shake her head. Then she remembered some long pillow conversations back when she and Longarm had first been getting to know one another. "I seem to recall a Mexican bandit leader who was called The Cat because he could see so well in the dark. Obviously, whoever you may be, sir, nobody ever told you it was customary to knock before entering."

El Gato sighed. "Alas! I was brought up by people of gentle manners. *Pero*, in the end, they were burned out by the *rurales* anyway. I do not consider myself a bandit. I consider the monster in Mexico City, *El Presidente* Diaz, the bandit. But I did not pick the lock out front for to discuss such matters."

"Wouldn't it have been as simple to just knock?"

"*Pero*, no. I do not like to linger in hotel hallways. I am a man with a price on his poor head on either side of the border."

"So that's why you came to call on a federal lawman?"

"I see you feel some awkwardness as we converse this way, Señorita," El Gato said. "You really shouldn't. You have a most beautiful body. Would you feel more comfortable if I waited out in the other room until you finished your bath?"

She said she wouldn't mind at all. El Gato stepped out, shutting the door behind him and, more importantly, leaving her her guns.

Jessie pulled the plug and rose from the tub to grab a towel and quickly dry off. She knew her .38 would ruin the line of the navy blue kimono she'd taken into the bath with her. She would look even sillier with a gun rig strapped on *over* a kimono. On the other hand, she had slipped her derringer into a sleeve pocket of the kimono almost without thinking. Now she was glad she had thought of it as she slipped into the kimono and went out to join her mystery guest, more armed and dangerous than she might look.

El Gato was standing with his back to her, gazing out the French windows to the balcony as she stepped out on the rug in her bare feet. He heard her anyway. He turned with a smile and said, "*Que linda!* Do not take me for a forward man, *por favor*. I would not wish for to steal you from an old friend even if I thought I could. It is simply that I feel more comfortable in the company of a lovely woman if I feel she knows I find her worth killing for."

161

Lone Star moved to the dresser on her side of the bed as she smiled and said, "I don't think I'd better tell you how good looking you are. You obviously already know. We have Kentucky bourbon and that awful Maryland rye Custis likes. I'm sorry we don't seem to be stocked up on tequila, but . . ."

El Gato shook his head. "I can't stay long enough to get drunk with you, either. My black stallion and some other friends are waiting for me in a nearby alley and we have far to ride, in some hurry."

"What *can* I do for you, then?" she asked.

El Gato ran his gaze up and down her wistfully. "Alas, I am in a hurry, and Longarm once saved my life. It is for to save *his*, perhaps, I am here. I do not know for why he is once more approaching the border. I have no wish to know. I came to warn him it would be suicide, right now, for any gringo to venture more than a mile or so south of Tijuana!"

She looked bemused. "Why on earth would we want to head that way?"

He said, *"Quien sabe?* I know Longarm has standing orders not to start any more wars with Mexico. Perhaps he is like me in that he can't refuse a dare. But you must tell him that this time he must avoid temptation. As you can see, I am a Mexican of some character and, at the moment, Mexico is too hot for me and my not-too-small guerrilla band. The Indians have once more risen in the hills south of Tijuana. I do not say they are in the wrong. I would be glad to help them fight the current Mexican government if only they did not enjoy killing all outsiders so much. As Longarm knows from having ridden with me down there in the past, *los rurales* are for real fighting men to spit on. Wild Indians can sometimes be avoided. But now a whole brigade of federal cavalry has been moved in for to restore order and while *los federales* are not much tougher than *los rurales,* man to man, we are talking about over a thousand of the *cabrones!"*

Lone Star nodded soberly and said, "In other words, the

162

country to the south is boiling over with rural police, federal troops, and wild Indians, none of whom like Anglos at all."

El Gato smiled crookedly. "They do not even like me and mine at all. The far west of Mexico is savage country, even when things are more peaceful. Even simple villagers turn a hard eye to strangers, any strangers. They have long-standing reasons to be hard and bitter. It is a hard land, a bitter land. Life there would be distressing enough, even if one knew a peon father could send his daughter to the well without wondering if he'd ever see her again."

Lone Star nodded. "I'll tell Custis I don't want to buy any cactus candy or a straw *vaquero* in Tijuana when he gets back."

"In that case I beg your permission for to leave, Señorita," El Gato said. "I shall carry this image of you in my heart as I ride off to meet my fate!"

She escorted him to the door and held out her hand to him. He bent to kiss it, put on his hat, and moved silently away as she called after him softly, "Go with god, *caballero*."

Then she shut the door and locked it so she could get some much-needed sleep.

But she had barely slipped under the covers, naked, when the door opened again, more lawfully, and Longarm stepped in, looking confused as well as tired.

He said, "I just read the damnedest wire from Billy Vail. It was waiting for me at the Western Union down the slope when I got there to wire him more fibs."

She yawned. "That's no mystery, dear. You wired him from up north that you were on your way here, remember?"

He sat on the bed beside her. "Sure, but that was all a lie, I thought. Now the home office tells me I used my head so swell they can't get over it. You remember that other mess of mean Japanese, up around Frisco?"

"That renegade officer, Nakamura?"

"That's the cuss. I'm ashamed to say I'd almost forgotten about him, playing games with the ones after *you*. But now they've wired me I'm right on his heels. For just a few minutes ago a gang as answers to the same dumb description stopped a stage up near El Cajon. That's in the Coast Range, so near here we should have heard the gunshots. The alert out on 'em says they shot hell out of the stage crew and half the passengers, then rode off with a pretty female passenger, laughing fit to bust and yelling in what one survivor feels sure was Japanese. He was Chinese, so he ought to know."

Lone Star said, "Speaking of bandits, one was just here. I had quite a conversation with your old pal, El Gato."

Longarm blinked in surprise and looked concerned. "Are you all right, Jessie?" he asked.

She laughed. "I couldn't even get him to touch your Maryland rye. But I wasn't sure he was your friend until he left me pure, with a warning for you."

She brought him up to date on her conversation with the handsome young Mexican. Longarm dismissed the warning about Mexico as unimportant. "Damn, I wish I'd had a chance to talk to him before he rode off. Once that old boy's riding he's hard as hell to have a word with."

"You don't suppose his gang could have had anything to do with that last stage robbery, do you?"

"Hell, no, carrying off women ain't El Gato's style, no matter how flirty he talks. Besides, that Chinaman says them other polecats talked Japanese. The timing lets El Gato off as well. El Cajon is close to San Diego, but not *that* close. I make her about a two or more hours' ride, and that stage got hit less'n an hour ago."

He got back to his feet to draw his sixgun and reload it with fresh rounds, muttering, "It only occurred to me as I was out, just now, how a sneaky Black Dragon might have thought to spill some powder before giving us back our hardware. Damn, I wish I'd known El Gato was in town before he left. If we'd had *him* along last night, things

164

might have gone a whole lot better. That old boy can see where I'm blind as a bat, and they say *I* got good night vision."

"Where are you going now?" she sighed. "Up to El Cajon to investigate that robbery?"

He took off his gun rig as well as his hat and coat while he explained, "That's what even Nakamura will be expecting me to do. By now them chaparral-covered slopes will be crawling with lawmen and local vigilantes who know the country better. I'm sure sorry about that poor gal they carried off. But if the more polite gents on the scene ain't cut her abductors' trail by this time, I suspect they never will. So far, Nakamura ain't left no sign. He rides slick as well as disgusting. He hits here, there, and everywhere, like a real pro. Only way anyone figures to catch him is by figuring where he'd headed next and getting there first."

He sat down on the bed again and began to shuck his boots. "I like to eat apples a bite at a time. First I got to get you and Ki on a Texas-bound train. *Then* I got to go get the rascals they sent me out here to get."

She sighed and said, "I wish we had El Gato working with us, too. For I don't see how we can try to contact Ki, or how he can get to us, if the Black Dragons are able to see at all."

He finished undressing and got under the covers with her. "You're making two problems out of one, old pard. Ki don't *have* to contact us, even if he knows we're here. Once he makes it to other friends we hope them lizards don't know about, he'll have money, arms, and new duds, and anyone in such a fine condition can surely get back to Texas on his own."

She shook her head as he slipped a naked arm under it. "You don't know Ki as I do. They're sure to tell him at the silk warehouse that I'm in town. He'll never leave without me. He won't know Togo has us under observation."

"It's early yet," he soothed. "Nobody figures to make any moves this side of sundown, and the two of us are so

165

sleepy we might not be thinking straight. Meanwhile we all seem safe enough for now, and I got other notions as don't involve such deep thinking."

"Why, Custis, are you suggesting what I think you are suggesting, bless your heart?"

"Ah, I hope you won't take this wrong, honey. But if it's all the same to you, could we get some infernal sleep, first?"

"I love you. You're so understanding."

★

Chapter 13

His friends and foes were wrong in thinking Ki had
escaped. It was true he was loose, but he was still on the
consulate grounds. It was broad daylight, with sunset hours
away, and as he crouched in a clump of foundation plant-
ings less than a hundred yards from the tool shed he had
messed up so untidily. He could tell the Marine he had
killed had been missed, for others were dashing all over the
place, calling out his name in vain.

Ki was still wearing the dead man's uniform. He knew
he might still be able to pass for a member of the guard
garrison to one or more of the civilians inside the walls.
But he would never fool anyone attached to such a small
military unit.

The scant cover he had chosen at random when he heard
the alarm sounded was hardly the sort of cover he'd have
chosen if he'd had more time, or had meant to stay there
any time. The wooden wall the bushes grew against was
that of someone's private quarters. It was built in the Ori-

ental style, on posts, with no basement. Ki flattened further and saw that while the crawl space under the house was shallow indeed, he could just make it. So, his back to the bare earth under the house, Ki commenced to inch his way deeper under it. He did so until light ahead warned him he was now as close to the inner garden as to the outer walls. So he just stopped and lay doggo, hoping the pounding of his heart could not be heard through the thin flooring just above him.

He could most certainly make out the soft padding of canvas soles on straw matting, right over his sweating, dirt-stained face. It sounded as if a maid was laying out a tea service. He could use some tea or, better yet, a slug of saké right now. But as he hadn't been invited, he thought it wiser to lie still and try not to breathe too much as at least two men entered the room above and sat down right above him, had they known it.

Ki heard the soft clink of pottery as his tormentors mucked about up there and made small talk before getting down to anything worth listening to. Ki knew his mother's people well enough to know that a Japanese murmuring nice things about a host's teacups could have anything from murder to simply enjoying a nice cup of tea in mind. So he paid attention. Finally, one of them said, conversationally indeed, "I have been thinking about that body in the gardner's shed."

Someone else sucked tea loudly and murmured, "I confess I have as well. It was very rude of even an unwilling guest to kill one of our brave guards, don't you think?"

There was a long silence. Then the first one said, "If we had to report it as a killing by an escaping guest of the Chrysanthemum Seal it would occasion loss of face by our dedicated military men."

"*Hai*, that would not be at all desirable. But surely we shall be required to report *something*. Due to the sergeant's careless haste, the entire garrison now knows of the unfortunate incident and, I regret to say, many of our modern

168

youth seem to feel they owe their loyalty to the official government."

"There may be a way to save face for everyone at all important," the other said. "The medical officer says that Okinawan was not killed last night, after all. He feels the man was killed with a ninja blow not more than a few hours ago. More important, he is willing to so state, officially."

The one who seemed to be the superior now asked, "Who could have done such a thing, then, if not that unpleasant half-breed?"

"The man was obviously murdered by someone he knew much better," his informant said. "He was found stark naked. There was no sign of a struggle, and the medical officer feels his uniform was removed before he died."

"*Hai*, I have killed often enough to know about such delicate matters. You are suggesting, perhaps, the victim took his clothes off willingly before he was taken by surprise?"

"Alas, it seems to be so. You know how Okinawans are. I have taken the liberty of questioning his fellow squad members. They told me he was inclined to disgusting practices. On more than one occasion he is said to have made improper and unwelcome advances to other men. His sergeant had warned him about his vices. He would seem to have learned to control himself better after his last beating. But perhaps this morning he lost control of his desires again, and this time, did not choose his intended partner at all wisely."

There was a long silence above. Ki grinned wolfishly in the darkness under them. Then the superior official said, "Forgive me. I know you mean well. But your idea is more disgusting than reporting him killed by a guest."

The other sipped some tea loudly before he said, "It shall of course be reported any way my elder and wiser host finds desirable. But may I humbly point out no face is lost, my way?"

"How can you say that?"

"*Hai,* I have given long consideration to how it may look on paper. In the first place, should we report a guard killed by a fleeing guest, it is most possible someone in Tokyo may wish to know why we were holding that half-breed to begin with. Even if Tokyo is satisfied with the charges we invented, there is still the loss of face to the guard detail that let such a thing as an escape happen!"

"They *did* let it happen. They *should* feel loss of face!"

"They do. But those on our side are positioned too valuably for us to spare. On the other hand, that disgusting Okinawan would never have been recruited as an Imperial Marine under the old system. Before the overthrow of the shogunate no Okinawans were even allowed to bear arms. Is it the fault of his officers and brave comrades that some misguided fool in the *new* government allowed the recruitment of lesser breeds?"

His superior gave a deep, pleased groan. *"Hai!* It was all the fault of the new government in Tokyo! No true Japanese lost face by dispatching such a brute as he deserved. In the good old days a fighting man was *supposed* to kill someone who insulted his manhood. You shall report the death as closed. A matter of personal honor."

"With your permission, master, it would look just a little bit better if we worded it more delicately. I told the dead man's corporal he could wipe out the dishonor to his squad if he confessed that he was the one who dealt with the degenerate himself."

"He is willing to sign such a confession?"

"He already has. It says he took the Okinawan aside to beat him privately for behaving so in public. The brute fought back. The corporal only did what he had to, then. He agrees the loss of one month's pay and confinement to the post, with no demotion, is just punishment for his failure to report the matter to his sergeant before the body was found."

"That seems more generous than he deserves, but let it

170

stand. What about the matter of the missing uniform?"

"Who is likely to ask, if nothing about it is reported to headquarters in Tokyo? Between the two of us, it seems likely one of the privates who found the body found extra clothing desirable, since they have some difficulty keeping up appearances on such a modest salary. May we get on to more important matters, now?"

"You mean that American woman and her domesticated ape in the brown tweed? What about them?"

Ki perked up. "They are at the General Grant, as they were sent. The man went to a telegraph office a few minutes ago. Our agent was unable to learn what messages he might have received there. But he got close enough to see that Longarm *sent* none. After that, Longarm returned to their hotel. Neither has been out since. They may suspect they are under observation. It won't help them much if they decide to make their next move after dark. The street out front is brightly lit at night."

"What if they decide to leave by the back way?"

"I hope they do. It would not have been desirable to kill two U. S. citizens on Japanese diplomatic property. But who is to say what might happen to innocent travelers in such a notorious seaport? Our agents report Mexicans moving freely in that part of town, even in and out of the hotel itself. We are in a position to prove they left here this morning, guns and all. Can we be held responsible if Mexicans or even American sailors rob and kill them in some dark alley far from here?"

The one with the final say growled, "You are not thinking like a Go master. Jessica Starbuck is no use to the dragon lying dead in some alley. I desire those orders changed at once. I want them followed, not killed. For they shall lead us to the one called Ki. And once we know where all of them are on the board, we can start the game again!"

Ki didn't like the sound of that at all. The man above him must not have, either. "I do not understand, honorable

171

master," he said. "I assumed this particular game was not going well and that it was time to cover the board with blood and perhaps start a new game, with less skillful opponents."

His superior groaned in discomfort or courtesy. "I am not the master dragon. Like you, I exist to obey orders, and we were ordered to gain a controlling interest in Starbuck Enterprises, not to enjoy a bloodbath."

The wiser head above Ki's own protested, "The white girl knows too much, now, and with both Longarm and that Ki backing her——"

"We have our orders," his superior cut in. "Nobody told us it would be easy. They told us what to *do*. If you wish to withdraw, I shall be honored if you ask me to be your second when you take up your ko-dashi, wrapped in fresh rice paper!"

There was a long silence. Then Ki heard, "I am not ready to commit seppuku yet. I feel our chances of coming out of this confusing game with honor would be better if we could at least eliminate two of her pieces from the board. Both Ki and Longarm only serve to confuse the girl's blonde head. If we could only take *them* out . . ."

"Do it," his superior commanded. "We have no orders about them at all. The abduction of Ki only caused us trouble without bending her to our will. Longarm, as you say, is as dangerous as her usual bodyguard, and seems to encourage her willful ways. *Hai*, wait until we get them all together, kill both her men, and we'll see how defiant she is."

People who dwelt in paper houses didn't waste much money on door locks. Japanese rich enough to burglarize had hired guards to watch their property when they went out. In this case, they had a detachment of Marines posted all around their private quarters. So Ki found it childishly simple to snake his way into the interior patio of another dwelling, where nobody seemed to be home, and simply

172

slide a shoji open, calling out politely just in case.

There wasn't even a maid on duty. An American burglar might have assumed there was nothing in the bare spartan rooms worth stealing. Ki knew the carpentry of his mother's people held some surprises. The people who didn't seem to be home this afternoon weren't being sneaky. They simply felt anything not in use at the moment should be out of sight. Ki found what he was looking for after sliding only three or four panels open.

The civilian suit was too small for him. It couldn't be helped. The hat and shoes made up for it a little by being too large.

Ki had planned to hide until dark and then go over the wall. Now that he knew the Black Dragons were watching Jessie and had assumed he was long gone, Ki couldn't wait. He knew the Yamaha warehouse was still safe. At least he hadn't heard it mentioned by the plotters. If he could somehow make it that far and then get word to Jessie and Longarm, the dragons wouldn't move in on them before they knew where he was.

He didn't want to get his new outfit dirty, silly as it must look on him, so he stepped boldly out the front way and headed for the front gate.

Ki knew the consulate had many visitors during daylight hours, of all sizes, shapes, and races. He knew the guard at the gate would surely demand to see credentials before letting anyone on the grounds. He hoped, like most Japanese servants, the guard would pretend to be invisible to anyone he assumed to be a guest on his way *out*.

Ki worked his way around the main building, bowing to a pair of kimono-clad ladies he passed. They only giggled. The gate was in view now. Better yet, the guard was examining the papers of some Mexicans with a cartload of firewood. Ki took a deep breath and walked boldly through on the far side of the firewood cart. The Marine posted there shot him a curious look but said not a word.

Ki walked across the avenue, trying to ignore the itch of

the bull's-eye he was feeling just between his shoulder blades. He got to the far side, turned right, and strolled under the shade of the pepper trees some early Spanish saint had planted for him so considerately. Ki swung around the first corner and kept on until he came to a men's store. He stepped inside and, as the shop clerk responded to the bell over the door, Ki said, "I need a whole new outfit."

The older man nodded. "That's for sure. What happened old son? Get caught in the rain?"

Ki smiled sheepishly and said, "Close enough. One thing we have to settle first. I'm as unlucky at cards as I am at picking mail-order duds. So he'd better discuss my credit first."

The older man shot him a keen look. "I admire a gent who don't beat about the bush, old son. Is your credit any good?"

"It is. I'm ramrod of the Circle Star, a well-respected Texas outfit. I can't prove it, but if you're willing to take my word I'm willing to pay double."

The canny old merchant looked him over a long time. "I'm a gambling man, myself. But double or nothing hardly seems fair when the odds are this risky," he finally said.

Ki nodded in agreement. "I only want to look cow, not high society. I need a work shirt, a pair of jeans, a hat, and a pair of boots. You write it up and I'll wire you three times as much as soon as I can."

"Well, you mind if the boots is secondhand? I got a pair of Texas boots as security off a man who never come back after I grubstaked him to a prospecting trip south of the border."

Ki said, "If I can get them on I'll take them. Do we have a deal?"

"I reckon so. Don't tell my old woman if she come out of the back, though. I promised her I'd cut down on my drinking, too, but damned if I don't think you're a good sport."

A few minutes later Ki was back outside, attracting much less attention, now, since his face was shaded by the brim of his new black Stetson and he was built much like any other cowhand. The boots were more than used. They were just about done for. On the other hand, he didn't have to worry about breaking them in, and he had a long way to go in them.

He went first, of course, to the Yamaha warehouse a quarter of a mile down the waterfront. He stood in the shade across the way for a while, not seeing much. The shoreward doorway gaped open and he sensed movement in the dark interior. He was still on the prod when a familiar figure came out, wearing an off-the-shoulder Mexican-style blouse and a bright green skirt. As she crossed to his side Ki headed her off, softly calling, "Yoko-San?"

The girl turned with a frown. "That's Concepción to you, cowboy. I hope you don't mean to make that dumb remark about Oriental gals, for I'm only half Japanese, and it wouldn't be true in any case." Then she saw who it was and gasped, "Ki! What are you doing here? Don't you know a whole Japanese army is looking for you?"

"I'm glad you remember me, Yoko-San. Last time I saw you you were just a little thing."

She moved closer, took him by one arm, and said, "Never mind that 'San' business. Start walking this little thing away from here as if we were sweethearts." She sighed. "That ain't hard, for me, at least. Of *course* I couldn't forget you, you big goof. How many of us are there?"

He started to ask what she meant by "us." But, of course, they were both half Japanese.

Yoko was going on about Jessie being in town and at the General Grant.

Ki hushed her. "I know all about that. I got to eavesdrop on the local head of the Black Dragons. I sure wish I'd gotten a better look at his face. But let's not worry about that now. Yoko, I need some weapons, some money, and a good mount, in that order."

175

"You've got them. Fortunately, I don't live at home these days. My father's a dear, but a Japanese father in a kimono and tabis can sure discourage gentleman callers. We're headed for my shack in the Mexican quarter. First we'll get you out of this hot sun and then I'll sneak all the things you need in to you. Horses are no problem. I know my dad will give me money for you. As to weaponry, I ain't so sure. Dad has a brace of old cap-and-ball revolvers at home, but he mostly relies on those funny Japanese creations he brought over here with him years ago. You'd never know it, just looking at him, but one time, when I was little and they were beating up on Chinese for some reason, a mess of waterfront toughs came in the shop to pester us and . . . well, the harbor was close and there wasn't really that much blood to clean up."

Ki smiled grimly and said, "Guns can be noisy. I can fashion a fighting *bo* from any handy stick. Ask your father if he can spare me a knife and perhaps a dozen *shuriken* stars."

"I'll bring the revolvers, too. That's my place ahead, the mustard-yellow shack with the white picket fence. Where are you figuring on going after I get all that stuff for you, Ki?"

"Texas, if I can get word to Jessie that I'm running free for the Circle Star and that she should do the same. The Black Dragons are expecting us to meet up closer and head home together. We may throw them off if we each cut out solo, see?"

Yoko said, "Up to a point. They'll surely be watching the rail depot, and even a good horse won't be much improvement. There are only a few passes over the Coast Range and even fewer safe trails across the Colorado desert on the far side. I may be just a girl, but I'll bet *I* could bottle one rider up in this corner of the California coast pretty good."

She led him inside. "I know," he said. "My best bet would be a night ride south."

She sat him on her bed, about the only substantial piece of furniture in her tiny one-room shack, as she poured saké for them both and said, "You must be loco, Ki. My mother went to a lot of trouble to get *out* of the Baja. Besides, Texas can't be *that* way!"

He accepted his small cup. "Sure it is, in a way. I can work my way home by way of Mexico easier than I can beeline with that gang setting up ambushes all the way home. My God, what did you spike this saké with, Yoko?"

She sat beside him. "Pulque. The bottle was running low. We have to make the best of both worlds. I know my mother's country better than you, if you think you can get to Texas by way of Mexico. Forgetting that the Baja can be injurious to one's health, you'd have the Sonora Desert to cross at this time of the year and, even if you could, the Sonora Hills beyond are infested with Yaqui. They're a lot like your Apache, only ten times meaner. Even if you got through Yaqui country, you'd still have *los rurales* to worry about all the way to, say, El Paso. I know you mean well, Ki, but you don't look as Mexican as me. *Los rurales* would be only too happy to gun a lone gringo for his hat and boots. Hat, at least, in your case. Do you want me to see if I can pick you up some decent boots?"

He shook his head. "No, thanks. Just what I asked for, and I'll make it right by you and your dad once I get home. I'm open to suggestions as to how we can get that message to Jessie at the General Grant. If they're watching her, they'll be sure to notice anyone who looks at all Oriental."

Yoko said, "That's easy. We have a couple of old Anglos working for us. Just tell me what you want one of them to tell Jessie and I'll have him drop by at quitting time, when the streets are crowded."

He finished his disgusting drink. "That's great. All Jessie needs to know is that I'm all right and headed for home by way of the Baja. You'd better not write it down. Anyone should be able to remember a message as simple as that."

Yoko tried to press more of her odd drink on him. Ki shook his head. "I'd better not. I have a long night ahead of me, and I didn't get any sleep last night, either."

"Why don't you stretch out here, then? My Mexican neighbors all around are enjoying their siestas about now. So why should you be different?"

"That's really a tempting offer, Yoko. I could use a few hours' sleep, and I can't make a move before sundown, in any case."

She rose, patted his shoulder, and said, "There's nothing to stop you, then. I've got a key. I have to, in this part of town. I'll lock up after me and you can get undressed and sleep until I get back with all the things you need."

He told her she was an angel. She dimpled and said, "As a matter of fact, my full name is Yoko Concepción Angelita Asada Tahara. So *sayonara*."

She left him laughing and as she locked the door behind her Ki got undressed, pulled down the counterpane, and lay on the bed. She was a pretty little thing, but sort of forward for a properly-brought-up Japanese girl.

Then Ki grimaced and said aloud, "Damn it, you're doing it yourself and you, of all people, should know better!"

Like him, Yoko was a neither-nor, a foot planted in two very different cultures as she tried to decide which set of rules to live by. And, like him, she had to make her own rules up as she went along. What mattered was that she was on his side. Neither-nors didn't have enough trustworthy friends to be picky about them. She had accepted him as he was. The least he could do for her would be to accept her the same way.

★

Chapter 14

San Diego would always be admired for its unusually fine
weather. But into each Eden *some* rain had to fall, and that
unseasonable typhoon out in the Pacific was a whopper.

Longarm and Lone Star were wearing rain slickers as
they strode boldly out the front entrance of their hotel late
that afternoon.

They knew their bright slickers stood out, even in the
quitting-time crowds running for home in the increasing
downpour. But, as Longarm had pointed out, there was no
way to sneak away from a staked-out hotel in any case.
Both of them were wearing their gun rigs under the stiff,
fish-oil-scented yellow poplin. Both had long since removed the linings from the side pockets in order to get at
the same should the need arise. Lone Star had taken further
advantage of her unfashionable outerwear. A lady in a big
town attracted undue attention striding about in men's
pants. But who was to say whether she had anything on at
all under the ankle-length, shapeless slicker? So her

shapely form was dressed for serious action in a man's hickory shirt and skin-tight denim jeans. Not wanting to stretch her luck, she had put her spurs in a side pocket. A lady had a right to wear high-heeled boots and a broad-brimmed hat in a rainstorm, didn't she?

They separated at the corner to attend to different chores, whether it confused anyone tailing them or not. Longarm went to the Western Union to find yet another message from Billy Vail. This one was less politely worded. Western Union had deleted a good third of the words in the interests of public decency. But, as far as Longarm could make out, Billy seemed curious if not chagrined about Longarm's failure to join the posse up near El Cajon.

Longarm picked up a yellow telegram form to wire back: "ANY FOOL CAN SEARCH FOR STALE SIGN IN GULLYWASHER WE AINT ENJOYING OUT HERE STOP AM INVESTIGATING OTHER LEADS STOP LONG."

He handed his message to the desk clerk and said, "Send this day rates, collect. That ought to hold him."

Meanwhile, Lone Star was at a livery she knew from earlier dealings to be as reliable as such dismal outfits tended to be. She demanded to speak with the owner rather than the stableboy who usually picked mounts for townee riders. She told the older man who she was. He seemed impressed even before she produced a bankroll to back her brag. "I don't want to hire any mounts," she said. "I want to *buy* two good ones. I don't know when, if ever, I'll get a chance to return, either. But if I do get back here, and you've sold me crowbait, watch out. I don't cheat at business and I don't like to be cheated. I'll need two stock saddles and bridles as well. Center-fire and Spanish bit for me. Double-rig roper and army bit for my friend. He's sort of sentimental, and big enough to get away with it."

The stable owner led her back to the stall and ordered his helper to run Old Buck and Ribbon out in the paddock for Miss Jessie's inspection. Neither critter liked it much.

But as they milled about in the rain she could see they both had four legs, and all eight seemed to work right. It was easy to see why the bigger buckskin was called Old Buck. She asked why the more graceful black Morgan mare was called Ribbon. "She won a blue ribbon at the state fair one time, Miss Jessie," they told her.

"I suspect that was some time ago. I make her about twelve, and I'm being polite to another lady," she replied.

The old horse trader chuckled. "Anyone can see you has an eye for horseflesh, ma'am. But you said you wanted serious mounts, and there's enough left in that old Morgan to get you a mile or more at serious speed."

"She does have nice lines, and look at her frisk in the rain. She won that ribbon as a show horse, right?"

"Not exactly, Miss Jessie. They had a bucking contest up in Sacramento that time and they had to give the prize to someone in the end. But, like you said, that was in her younger days. She ain't hurt nobody, serious, for at least a year."

Lone Star raised an eyebrow. "I'll shove Ribbon on the back of the stove for now. What's the bad news about the buckskin?"

"Oh, Old Buck's a fine stud. Gentle as a lamb, even though he was never cut, and worked many a roundup for the Hash Knife, other side of the mountains."

"What's he doing in a riding stable if he's a trained cow pony?"

The old man hesitated, then said, "Them's the two best mounts I can sell you on such short notice, ma'am."

She said, "I didn't ask you that. I asked what's wrong with the buckskin stud."

"Well, he's sort of willsome, ma'am. As you can see, he's big for a cowpony, and it takes a big man to handle Old Buck when he takes it in his barrel head he'd like to knock off early, or . . . There's no delicate way of putting it—get sort of forward with a mare or, failing that, a range cow in heat."

Lone Star tried not to laugh. "He may be well matched

181

for his rider, after all. You're sure there's nothing wrong with his wind?" she asked.

"Oh, no, ma'am. They tell me he once chased a female mustang thirty miles after throwing his rider and licking her wild stud in a fair fight. That could be why they sold him to us, after. You won't have to worry about him and Ribbon, though. They don't like each other, even when she's in heat, and she ain't due for a month or more."

Lone Star stared soberly at the unlikely pair from under the dripping brim of her hat. "To tell the truth, I hadn't planned on a mean-streaked mare and a lovesick stud. But they both look lively, for livery plugs, so let's talk money."

He wanted way too much for two unreliable mounts and well-worn tack that looked more repaired than "broken-in," as he insisted on describing it. Alex Starbuck had left his only child well provided for indeed, but before he had died he'd lectured her on the value of money more than some rich fathers tended to. He'd told her more than once, "I intend for you to grow up smart as well as rich, kid. So always remember, *losing* money is a whole lot easier than *making* it. Never peel off a dollar bill without picturing the one hundred copper pennies it stands for, and don't ever forget how much a penny means to a poor kid. You'll never want for penny whistles or ribbon bows, Jessie. Some day you'll be eating in fancy places where a steak costs as much as some less fortunate gals see for a whole hot day in a cotton field. Go ahead and enjoy the fine wine and fancy food that comes with the good life I've planned for you. Go ahead and tip the waiter generous, for I've raised you to be generous. But don't ever let 'em sucker you with flattery into tipping more than ten percent. For a fool and her money are soon parted, and I haven't raised you to die poor!"

Remembering her dad's advice, Lone Star beat the horse trader down by half and told him he was still taking advantage of a helpless woman.

In the end they shook on it, with him saying sadly, "I'm

182

glad it's such a slow rainy day. For I'd never live it down if the boys knew I'd been skint-so by a girl-child young enough to be my own. Can I at least say I gave in because you was so pretty?"

She thanked him for his rough gallantry and helped him bridle and saddle the two mounts. Ribbon tried to bite her hand, but a hard left jab to the nuzzle made the mean-streaked mare reconsider her smaller than usual enemy. Only Ribbon remembered the cruel stableboy of her youth, who had convinced her all mankind was her sworn enemy. Since then, Ribbon had learned to bide her time with riders who seemed as alert as she was to the advantages each side held in the eternal love-hate relationship between two species that had little else in common.

Ribbon made her next move halfway back to the General Grant. As Lone Star rode her in the rain, leading Old Buck, Ribbon waited until they were passing a cast-iron lamppost before she danced sideways, her steel-shod hooves sparking on the granite paving blocks, to see how Lone Star felt about a broken knee.

The born horsewoman wasn't hurt as much as her mount when they crashed broadside into the solidly set lamppost. She'd kicked her right foot free of the stirrup and swung her leg back to stand in the left stirrup like a ballerina as they hit. She yanked back hard on the Spanish bit. Trained to ride by *vaqueros*, she knew the wicked-looking bit they preferred could be gentle in the mouth of a willing mount and as cruel as it looked if need be. Ribbon froze in place obediently, as any horse on earth would have done with cruel steel cutting into the roof of its mouth. But Jessie wasn't finished. She swung gracefully from the saddle, holding Ribbon firmly under control with the Spanish bit, until she could clamp her free hand over the mare's muzzle, pinching both nostrils shut.

Now, as anyone should know, no animal at all related to the horse family can breathe through its mouth. Unlike humans and other more fortunate critters, the mouth of a horse was designed only for eating and the nose only for breathing. The two passages are not connected. So, despite their different sizes and strengths, Jessie was strangling the mean-streaked mare as surely as if she'd been a giantess big enough to get her hands around Ribbon's big throat. The willful mare struggled, of course. Even Old Buck nickered nervously at the end of his lead line as he sensed the dismay of his stablemate. But Lone Star had them both under control as she stated flatly, "I can be a bitch, too, Ribbon. So are we going to act like ladies, or do you want me to kill you, here and now?"

The words meant nothing to Ribbon, but there was no mistaking their intent. Had she been able to reply, Ribbon would have been saying she was sorry and that she'd never do it again. All she could manage was to go sort of glassy-eyed as she tried in vain to breathe. Lone Star waited until she saw the mare was about to collapse. Then she let go of Ribbon's muzzle and reached in her slicker with her free hand, saying pleasantly, "That's better, dear. Do you promise to be a good little girl if I let you out of the corner?"

Then she fed Ribbon the lump of hotel dining-room sugar she'd brought along with just such an emergency in mind. Ribbon liked the sugar. She was still confused as hell as Jessie remounted and spurred her forward again. Old Buck followed, as amused as his dim understanding could make a horse feel. He didn't know what the small human had done. But he was glad the mare he knew better had somehow been made to behave. The pretty black creature had bit him more than once, and she'd been stupid to kick that stableboy that time, before they'd all been fed. Any creature in their position had to know one hurt the small master beasts when there was a good reason, not when they were trying to feed or water one.

Lone Star made it back to the hotel without further incident. As she dismounted to tether both mounts to the hitching rail out front, a shabby stranger approached her in the rain. She repressed a grimace of distaste and reached in

184

her jeans. For though her dad had taught her to be careful with pennies, a beggar out in such a driving rain had to be truly desperate.

But the old bearded Anglo she'd taken for a beggar ticked the dripping brim of his cap at her and said, "They wouldn't let me wait inside, Miss Jessie, so I been waiting here."

"Do I know you, sir?" she asked.

"I doubt it," he answered, "but I've seen you afore, talking business at the warehouse, and you ain't easy to forget. I wasn't always this old and ugly. I wasn't sent here to admire you, though. Miss Concepción sent me here with a message for you and that deputy pal of yourn."

"Concepción? She says she knows me, sir?"

"Oh, that's right, she used to be calt Yoko afore she got so fancy. Seems like yesteryear she was just a bitty girl-child playing hide and seek amongst the piled silk bales. Anyhow, she told me to tell you some Kiowa is safely in the box, whatever that means."

Lone Star frowned and said, "That doesn't mean anything to me, the way you just worded it, sir. Are you sure she didn't say Ki, not Kiowa?"

He wiped his dripping nose. "Yeah, that was it. He wants you to know he's all right and hiding in the box, or on a box, or some such thing. Miss Concepción said that was all you needed to know. So that's likely why it was all she told me to tell you."

"I don't understand the part about the box. He can't be hoping to ship himself all the way back to Texas in some crate!"

The shabby old man shrugged. "I thought it sounded dumb, too, but I just follow orders from my betters. So now I've told you all I know and I'd best get out of here. They said I might be getting watched by someone and that I was to talk to you inside. But that snooty desk clerk inside chased me out. So here we are, and now I'd better go."

Lone Star agreed but said, "Wait. I'd better give you the money you just asked for."

He protested, "Lady, I ain't no infernal beggar. I may look like one. But I *work* for my drinking money, most days, anyway. Sometimes I get to feeling poorly, but the old man I works for is an understanding cuss."

Lone Star pressed two bits on him anyway. "Anyone can see you're a proud working man, sir. But in case we're being watched, can't you *pretend* to be a street beggar for me, just this once, sir?"

He grinned at her, exposing a dreadful need of dental care, and ticked his brim to her again. "All right. I mean to spend it well, drinking to the health of a great lady, if you don't mind."

She smiled at him and told him she felt honored. As he shuffled away in the rain Longarm came into view from the other way. He joined her and asked what was up. She repeated Yoko and Ki's odd message. He said, "Let's study on it out of this rain. It don't make sense, wet or dry. I hope that bigger horse is for me?"

"Yes. They tell me *he's* too horny for his own good, too. Never mind the damned mounts, Custis. What on earth do you think Ki's up to?"

They were in the lobby by this time. The desk clerk shot them an annoyed but resigned look as they dripped their way across a rug that was already wet and muddy enough. On the stairs, Longarm said, "One thing's for sure. There's no mistaking *Billy Vail's* intent. I got to get you out of this fix so's I can chase that Nakamura gang some more, sudden. Billy knows Western Union tends to cross out the worst things he calls me over their wire. But he knows I still know what blankety-blank-blank means."

"If only they'd sent that old drunk with a written message instead of entrusting it to his rum-soaked memory. He got Ki wrong, calling him a Kiowa. Lord only knows what he might have turned into a *box!*"

Longarm said, "If that Miss Yoko is part Mexican

there's no saying how *she* might mangle English. The first thing that makes sense if Baja, but not when you really study on it. The Baja is what they call the country south of Tijuana, but Ki would be dumb to head that way, even if he don't know El Gato."

"He could be planning to work his way back to Texas by way of Mexico, don't you think?" she asked.

"Not if he knows Mexico half as well as I do. I told you, once, about the time I checked out the Laredo Loop, running stolen cows from Texas to Arizona by way of some awful country. I damn near wound up killed, and I only had to worry about mean Mexicans and Yaqui. Ki had to know he has them lizards trailing him and, once he's out on open desert, that big breed will be visible for many a mile."

They had reached their room by now. She started to peel off her wet slicker. "Of course, if Ki meant to hide in some kind of shipping crate or chest—"

"El Cajon!" Longarm cut in. "Don't take that slicker off! We got to get our gear together and check out to do some soggy riding. Lord knows what in thunder Ki aims to do up in El Cajon, but, do the vigilantes wonder about his looks he could wind up rope dancing for what them *other* Japanese done this very day."

She started to ask what he was talking about, but she spoke Spanish better than he did. So she nodded and said, "How stupid of me! I'd forgotten how Mexican little Yoko likes to act and, of course, El Cajon means 'the chest!' But why do you suppose they call a mountain stage stop a chest, dear?"

He said, "Box canyons up that way. Keep packing. It ain't far to ride. But I'd sure hate to meet up with Ki again, hanging from a canyon oak."

She worked fast, rolling her things into a tight saddle roll on the bed. "I'm going as fast as I can. What about these yellow slickers, dear? Wouldn't we be harder to follow if we weren't wearing them?"

He said, "We'd be wetter, too. There's no way to leave this fool hotel without being noticed, Jessie. On the other hand, I've put many an Indian off my trail in hilly chaparral, and how good could an infernal lizard be at trailing in the dark?"

As they were debating this, the old man who had delivered Yoko's garbled message was having his own problems, a few blocks away, in a dark alley. The two black-clad Japanese who had dragged him in off the street had been cruel village bullies even before the Black Dragon had recruited them and given them ninja training. So the old man was in considerable pain as one held him, helpless, for the other to question. As he was kneed again, the old man gasped and insisted, "You got the wrong man, damn it! I told you. My name is John Hall and I'm on the beach with a bad-conduct discharge from the Pacific Fleet out yonder. You know I got no more money, now that you've turnt my pockets inside out!"

His questioner hissed, "We were not robbers. You know what we want, you old fool!"

Their victim groaned. "I'm old and ugly even if I went in for such things."

The dragon slapped his face again, just soft enough to keep from knocking him out, but hardly gently, as he insisted, "You will tell us what that message you just delivered was. *Hai*, and you will tell us who sent it, and where they might be right now!"

"I don't know what you're talking about, gents. I asked a nice lady if she'd stake me to a cup of coffee, and you *got* the two bits she gave me. So lemme go, damn it!"

His questioner placed the blade of a throwing knife against the old man's scrawny throat and insisted, "We do not have time to play games with you, John Hall. You know we know the woman we saw you talking to just now was Jessie Starbuck."

"Do tell? Well, whoever she was, she was a gracious lady who called me sir. So, if you ain't friends of her'n, I got nothing to say about her to the likes of you."

The tip of the blade drew a dotted line of blood beads across the old man's throat as its owner hissed, "Sing, damn you!"

The old man shrugged and said nothing.

The black-clad dragon swore, drove the blade into the old man's guts, and twisted. As they let go of him to vanish down the alley he groaned and muttered, "I figured they meant to end it something like that." Then, clutching at his ripped-open belly, he staggered back to the street and collapsed under a streetlamp. He was still breathing when a copper badge who'd run him in many a more pleasant evening shook him by the shoulder and asked, "Who done this to you, Matty?"

The dying man coughed blood, swallowed some, and muttered, "A couple of ninja boys. Bad Japs. I know about such things because when I was still alive I worked for some *decent* ones. It's a funny thing, Ryan. But once you get a job with a decent Japanese he never fires you, no matter what you do, as long as you show him *some* loyalty."

He coughed again and added, "I reckon I just did and, guess what, a pretty lady smiled at me, and called me sir, tonight. I reckon that makes all this worth it, don't you?"

★

Chapter 15

Ki was neither in the Baja nor El Cajon at the moment. He was in Yoko's bed. He would have still been sleeping, but Ki was a hard man to move in on, even when he wasn't on the alert. So Yoko almost got her neck broken as she climbed in bed with him. But Ki figured out, just in time, who she had to be. He let go of her long hair and grunted, "Don't ever try that again. It's a good thing you're naked. I was about to kill you until I realized that. Why are you naked, by the way?"

She nursed her bruised upper arm in the darkness. "I'll just bet those finger marks show in the morning, you mean old thing. How many damned hands have you got? It felt like I was mixed up with a devil-fish just now."

"I just told you how lucky you were. That's not the question I asked."

She lay down beside him as she said, "Well, hell, it's my bed we're in, after all. I got the horses tied out back. I brought everything else in with me. It's raining fire and salt outside, and I got so wet running your errands that I decided I'd better change. Then, as long as I was undressed anyway..."

"Where do you think you're going with that hand, Yoko-San?" he cut in.

She giggled. "We'll know when it gets there, won't we? I told you not to talk so formal to me, Ki. I told you I've felt more Mexican than Japanese since I've been old enough to feel my sort of hot blood taking over."

He sighed and said, "Stop the foolishness, Yoko. I'm trying to remember your father is a friend and that you're ... what, sixteen?"

She said, *"Going* on sixteen."

"This isn't fair," he said. "This is the *second* damned night I've had to do without a woman."

She swore in Japanese and Spanish before she added, in English, "Son of a bitch! I got him horses, I got him weapons and money, I damn near got killed, and now he won't do as I want!"

Ki laughed, but said, "I hope you didn't get the things I asked for by almost getting killed."

She said, "I didn't have to. I just had to tell my dad who I wanted 'em for."

Ki got off the bed, with Yoko still clinging to his hand. "Maybe you'll change your mind when we're riding south together tomorrow," she pouted.

He asked her what on earth she meant by that, explaining, "I planned on riding south about midnight, alone, Yoko."

"Don't be silly," she said. "It's far too dangerous, Ki."

"That's what I just said. I'd be a fool even to consider taking a slip of a girl like you as far south as Tijuana!"

She said, "You'd be even sillier trying it alone. My mother was from the Baja, *querido.* I have friends and relations down that way. You don't. To them you'd just be a strange, rather spooky-looking gringo. You have to let me help you, at least as far as Sonora."

Ki didn't answer. When she took his hand and murmured, "Ki?" he said, "I'm thinking about it."

192

The California Coast Ranges were old and tired, with a lot of their rough edges rubbed off by Father Time and Mother Nature. What Californians insisted on calling canyons looked more like glorified gullies to a rider who'd seen the real canyonlands of the Four Corners country. But Longarm warned Lone Star to take care, anyway, as they followed the winding wagon trace up to El Cajon in the rain-swept darkness. It hardly mattered whether a horse and rider went over a sheer cliff or a mighty steep slope in the dark.

It was a hell of a way to get to know untested mounts, they both knew. They could barely make out the rutted wagon trace they followed and, while horses had better night vision, they didn't know the twisting mountain road any better than their riders. In some places it would have been treacherous enough on a bright sunny day.

They were walking their mounts around a bend with a roadcut rising sheer to their left and the other side dropping off into the darkness to inky nowhere when Lone Star said, "Listen. I think there's someone on the trace behind us!"

"No you don't," Longarm said. "They're there for sure. I make it three riders or more. The question before the house is whether they're following us or just using a public right-of-way."

Jessie said there was one way to find out and spurred her mare forward. Longarm cursed and followed, since he had no other choice. He and Old Buck chased Lone Star and Ribbon around the scary bend and caught up a quarter of a mile on as Lone Star reined in.

He said, "Jessie, this is no time and hardly the place to lope a pony." Then he cocked his head to listen, too, and said, "You're right. They're pacing us. I hope you scared them as much as you just scared me. Now they're sitting their mounts, mayhaps half a mile back. Sneaky sons of bitches, ain't they?"

"Plenty of places to set up a warm welcome for them, dear," she suggested, pointing to a clump of scrub oak on the uphill side of the trail.

"Sounds tedious as well as soggy, Jessie," he said. "Listen tight and you'll hear they're back there waiting for us to proceed. I'd say they had orders to follow us, not to move in, till we lead them to Ki, at least."

She sighed. "I think you're right. So what do we do? I'm not about to lead anyone but you to Ki and I'm getting wet just sitting here."

"Hell, girl, you've *been* wet since we rode through that chaparral just outside town to see if we could throw 'em off. As we didn't, we'll have to do it another way. Ride on. Let's jar 'em back to feeling smart some more."

They did and, sure enough, they could make out the sound of hoofbeats moving at the same speed well behind them, but not as well behind them as before.

"They've closed the gap some," Longarm said. "We must have worried them with that long moment of silent prayer. Steady as she goes, and let's see if they mean to keep their distance or if I got a night fight on my hands."

She patted the stock of her saddle gun grimly and said, "You mean if *we* have a night fight on our hands, don't you?"

Longarm had his own old Winchester aboard his new saddle, with his throw rope hanging next to it. But he said, "They seem to be pacing us discreetly enough. They're too slick to ride into the usual bushwhack and, even if they wasn't, I don't like the odds."

"Pooh, we've won a fight or two at worse odds than two against three or four at the most, dear."

"I know. I still have nightmares about 'em. The hills all around are built wrong for a stand, Jessie. No matter where we forted up they could circle through this soaked-soft chaparral and come at us every way at once. I got a better notion. Here. Take my reins a spell while I unlash this fool rope. Ain't wet latigo leather a bitch when it's knotted, though?"

She did as she was told and led Old Buck as Longarm freed his rope and Winchester. She didn't ask what he was

194

planning. It was obvious to even a ladylike fighting Texan. Longarm waited until they were nearing another hairpin turn. Then he said, "All right, Jessie. Ride like hell and don't stop till my Winchester tells you to stop. Don't come back. I'll join you up the trail if I win and, if I don't, you won't want to tangle with anyone who can get the drop on *me* in the dark."

She said, "I can't stand false modesty. All right, ponies, we have some ground to cover. *Move,* damn it!"

They did, fast, as Longarm rolled out of his saddle on the high side, throw rope in one hand and carbine in the other.

As Lone Star tore on through the darkness with both mounts, Longarm heard other hoofbeats coming at him fast from the other direction. He leaned the Winchester against a handy oak and shook out a community loop to rope another across the trail. Then he wrapped the loose end around the one his carbine was resting against, picked up the same, and moved upslope to await further developments.

They were interesting. He could barely make out the trio of riders taking the hairpin at full gallop in the dark. They failed to see his rope at all until the first two ponies, loping abreast, tripped over it at the same time. They pitched headfirst into the black gulf ahead, riders and all, and vanished in a confusion of crashing and screaming, animal and human. The third rider reined in in time, doing some screaming on his own until Longarm blew him out of his saddle. His spooked mount bolted blindly, hit the same trip, and then it was over the side as well.

Longarm muttered, "Sorry, horse," as he broke cover to have a closer look. The one sprawled face down on the muddy wagon trace was dressed like a cowhand but, when Longarm rolled him over, his face was more Oriental. Longarm wasn't too surprised. He patted the body down for I.D., found none, but figured the thirty-seven dollars and six bits was his now.

He rolled the limp cadaver over the side with a few

good kicks and recoiled his rope. Then, figuring he'd left the wagon trace neat enough, he worked his way down the steep slope, rope slung over a forearm and Winchester cocked, to see how the first two had made out.

They hadn't done too well. He found them at the bottom, sprawled with their busted-up mounts in the running whitewater of a sometime stream. He found no I.D. and collected close to another eighty dollars. By the time he had cursed his way back up the steep slope, clinging to wet bushes that smelled like drug stores, he figured he'd earned it.

Lone Star and their two mounts were waiting for him on the wagon trace. She put her saddle gun back in its scabbard when she saw who had won and asked if he was all right.

He said, "No, I'm mad as a wet hen. Partly because I'm wet as hell and mostly because I told you not to come back till you knew it was safe."

"I heard one shot," she said. "Wasn't that the signal we agreed upon, dear?"

He said, "All right. You ain't just a dumb old girl. I had to gun one because he refused to fall off a mountain in the dark. All three were dressed American and rode stock saddles, even if they did have the stirrups too high. They had no I.D. and their sidearms wasn't worth salvage. One had some of them throwing stars Ki plays with in his saddlebag. All three had throwing knives stuffed in their belts. I make 'em as Japanese windjammers we figured might be trailing us."

She said, "The word is ninja, and I think you're right. Do you realize what we've done, darling? We've thrown the Black Dragon off Ki's trail as well as ours!"

He remounted beside her. "We'd best catch up with him before the vigilantes do, then. He sure picked one hell of a spot for a gent of Oriental persuasion to head for this evening. Of course, he had no way of knowing the Nakamura gang just stopped a stage and stole a white gal where we're going."

"I still don't see why he'd want to head for El Cajon in the first place, Custis. What sort of a place is it?" she asked.

"Tedious, when bandits ain't about. El Cajon's just a wide spot in the road over these mountains. Less important now that the rails have been laid to the south. The stage and freight wagon route still serves a gold mine here and a sawmill there. Don't go too far down the far slope, now. Hell of a desert on the far side. Mayhaps Ki chose to meet us in El Cajon because it's such a dumb place to be he figured them lizards wouldn't think of it."

Ki would have been the first to agree that El Cajon was a dumb place to head for, had anyone asked him. So, as his friends rode east-northeast to meet him there, Ki was riding south-southeast in the same rain. He would have felt even more lost in the dark had not Yoko, in the lead, kept insisting she knew where she was going.

The more civilized way to Tijuana followed the coastline half a night's ride south of San Diego. Yoko had explained and Ki had agreed that a security officer stationed that close to the border had to know the main road, but might not know the smugglers' trails threading southward through the brown hills farther inland. Ki felt better, or less guilty, about letting her tag along once he saw who was doing most of the tagging. As they stopped to rest their mounts atop yet another rise Ki looked back the way they had come and told her, "If this goat trail's really going anywhere, we seem to have it all to ourselves. But won't we have to swing over to the main route as we cross the border, Yoko?"

She asked, "Why? Do you really want to go through the official crossing?"

"Not really. Togo would only have to have one agent posted there to make this whole detour a wasted effort. We can't bank on *every* Black Dragon being Japanese, either. The dragons know as well as we do that Orientals attract attention in these parts, and I've met many a white man

197

who'd sell his mother's false teeth for drinking money. Is there a way into Tijuana perhaps less brightly lit?"

She laughed. "Silly, we don't want to go anywhere near a border town if we don't want anyone to know we're jumping the border. This is not Texas. There's no river to worry a discreet traveler. The border, out here, is only a line on the map. It was drawn by a ruler, across much more complicated land. They keep saying something about a fence some day. Meantime it has not been strung, and neither the Yanquis, *rurales*, nor coyotes can cover every trail through these hills at once."

Ki frowned and asked, "Do you worry about *coyotes* out here, Yoko?"

She laughed. "Not the ones chasing rabbits on four legs. A breed of vermin who haunt the border to prey on the innocent but perhaps sneaky traveler," she explained.

"You mean bandits, then," he said.

She shook her head. "I mean coyotes. They are not manly enough to call bandits. Some are smugglers. Some act as guides who, like me, can lead one across where fewer questions may be asked. Some coyotes will kill you for your boots if they think they can get away with it. Most are all three. They are a sort of hill tribe that has claimed the border country they know so well as its own. But don't worry about them. I just told you I know these hills well. I have often visited my maternal relations in the Baja, and the official crossing can be tiresome."

He shrugged and suggested they move on. As Yoko took the lead again through wet chaparral brushing their stirrups on either side, Ki reviewed the weaponry he had to work with.

The ninja weapons Yoko's father had brought from Japan so long ago were now antiques. While long preserved in oiled rice paper, they could use some sharpening as soon as he got the chance. Unlike an American Green River axe or cavalry saber, Japanese tools and weapons depended more on edge than mass and required constant

198

retouching. The antique Walker Colts had been a more pleasant surprise. For though they dated to before the War between the States, both had been converted from cap-and-ball to fire regular cartridges and Yoko, bless her, had thought to bring along a box of .45 rounds. Ki of course had a well-balanced if somewhat dull throwing knife tucked in his jeans under the gun rig. An outwardly nondescript canvas bag filled with throwing stars, older than he was, was slung to ride just behind his right-hand gun. Both guns were hung cross-draw, partly because that was best for fighting mounted as well as afoot, mostly because that was the way the old gun rig had been made, years ago.

Less obvious was the need for the two heavy water bags slung from the saddle skirts of his bay gelding. Yoko had insisted on packing as much water aboard her painted pony. Ki had been south of the border before. The desert was a bitch, but up to now he'd always felt safe enough with a couple of canteens and, damn it, this coast chaparral was so wet that a water emergency was the last thing he was worried about.

Yoko was worried enough to rein in on the next rise. As Ki joined her there he didn't have to ask why. Despite the rain a campfire was burning brightly in the valley ahead.

He said, "Looks like a cow camp."

"Quien sabe?" she replied. "I know of no cattle outfit this close to the border."

He grimaced. "It might be a dumb place to keep cows one was at all attached to. Border patrol?" he hazarded.

She shook her head. "Not in this weather. They don't take it that serious. We're a little too far north of the border, in any case. It can't be *los coyotes.* They would never build such a large night fire, even this far off the coast road. Whatever it is, we'd better work our way around it. Let me see, now. Ah, *bueno,* I know where we are. We must go back a mile to a fork I know."

Ki said, "No. I've two reasons. I like to know who I'm dodging, and I'm already tired and wet enough. Wait here.

I'm going in to scout that big fire."

He handed her the reins of his bay. She started to protest. But Ki had already vanished in the darkness, so swiftly and so silently she didn't know in which direction. Yoko swore in three languages and asked herself for the hundredth time what on earth she was doing here. She was soaked to the skin. If she didn't catch her death of cold and the hot sun of the Baja didn't kill her, Ki was sure to get her killed some *other* way. But, *Madre de Dios,* he was the first man she'd ever been in love with, and she still hoped to get a chance to prove her love, in spite of his insistence she was too young.

Meanwhile Ki was moving like an Apache, or perhaps like a man the Apache could learn a thing or two from. The patter of raindrops and the drip of rain-soaked chaparral would have disguised any noise he'd made in any case, if Ki was in the habit of making any noise in even dry brush. As he worked his way within pistol range of the still forms lying around or on the blazing bonfire, he saw his efforts had been wasted. There were eight of them. The smell of burned human flesh mingled with the reek of charred wool, canvas, and tanned leather. The bodies had been stripped as well as mutilated. He hoped the two thrown on the fire had been killed first. He could still tell they had been Indian or dark Mexican. A big straw sombrero, painted barn-red, lay near the bare feet of a headless hombre. Everything else they'd owned, if not stolen, had been tossed on the fire. Six or eight wooden *vaquero* saddles—it was hard to tell—made a quite a blaze. Ki didn't see any sign of the horses that had to have gone with them. He eased back up the slope to Yoko and their still accountable horses. He remounted and told her, "Eight of your mother's people. All dead, killed ninja style, with blades, not bullets. I suppose it could have been Indians. What kind of Indians are we talking about in these hills?"

She frowned. "Diegueño, sort of like Yuma or Mojave, only meaner if they're not Mission. I've never heard of

200

Dieto raiding this far north, though. Mission San Diego was built with that in mind. You say the men they killed were Mexican?"

"They rode *vaquero* saddles and one at least owned a big red sombrero in his happier days."

Yoko gasped. "That sounds like Sombrero Rojo! You say he's dead?"

"Somebody who wore a red sombrero sure is. Who are we talking about, Yoko?"

"A coyote. A bad one. That must have been his camp, down there. That east-west valley leads down to the coast road."

"And somebody even nastier jumped the gang," Ki cut in, musing on, half to himself, "All right, we're talking about a bigger or at least a better gang of outlaws, if they got the drop on a local boy in his own hills. Do those coyotes fight among themselves often, Yoko?"

She shrugged. "Do weasels hunt weasels in a world so full of chickens? You say they were cut up ninja style. I say we should turn back, now. Because it's beginning to look as if the Black Dragons may be *ahead* of us, and it was bad enough when I thought they were *behind* us!"

"That was the first thing I thought of. It doesn't work. Togo's ninjas are after Jessie and me, not out to do the world any favors."

She insisted, "They could have guessed we were making for the border and ridden ahead to cut us off. They could have run into coyotes and had to fight them whether they wanted to or not, see?"

He said, "No. Those Mexicans never had a chance to pick a fight with anybody. They were taken by surprise in their own out-of-the-way camp, by experts. If Togo was out to cut us off he'd tell his men to take the easy road and beat us to the border. He'd have his men spread out along it, waiting. He's a strategist, a clever one, not a wild man."

"You said he was a dirty fighter, though."

"Oh, he's *dirty*, all right. I told you how he slickered me

201

into killing his superior so he could move up a notch with no risk at all to himself. That's why I can't see him allowing his men such a free hand. I'm sure he'd tell them to avoid needless bloodshed, and that mess down there was bloody as hell."

Yoko sighed. "Well, if I can't get you to turn back, we'd better go on, then. Are you sure the people who butchered those coyote butchers have gone on?"

"No. I *think* they have. I don't *know* they have. Whoever they are, they're bad news. We'd better backtrack to that other trail you told me about. I wouldn't want a pretty little thing like you meeting anyone like them in the dark. Come to think of it, *I* wouldn't want to meet them in the dark, either."

★

Chapter 16

Longarm and Lone Star were more surprised than Ki would have been when they didn't meet him up at El Cajon. It didn't require a whole lot of searching to suspect their friend wasn't in town. El Cajon was a tiny mountain hamlet. The only night life consisted of the tap room at the stage station and the tapping from the smithy next door. The blacksmith would have been in bed by now, too, had not a couple of posse riders thrown shoes riding in circles over slick rock on the ridges all around.

Most of the posse, tired and wet, were now trying to recover their health with medicinal beverages in the tap room. When Longarm and Lone Star squished in to join them, they drew a few thoughtful glances. But since neither looked at all Oriental and Lone Star's figure was hidden by her shapeless yellow slicker, nobody asked any serious questions as they bellied up to the bar to recover their own health.

The barkeep also served as night wrangler of the whole

shebang. So while he served them willingly enough, he leaned forward across the bar to confide to Longarm, "We don't usually serve ladies so informal. But the dining room is closed and I can see you and your wife has had a long, hard ride. Wouldn't the little lady be comforted if we was to mayhaps send some hot toddies up to your room, though?"

Longarm doubted he could look at her without laughing. He nodded soberly. "That do seem more genteel and proper. But before we dry off and warm up I'd best inform you I am law, federal, and that we come up here looking for a sidekick."

The barkeep called out, "Hey, Roy? There's a federal lawman wants to jaw with you down this way!"

That hadn't been what Longarm wanted. But he saw no harm in it as a rain-soaked older man with a county star joined them, name of Roy Lopez.

"We sure could *use* some trained federal help," he said.

"This here's Jessie. Do you have a telegraph office in this town, Roy?" Longarm asked.

"Not hardly. They're talking about closing down the stage line. Who was you figuring on wiring, the army, now that we've found the gal's body, at least?"

Longarm said, "My office. I don't like to feel missed. But it can wait. You say you found a body, Roy?"

Lopez grimaced. "What they left of it, the sons of . . . Sorry, ma'am. I was brung up proper, but what we found up to Pine Valley has me sort of rattled." He told Longarm, "Her name was Sally Moran. She got on that stage seventeen years old and, according to the doc, a proper maiden. She'll never get any older, now, and the doc says it looks like at least a dozen men . . . ah, never mind. They cut her up with mighty big carving knives as well, afore they left her there for us to find. We never found her duds at all. She was left alongside Pine Creek. We figure they throwed her duds in the creek, first. If so, they're on their way to the Salton Sink in this weather. Pine Valley's up on the divide, you see."

Longarm said, "It would have to be, if it drains into the desert to the east. You'd have noticed if they'd left other sign up there, of course."

"In this unseasonable rain? They could have rid off on spiked stilts for all the good it would have done us! The forest up yonder is thick as a rug. A soaked-through one. Come daylight and a break in this weather, it'll all be packed down the same, whether an elephant's been walking across it or not. Them Mex-dressed Japs are long gone, the sons of . . . Sorry. What really got my dander up is the wolverine way they acted. I mean, sure, a road agent needs money, same as everyone else, and I hope I can say in front of a married lady that some gents just can't behave around pretty gals. But it just wasn't natural to gun unresisting gents just to laugh at 'em, and what sort of animal would do that to a gal, for Pete's sake?"

Longarm said, "I know I wouldn't. I can see you boys are upset at them Orientals this evening, and I don't blame you. But I hope you ain't confused enough to string up any laundrymen or harmless farm workers you may run across."

Lopez shook his head and said, "Matter of fact a decent Chinese put us on to them bandits being Japs. He says he knows because they act much the same where he hailed from, original. I ain't never met nobody from the Japans before. They sure make Chinese and even Diegueño look civilized! I sure wish I was President Hayes tonight. For if I was, I'd send the fleet out to sink their whole country."

"Well, if it's any comfort, there's three of 'em dead down a canyon about five miles down the road to San Diego. I took the liberty when I caught 'em following me and Jessie, here."

Lopez brightened. "I don't blame you. On the Diego road, you say? Well, I don't see how they got through us. But that's *three* of 'em accounted for, at least."

The last thing Longarm had wanted to do was what he saw he had just done. But he didn't want to explain what he'd been doing inside the Japanese consulate when he was supposed to be up here chasing *other* mean Japs. On the other hand, since the dragons were dead and Nakamura long gone, he contented himself with saying, "You'll want your witnesses to look the ones we run into over, just in case."

"Thunderation! Are you saying there could be *two* such gangs to deal with?"

Longarm owed neither outfit any favors. "It's worth considering, in moderation. *All* of 'em can't be bad. As a matter of fact I have a part-Jap pard sort of working with me on this complicated case. He's tall, more American than Oriental looking, with a droopy moustache. He answers to Ki. I don't imagine you and yours have seen anyone like that in these parts lately?"

Lopez said, "Never seen him. He'd be staying *here* unless he has friends in town. Ain't no other place to stay."

Later, Longarm and Lone Star wished there was. For the room they hired upstairs was just passable if they'd paid a third of the price. As he locked the door, Longarm explained that while *they* were no doubt tough enough to go on in the rain, it was rough on horseflesh to be needlessly chilled and, of course, dry stalls and oats for a traveler's mount came with the room for the night.

Jessie told him to stop talking so much and help her out of her wet duds, so he did. Her damp skin was chilled to the bone and clammy to the touch. Or it was until they'd been under the wool blankets long enough to throw them off and really get down to serious loving.

Later, as they lay once more under the covers together, sharing a cheroot, she said, "That was lovely, but what about poor Ki?"

"Let him get his own gal. This can't be the box he said he was heading for, after all."

She insisted, "That's what I mean. Unless Ki's hiding out up here for some reason, we just made a horrible mistake!"

He held her close. "Ki's not dumb enough to hide from

us after sending word to us he'd be here," he assured her.

"That's what I mean!" she insisted. "Ki couldn't be worried about the Black Dragon with the whole town filled with lawman on the prod for Orientals, and he'd know we'd come here to this stage station if we came at all!"

"I know he can't be here in El Cajon, Jessie. I wish I could tell you where he might be, but I can't. So what say I get rid of this fool cheroot so's we can put our heads together some more?"

She sighed. "Please don't, Custis. You know I can't think straight when we're making love, and this is serious! I don't know what on earth we're going to do now!"

"All right, let's study on that box old Ki said he was getting into. We agreed a packing crate sounds dumb, even for Ki. The only other notion I can come up with is Baja, and that sounds even dumber."

"But, Custis, Ki never heard El Gato's warning about the situation down that way."

He shrugged. "It's never a good situation in the Baja. But Ki might not know that and, cuss my big mouth, I do recall telling him about that time I traced the Laredo Loop south of the border and made it through alive. Ki's always acted as if he thought he was tougher than me. If he's headed back to Texas by way of Mexico, he'll surely get to prove it!"

She said, "We can't let him try it on his own, dear. We're going to have to catch up with him somehow."

He shook his head. "Jessie, I know you can lick your weight in wildcats and ride anything on four legs through fire and salt. Now I want you to listen to me. I ain't taking a woman into Mexico with me while Indians are on the warpath and both rural and federal Mexicans are raping and shooting women just to show how brave they are!"

"I heard what El Gato said. He was talking to me at the time."

"I wish you'd listen to *me*, then. The Baja is primitive, even for Mexico. The folk there stare at even regular Mexicans as if they come from some other world. A gringo like me would have enough trouble down there, even in peace-time. Let word a blond American woman is about, and people will line up for miles just to get a glimpse of her. That's the *friendly* people I'm talking about. Them crazy *federales* are as likely to lob a shell in your general direction. They don't seem to understand this in Washington, but no Mexican government since the time of Juarez has liked Americans at all, and I suspect he had his doubts."

She said, "I was brought up on the Alamo, dear. But just the same . . ."

"It ain't the same," he said gruffly. "Texas won. It ain't never the same to the folk who lose. Winners can afford to be generous. Winners can forgive what happened and build a monument. Down in Mexico City they got a monument to brave Mexicans, Mexican kids, the young cadets at the military school there, who held off the United States Marines till the U. S. Army blew 'em away with artillery fire."

"Custis, that's all ancient history," she protested.

"Did you ever try to tell one of the now-old men who fought for Texas that the Alamo was ancient history? Have you ever requested 'Rally 'Round the Flag' or 'Marching Through Georgia' in a saloon Confederate veterans hang out in? We screwed Mexico, Jessie. They let Anglo settlers claim land in Texas, hoping to have a buffer of tough Yan-kee fighters between them and the Comanche. With all due respect to a great man, men like your dad paid Mexico back by taking Texas away from them."

"Now see here, there was more to it than that!" she blazed.

"Sure there was. But all most Mexicans know is that they invited us in and we wound up taking the house. I can read. I know there was more to the Mexican War than a land grab. But few Mexicans can feel too good about the land we grabbed off 'em, every time they look at a map. We marched to Mexico City and humiliated the survivors, Jessie. Then we gave 'em a break and just took most of what we now call our West away from 'em. We found gold enough to finance the War between the States in the one Mexican territory of California alone. They're poor now, Jessie. How do you think they feel about being poor, knowing how much gold, silver, copper, even lead we've dug from land that was once their own?"

"You sound like you had to dig most of it yourself," she answered dryly. "Are you suggesting we give everything back?"

He smiled thinly. "Hell, no! We fought for it. I'm only trying to make you see how they feel about us, honey. They like us about as much as our South would like our North if the Yanks had pushed all the losers down into Florida and called everything else New England."

"I've always gotten along well with most Mexicans," she insisted.

"I ain't talking about friendly Mexicans. I'm talking about the troops of a Mexican dictator who hates our guts. Wild Indians hate everybody. So here's what I want you to do. I want you to head back to the Circle Star and fort up."

"Not without Ki!" she protested.

"Hell, girl, if he ain't dead he could be waiting for you there. Meanwhile, since I *have* to head down into the Baja in any case, I'll keep an eye out for him and do I see him stuck in a cactus I just may pull him out."

She sat up in bed, the covers falling from her beautiful bare breasts as she smiled down at him radiantly and said, "Oh, Custis! I knew I could count on you!"

He was about to point out that Billy Vail was counting on him as well, and that the Nakamura gang was even more likely to have jumped the nearby border than Ki, having proven *they* were crazy. Then he wondered why anyone would want to say a dumb thing like that. She was all over him, kissing him and sobbing about how brave he was. He took the lovely girl in his arms and tried to show her that whether he was brave or not, he surely could be as active as she was right now.

• • •

"Welcome to Mexico," said Yoko as she led Ki, as far as she could tell, over yet another monotonous rise.

The rain was letting up. A pale moon was rising above higher mountains. They were still tired, cold, and hungry, in that order, and it would be hours before the sun came up to dry their wet clothing and warm their clammy flesh.

Ki was used to ignoring discomfort, but the border crossing struck him as a letdown, just the same. He chuckled and when she asked him why he said, "I was thinking of the day I became twenty-one."

"Oh, I wish *I* were twenty-one, so people would have to treat me like an adult instead of just a silly child."

"Nothing happens. One night you go to bed still only twenty. The next morning you wake up twenty-one. You don't feel any different. Nobody *treats* you any different than they did the day before. Some still call you Kid and others were nicer to you to begin with. You feel you ought to at least get to shoot up the town or something, but that would *really* make you a kid. So you just have to get on with it, wondering why you feel so odd about not feeling at all odd."

She said she didn't understand what he meant and asked if they hadn't at least given him a big birthday party.

He shrugged and said, "I had an unusual childhood. But look on the bright side. Perhaps it doesn't hurt as much to wake up sixty either."

"I don't ever want to be sixty," she said. "I just want to be twenty-one so people will have to treat me like a grown woman."

Ki said nothing. He was tired of the subject.

She said, "We shall soon be at the old 'dobe I told you about."

"How do you know nobody lives there now?" he asked.

"Silly. It has no roof. *Los rurales* burned out the people who lived there years ago, and who would move back into a burnt-out shell with no roof, eh?"

He started to ask why they wanted to go there at all in

that case. Then he remembered. She chattered so much it was hard to remember all she said. Only some made sense. The part about fire-hardened 'dobe walls did. There was a well there. They could build a fire safely if they built it small enough, in a corner. Ki wasn't at all thirsty, thanks to the rain. They hadn't touched their water bags yet. But the thought of a fire made him want to fire his gun at the moon and the more water they drank along the way, the longer their water bags might last. The country was flattening out now. They were crossing a cactus flat between brooding ranges to both east and west.

At least Ki thought it was a cactus flat until he spied what looked like a huge carrot standing on its head in the moonlight with a few tiny leaves where rootlets should be sprouting. He asked her, "What do you call those crazy trees?"

"Crazy trees," she answered. "They have no proper name. A gringo who came down here to write things in books, one time, said there was no such species of flora. It is unusual to see them this far north. There are forests of them farther south."

"The American botanist must have been thrilled. What did he finally decide they might be?"

"*Quien sabe?* Somebody killed him for his burro and his boots. It might have been *los rurales*. They are not paid well and they hate all gringos. On the other hand, the Diegueños hate everyone, whether they have boots or not, so maybe they did it. It was hard to tell whether the *pobrecito* had been arrowed or shot by the time the vultures led someone more nice to him."

They rode on for perhaps a couple of hours. It was hard to judge time with chattering teeth. When she at last pointed out the ruin she had been leading him to they were almost on top of it. Ki was glad. The nondescript black blob surrounded by open cactus flat was harder for a stranger to find than she had described it. But the trail they were following was distinct enough in the moonlight and as they reined in and dismounted, Ki sniffed and said, "Wait, I smell horse droppings. *Fresh* horse droppings."

But Yoko was already inside, calling out, "Oh, come in and get out of the wind! It feels so warm and dry in here, even without a fire!"

It hardly seemed likely they would be ambushed, now. Ki led their ponies in, tethered them to a charred post in a far corner, and sniffed again, saying, "It's no wonder it feels drier in here. Someone *had* a fire going in here not too long ago."

She said that sounded like a good idea.

"Go ahead, then. Keep it small. I'm going to scout around outside," Ki told her.

Yoko poked at the black pile in one corner, found glowing coals under the blanket of ash, and proceeded to toss greasewood on them until she had a bright little fire going.

Ki came in to rejoin her. "A large party, riding south, since the rain stopped. I make it about twenty horses. Moving at a trot. Meaning they're out to make good time but not being chased. *Rurales?*"

She said, "Perhaps two eight-man squads led by officers, no? Whoever they were, they are gone, and the sweet things left this place so cozy for us, too!"

He hunkered down by the fire, letting the warmth soak into his chilled flesh. Then he noticed a fresh tin can and a short length of clean pine. He pointed the can out to Yoko and said, "Someone just ate American beans here."

She shrugged. "What of it? I told you this was a smugglers' trail and people to the north drink tequila, too."

"Maybe. I know there are a lot of Orientals in California, Yoko. Are there any at all down here in the Baja?"

"Sure. There is even a colony of Russians mining copper down the coast. Some Japanese tuna fishermen who put in even farther south. Why do you ask?"

He picked up the stick and told her, "This looks like a homemade hashi."

She looked incredulous. *"Rurales,* eating beans with chopsticks?"

He said, *"Hai,* it makes one wonder, doesn't it?"

"But those men who just rode on could not be following our trail. We just got here, coming the other way."

He didn't answer.

She tried, "Perhaps some Chinese, going somewhere in a hurry?"

"That makes more sense than two squads of Japanese horse marines," he decided. "Ninja usually come in smaller doses. Neither would be trotting merrily ahead of us if they were chasing us. Unless, of course, they're planning to wait for us somewhere."

She asked how that would be possible.

He said, "If they know you're with me—and I can think of a dozen ways Togo could—they may know about Mexican in-laws of a Japanese subject. It's not as if they have to keep tabs on all that many, you know."

"I doubt they'd know about my Tio Pedro. He does not make a custom of reporting his movements to anyone on either side of the border. Once we get to this rancho . . ."

"We're not going there," Ki said. "I may be overcautious. I'm alive tonight because I've always been easy to spook, as an American lawman I know puts it with some justice."

"Then where *are* we going, if not to friends and relations who can help us?" Yoko asked.

"Nowhere near them. We can't take the risk. I mean *I* can't, that is. You should be safe enough if you ride on to your uncle's spread. They won't be expecting one girl, dressed Mexican, riding in alone."

She protested, "I can't leave you alone in the Baja, you maniac! Where would you go without me to look after you?"

He told her, "I'm on my way to Texas. Alone. That was the point of all this stupidity."

Chapter 17

Longarm waited until Jessie had repeated how little she thought of a grown man who sulked before he growled, "I ain't sulking. I'm riding alone. Like I told you back there at the stage station, I'm too polite to say how disgusted I can get with mule-headed women."

They were riding across a mountain meadow stirrup-high with wild mustard and tarweed, surrounded by pine-covered ridges. The tarweed was in yellow bloom, so the bees were buzzing at Longarm as well when she said, "This can't be the way to Mexico, Custis. Why are we riding east?"

He said, *"We* ain't riding *nowhere*. If the map Roy Lopez showed me this morning makes any sense at all *I* mean to have a look at where they found that young gal's body."

"I thought we were going to look for Ki in the Baja. Sheriff Lopez said his men read no sign left by Nakamura anyway, remember?"

"I can't remember. I wasn't with 'em. Even if they was

skilled trackers and not just excited cowhands, it was dark and raining. Things usually look brighter after a dark, stormy night."

She said, "Custis, these springy weeds have all perked up the same after a good watering and plenty of rest."

"I noticed. She was found alongside a creek, ahead. It ain't as unusual to find hoofprints in damp sand."

She protested, "Darling, you know at least a score of riders on our side must have milled all about when they found that poor girl's body."

"That's why I had word with the blacksmith in El Cajon after breakfast. He's the only one for miles around and, as I had hoped, he shoes all the local riders. He confirmed he uses mill-made shoes, all the same brand, and just hammers them to fit a particular hoof. I was too polite to notice he skimps on nails as well. I figured there had to be a reason more than one posse rider throwed a shoe on the same ride, but I reckon he figures he's entitled to make a living."

She brightened. "Oh, then we're searching for mayhaps a tailor-made shoe with honest nailing."

It had been a statement rather than a question. He still replied, "*We* ain't. *I* am. Damn it, Jessie. Them owlhoots slaughter gals!"

"Pooh, they can't hurt me if they're not around, can they? I thought you said they'd be in Mexico by now," she said.

"I said they *could* be. I said they likely *were*. Nobody can say for sure what a homicidal lunatic might consider a smart move."

They rode on until they came to the valley stream and followed it toward its appointed death in the Salton Sink farther east. Pine Creek was broad and shallow, paved with cobbles for the most part, with here and there a patch of glittering sand. Longarm grunted, "Fools' gold. Lots of it. That may account for all the dumb holes in the ground in these parts. Lopez says they never found much real color in

216

the old days, but some hit enough mercury ore to make it worth their while."

"Are you always that curious about country you're only passing through, dear?" she asked.

"I have to be," Longarm told her. "I has a nosy job. That must be where they found her, just ahead. Weeds are flattened considerable and you were right about the posse dancing their ponies all around the site. I sure find a novelty-seeking crowd a bother. Even when they ain't in your way, they mess the sign considerably."

He dismounted to mosey along the streambank, leading Old Buck and staring down intently. Lone Star glanced at the only tree at all near the site, a pretty young pine, and shuddered as she said, "Such a lovely spot to die so ugly." Then she dismounted too.

A tracker in her own right, Lone Star led Ribbon across the ankle-deep water to scout the far bank. Neither said much as they moved side by side but separated by the broad babbling creek.

Then, ignoring the cold water that sloshed into her right boot as she knelt on one knee, she called out to Longarm. He and Old Buck sloshed across to view her find. He stared soberly down and said, "Yep. At least a dozen mounts, single-file and leaving the sod torn up considerable where they came out of the creek, here. Soil's too sandy to record much detail. So who's to say how well that one clear hoofprint was nailed? But it ain't as skimpy a shoe as that cheap smith in El Cajon fancies. Even if it was, I can't see posse riders scouting for sign riding in single-file."

They both stared north, picturing the long line of riders in the night moving on across the flat toward the steep saddle rising beyond. Lone Star said flatly, "They're headed south. That old ruse is so stale I'd get rid of a foxhound who fell for it."

He had to agree, grudgingly. "It's the first dodge a fox cub or an outlaw with time to waste tries, and I feel a mite

217

insulted. Any damn fool can see nobody could take that far slope aboard a pony. I doubt they went as far as the slope. It's too easy to leave sign in pine duff."

"They turned east. Riding west would have taken them back to more settled country. The only question left is whether they crossed back close enough to matter or made for the desert farther down before they swung south."

He said, "The Salton Sink is rough on horseflesh, even in winter when it ain't as hot down there. Even strangers would see it makes more sense to follow the grain of the Coast Range south. There's nothing much worth robbing, high or low, between here and where the S.P. tracks cross through just above the border. So if Nakamura ain't planning a train robbery next, the Baja sounds like the best place to look for the rascal."

"And Ki," she insisted.

To change the subject he said, "You ain't a bad tracker if you know about backtracking, Jessie."

She shrugged modestly. "I was just a girl-child the first time some Comanche pulled it on me, or tried to. They hit one of our line riders for his pony and gun, then lit out for the border, as if we didn't know they always hid out in the Staked Plains to the west. There were six in the war party. They seemed awfully surprised to see us when we cut them off."

"*We* would have included who? Ki and your father?"

"No, dear. Dad and Ki were away on other serious business. But I had a couple of *vaqueros* with me, of course."

He smiled crookedly. "The poor bastards never had a chance, did they? But the Baja ain't the Staked Plains, Jessie."

"So El Gato mentioned. But how much worse than Comanche can wild Mexican Indians get?"

He swung up in the saddle, saying, "Nobody can get worse than Comanche. They've lifted more hair than any other nation. But like I said last night, Indians are the least of a stranger's worries in the Baja."

218

She mounted beside him. *"You're going, aren't you?"*

"I got to. I'm paid to act stupid by Uncle Sam."

"If I wasn't so stupid I'd either say no more often or marry you," she said.

"If I hadn't been fibbing about that when we checked in together you'd have to do as you was *told* for a change, woman!"

She dimpled sweetly. "Maybe that's why I keep letting you get away, then. I haven't had a mere man boss me since my daddy stopped trying, and I'm not sure I *ever* intend to be bossed by anyone with a legal right to boss me."

They rode on downstream. After a while Jessie said, "The weed-cover's been grazed, up ahead. It might make it easier to spy sign, don't you think?"

He snorted in disgust. "I don't mean to follow 'em sniffing every infernal tree. Was them Comanche you trailed that time wearing them sneaky long-tailed moccasins they favor?"

"Of course. That was how we knew they were Comanche. Kiowa would have left clear footprints, while Plains Apache wouldn't have left any sign at all."

He nodded. "You only have to guess who they might be and where they might be headed. Once they got down into the dry and dusty Baja they'll leave more than sign. I savvy enough of the lingo to sense what a Mexican might mean when he's saying 'they went thataway' in Spanish."

"My Spanish is better. I can pass for a native. Ki will find it harder to hide out down there, too."

Longarm shot her a sardonic glance. "Well, I have met blond Mex gals. But how many strangers of any sort do you reckon the Baja to absorb before somebody notices?"

Then he added, in a more serious tone, "No bull, Jessie. I really mean to play the rest of this game out by my lonesome."

"It's my game, too," she insisted. "The Black Dragon dealt me in before you sat down at the table, remember?"

He sighed. "I noticed. The table stakes are getting too high and there are too many jokers in the deck. Aside from wild Indians, *rurales, federales,* and Togo's lizards, Nakamura is a pure maniac."

She sniffed. "Yes, and I mean to give him a good piece of my mind when we catch up with him."

He growled, "Just make sure your mind don't wind up in a tree, wrapped in your detached skull."

"Oh, darling, does that mean you're taking me with you?"

"I ain't *taking* you anywhere, damn it. But I'm too fond of you to shoot you and I'll be whipped with snakes if I can think of any *other* way to keep you from tagging along."

Far to the south, Ki was having a similar conversation with his own attractive but unwanted companion. They were riding southeast across rolling country too dry to call range and too covered with unlikely vegetation to call true desert. Ki was in the lead, even though Yoko kept insisting she was showing him the way to Sonora. When Ki's mount stepped over yet another weird botanical specimen he called back, "What do you call these big cactus trees that want to crawl along the ground like snakes?"

"Serpent cactus. It's related to the saguaro trees of the Sonora desert ahead. So it looks sort of like one, lying down. Nobody knows why it grows like that. The Baja is cut off from the rest of Mexico by the terrible Colorado Delta and of course the Sea of Cortez further south. Lots of things here are different."

He said he didn't doubt her as he stared ahead at the notch in the volcanic ridge they were heading for. At least, Ki hoped it was a notch. As the air heated up everything more than a mile or so away shimmered too much to make out its outline.

They topped a gentle rise. Ki reined in and muttered, "Damn. That rain we had seems to have flooded a playa between here and that pass. We'll have to work around. I mean *I'll* have to work around. I told you to ride on to your

220

uncle's ranch if you don't want to go home, Yoko."

She said, "I won't go home. I love you and you need me."

"I need you like I need a ball and chain attached to my ankle, damn it. I said I was grateful for you for getting me this far. But this is getting silly, Yoko. I know where I am and where I'm going, now. You'd only slow me down, even if you didn't get hurt."

"That's what you think. To begin with, that flooded playa you'd be working around if I didn't know this country better is not exactly a flooded playa."

Ki looked again, glanced up at the morning sun, and swore. He wasn't swearing at Yoko. He had ridden desert country often enough to know a mirage when he saw one —or at least he did when a mirage didn't look this real.

"I feel stupid. I was fooled by all that rain last night," he said slowly.

"No, you weren't. The Diegueños call it Ghost Lake. It fools them a lot, too. It won't be there once the sun is to the west. Then it will be behind us. Ghost Lake is always somewhere on this flat, but it likes to move around a lot."

He relented enough to ask her what she might know about that distant notch. "It's a pass through the lava rocks over that way. You don't want to take it, though. You'd wind up in scab lands with the only possible trail winding on, in time, to the mud flats of the delta."

He said, "I have to cross the Colorado Delta to get to the mainland, don't I?" -

She shrugged. "Sure, where the ground is firm enough to ride on. The delta is big, and complicated. Some of it's dry and a lot of it is an awful mess. Mud flats are bad enough. Salt marshes are worse. What you really have to look out for is quicksand, covered over with dry dust from the deserts all around."

Ki sighed. "All right, you may as well be useful as you pester me. How do we get from here to the drier parts of the delta?"

"Follow me." She took the lead. The silvery sheet of

tempting water receded just ahead of them as they rode on and on over cactus pretending to be fallen logs and between cholla cactus pretending to be apple trees. As she led Ki through a tighter than usual spot Yoko called back, "Watch out for that cholla. It throws things."

Ki told her he'd met jumping cholla before. The harmless-looking fuzzy pads on the treelike limbs didn't really jump off at a passing rider. They just seemed to if one brushed against even an innocent-looking hair. Cholla thorns were barbed much the same as porcupine quills, albeit on a much smaller scale, and worked the same way. Once one thorn had a grip in anyone or anything, the whole pad came off to drop down and stab more microscopic thorns in. Only greenhorns made the mistake of slapping at what they took to be a ferocious attack by some fuzzy gray-green critter. But ridding one's hide of a cholla pad with even a delicate knife blade could be a problem for a hand who knew what he was doing. It seemed one always missed at least one thorn tip and, in time, they always seemed to fester under the skin like a glass splinter.

As ever in dry, open country, distances were deceptive, and the Baja was a lot bigger in person than aboard a map. So even though they were cutting across its long, skinny length, they didn't seem to be getting anywhere. The day wore on and their water bags kept flattening. Ki, or even Yoko, could have gone without water better than their ponies. Ki knew it made more sense to water well and hope for the best than to wind up walking, sooner, after riding a pony dry and down.

Fodder was no problem for either species. Yoko had brought tinned beans and tomatoes, as he'd asked. When they took a noon break Ki peeled some prickly pear for their mounts while Yoko cursed open their own grub. They didn't have to cook what was in the cans. That was why beans and tomatoes were standard cowhand fare away from the chuck wagon. They hunkered together in the slight shade of an unlikely if interesting botanical specimen

222

unique to the Baja and sort of inhaled the beans before washing them down with tomato preserve. Yoko belched, delicately, and said, "You were right. You don't need spoons or even chopsticks with such slurpy food. I'm still thirsty, though. Do you think our ponies could spare us just a tiny sip of water?"

He said, "You go ahead. Make it just one swallow. It's too hot to ride now. Maybe if I toss a tarp over whatever this big bush is it may cast some shade."

He rose, moved out to the tethered ponies munching pear, and unsaddled both, telling them, "I'd rub you down if I saw a drop of sweat on either of you. I'm sorry we can't invite you in with us, but there's more pears where that came from. So don't try to break free, no matter how cranky the heat makes you."

He unrolled his bedroll, tucked the blankets under his arm, and tossed the canvas over the bush. Yoko rested in the resultant shade.

He moved up the gentle rise to scout beyond their trail-break. He was American desert-hand enough to know not even an Apache would be out in this hot sun unless it was mighty important. He was enough of a trained warrior to know some people paid no attention to the weather when they thought it *was* important.

Ki stopped atop the rise to sweep the skyline in every direction with his keen eyes. Everything was shimmering, but he saw nothing really moving in any direction, at first. The mirage was off to the west now, covering the parched ground they had been riding across.

He frowned out across the dancing sheet of what certainly looked like blue water as he tried to recall passing a line of shimmering somethings lined up like a troop of horse marines. He couldn't. It was hard to tell if those dots were moving or simply another trick of the light. Whatever they were, whether they knew they were walking on water or not, they hadn't been there when he and Yoko had ridden the same stretch. He knew where he and the girl had ridden, of course, leaving distinct tracks in the desert pavement. The dots they'd never ridden past were perhaps an hour's ride out on the flat, either growing by the trail they'd left or following it.

Ki ran down to where he'd left Yoko, snatched up his fighting tools, and snapped, "Get up. Get ready to ride. I'll saddle the ponies."

He paid no attention to her wails of protest. She really didn't get to ask him what was up until they were both mounted and up on the rise. He looked back. "I was right. They do look closer now. A party of riders, a *big* party of riders, has cut our trail!"

She gasped, "Oh! *Rurales* or *federales?*"

"What's the difference? They're after us, whoever they think we are. We need slick rock, fast. If you know of any near enough to matter, take the lead and get us to it. Now!"

She did. Ki noticed she was beelining for the notch she had said led nowhere. He didn't ask why. She had told him the badlands beyond were old lava flows. They were leaving hoofmarks even a kid could have followed as they rode for distant slickrock. At quite some distance from their disturbed nap Ki looked back from atop another rise and said, "Damn. They've swung this way. I didn't *think* they were on their way to Sonora. Let's get out of this hot sun."

They were leaving less sign now as they rode over lava scree for the notch in the ridge. But of course anyone on their trail had to know they were making for the one gap in the now huge massif of coal-black rock.

They passed through and pounded on down a trail that seemed paved with rough cinders. Ki spotted another break in the nearly sheer wall to their left and called out, "Not that way, Yoko! Up this side cleft!"

She reined in, spun her pony, and followed as Ki took the lead and loped into the narrow cleft. He saw they were raising little dust and leaving no sign on the crushed black lava. But nonetheless he cut up yet another side canyon, riding up a steep slope with sky at the top. He topped the rise and loped down it into the open grass-lined bowl of what had to be a long-dead volcanic crater, with Yoko following him.

As he reined in, too late, a dozen figures dressed in charro outfits rose from the knee-high grass, covering him with American Winchesters and Oriental eyes.

Ki kept his mouth shut and his hands polite. Yoko rode down to join him. He'd been telling her she had no sense. One of the men covering them laughed boyishly and said, "You are alive for the moment because I am curious to know why Yankee cowboys shout at Mexican girls in Japanese. Would you explain that before you die?"

Ki replied in Japanese, "This is not a desirable time for even polite conversation. We are here because at least three times as many men as I see here are right behind us. Unless you happen to be oddly dressed Imperial Marines, you may find us more useful to you alive than dead right now!"

The leader snapped curt orders. Two of his followers dashed up the path to cover the cleft leading into it as another nimbly scaled the crater wall for a peek over the top.

The leader turned back to his surprise visitors and said, "I am Hideki Nakamura. Two-sword rank, of course. Perhaps you have heard of me?"

Ki hadn't. He knew nothing of Longarm's mission. So he found it easy to sound sincere when he replied, "I feel sure I shall, in time. Your clan is an old, distinguished one, is it not?"

Nakamura nodded curtly. "Very distinguished. Not as powerful as it was under the shogunate."

Yoko, who still had a lot to learn, sobbed, "Oh, no, they *are* Black Dragons, Ki!"

Ki felt like killing her.

Nakamura frowned up at her—he was very good at frowning—and decided, "This is turning out to be a very interesting afternoon after all. How would even a Japanese-speaking Mexican girl know about those pathetic dreaming dragons?"

Since he had just said what he thought of the Kuroi Ryu

225

faction, Ki thought it safe to say, "She is, like me, part Japanese, and of course all right-thinking people share your opinion of such silly people, Nakamura-San."

The renegade samurai grimaced. His boyishly handsome face might have looked nicer if he hadn't kept making such ugly faces. *"Hai,* silly old men dreaming of a bright tomorrow, perhaps fifty years from now even if they succeed," he snorted. "I, Nakamura, live in the here and now. You have my permission to dismount. I may not kill you and enjoy the woman here and now. It is early yet, and you interest me."

The bushi he'd sent up the crater wall slid back down to join them, looking puzzled. "They were telling the truth. A very large party just rode on past. Like us, they were wearing Mexican costume. But I heard their leader shout orders in our language, Nakamura-San!"

The samurai scowled at Ki. "I thought you said they were Imperial Marines."

Ki said, "I may have been wrong about that. They may have been dragons. Whoever they are, they're after me."

Nakamura led them all across the crater to where their own ponies were tethered and their camp gear spread out on the grass. He sat down and said, "We have no tea. I may offer you water, in time. First I desire to hear all about you and why you seem so popular."

Ki sat on his knees, with Yoko remembering her manners and kneeling well behind him as she was supposed to. Having no idea what so many other Japanese could be doing in the Baja, of all places, but sensing they had to be outlaws, Ki decided honesty was the best policy with tough crooks. When he had brought their captor up to date Nakamura reached in the grass at his side for a canteen and tossed it to Ki. "I have heard of this Togo. I think he is a bastard, too. Have you really been trained as a bushi? All my men are the real thing. Old family retainers who chose freedom under a real samurai to slavery under those fools who now rule in Tokyo, pretending to be Englishmen or something."

Ki modestly mentioned a few names. Nakamura tried not to look impressed as he grunted, *"Hai,* good teachers, at least. Do you fight in the proper manner of a samurai, or like a ninja in the night?"

Ki said, "I can fight any way I have to."

Nakamura grunted. "As you see, my army is small. You may keep your weapons if you find it desirable to follow my banner."

Ki didn't see any banner. He asked, politely, who they were fighting in this man's army.

Nakamura said, "Everyone we've met, so far. You find us resting here because yesterday we got to kill some Mexicans with badges and big gray hats. They were pathetic, for all their noise. Just the same, we have been hiding up here as we consider our next moves. Crossing into Mexico might not have been as desirable as I hoped. So many people seem to be dashing about with guns down here. We had much less trouble to the north."

"I have heard there's trouble in the Baja at this moment, too. Yoko, here, is a good guide. Perhaps if we all worked our way over to Sonora, where there are only wild Yaqui to worry about—"

Nakamura cut in to snap, "I'll make you a follower and her my mistress as well as our guide."

He waited to see how Ki would take that before he added with a sinister smile, "Unless, that is, you find her desirable enough to fight for?"

"I am always ready to fight any man, at any time, for any cause," Ki said. "But do you think this is a desirable time for us to fight over a woman, with enemies enough around us?"

Nakamura kept smiling, or grinning nervously. "I told you I live in the here and now. Those others rode on. They are no danger to us at the moment, and the girl is not at all undesirable."

Ki said, "Wait. She's not only pretty. As I told you, she's a worthy guide."

"Hai, I have a little pony for her to lead into the stable."

"Listen to me, damn it. Those others won't ride far before they're forced to turn back. The trail they took leads nowhere. They know we were on it. They'll know we foxed them by riding up a side canyon. On the way back, they'll be *searching* every side canyon. We just don't have *time* for a decent fight."

Nakamura said, "There is always time for a decent fight. What sort of action would you prefer? We can offer anything from swordplay to bare-handed."

Ki was somewhat surprised to hear such an offer from a two-sword noble. "I choose to fight *bojutsu*, then. It's usually over fast, at least."

Nakamura nodded pleasantly, clapped his hands for attention, and called out, "Miki! Break out two fighting staves. Our new bushi says he is a *bo* fighter!"

Miki was a husky, balding man with one gold tooth who whipped two heavy lengths of black varnished wood from his own bedroll with considerable enthusiasm. "Miki seldom gets a chance to practice these days," Nakamura said. "He holds a master's belt for *bojutsu*."

Ki rose. "Miki wasn't exactly who I had in mind, but that's the way things go, sometimes."

As Nakamura got to his own feet, Ki noticed the renegade had picked up an ancient, finely crafted katana to carry casually by its scabbard. Ki hoped it was just an heirloom blade Nakamura was careful about. All his followers seemed content with modern weapons, save for the pair of fighting sticks Miki strutted on ahead with.

They all moved down to the flat, sandier bottom of the crater. Miki handed a *bo* to a comrade, who moved over to present it to Ki with a formal bow as the others formed a circle. In English, Ki told Yoko to get behind him and stay there. She sobbed, "Oh, what will I do if you lose?"

He didn't answer. He took off his other weaponry and hat, handed them to her, and turned to face the *bo* master. Holding his own stave stiffly in front of him, Ki bowed to show he was ready. Miki bowed as well. Then, formality

228

out of the way, he charged.

A *bojutsu* match, friendly or not so friendly, was a noisy affair between well-matched opponents. The idea was to let the other man hit your stick, not your head, or ward it off with a chop when he tried to poke an end—either end —in your eye or your guts. To anyone unfamiliar with the deadly sport, it would have looked like two insane drum majors trying to twirl their batons in the same spot while they grunted at each other like pigs. But the men all around them knew the finer points and gasped with approval or dismay as one or the other scored a point.

Miki was good, and Ki had to admire his sportsmanship as well as his skill. The husky bushi fought clean as well as ferociously. He was out to kill. There was no mistaking his intent after Ki had warded off a few of his powerful blows. But his style was as traditional and correct as one could consider a fighting style that allowed a man to break any bone or stab any organ he could get at with a sawed-off flagpole. At one point Ki's booted foot slipped on treach- erously rooted grass, and as he dropped to one knee he braced himself for the expected blow. But Miki stepped back, bowed, and asked, "Would my honorable enemy not fight better if he took the time to bare his feet?"

Miki was wearing boots as well, albeit low-heeled boots that fit him. So Ki knew he was showing off as well as being a good sport. Ki got back to his feet, slowly, enjoy- ing the short pause for breath, and replied with a formal bow, "My greatest desire is to get this over with."

Miki bowed back, and said, *"Hai,* the sun is hot this afternoon, even up here in these hills." Then he came whirling in for the kill, perhaps a bit overconfident, for the next time they locked staves Ki was able to sweep Miki's chunky legs from under him with a heel kick. The sur- prised *bo* master landed on his rump, knees and *bo* up to ward off Ki's downward slash. The *bo* in Miki's hand broke in two with an explosive crack. Ki halted his own less than an inch from Miki's dismayed face, reversed ends

229

in a blur of lethal motion, and had his man pinned with the blunt end of his *bo* pressed down against Miki's throat. The husky bushi was quick enough to grab Ki's stick with both hands. But Ki didn't want the tip anywhere else. So Miki couldn't budge it. He relaxed, fatalistic to the end, and smiled sheepishly up at the death he'd been trained to accept as a man.

Behind him, Ki heard Nakamura laugh and say, "Get on with it."

Ki stared soberly down at the defeated bushi and asked softly, "Would a man who fought bravely feel too insulted to bear it if I gave him back his life?"

Miki's voice was just as steady. "I believe I could bear it. There is no shame in being beaten by an enemy who fights as well as *you!*"

"In that case, I do not find it desirable to be your enemy." So saying, Ki twirled his *bo* up into a formal salute as he stepped back and bowed again. "You were never really beaten in any case. Your weapon failed you, not your courage."

There was a collective hiss of admiration for both of them as Ki tossed his *bo* aside and held his hand down to Miki to help him to his feet. Nakamura was the only one there who did not seem pleased by the way the match had turned out.

As both Ki and Miki faced him to bow and signify the fight was over, the bloodthirsty young samurai sneered. "I need fighting men, not salve-selling boys. You call that a fight? Neither of you are even bleeding!"

"I am truly sorry," Ki said. "But now, if I may make a humble suggestion, we are running out of time for games. Those others will be reaching the dead end of that trail any moment now. We have to get out of here before they see the error of their ways and turn back."

"*I* give the orders here," said Nakamura. "I am not in the habit of avoiding fights. This crater seems a fine place to defend. One or two men in the cleft you entered by

230

could stand off an army of any size."

Ki smiled dryly. "An army trying to push through one entrance single-file would deserve to be defeated. But they may see they don't have to. They may simply surround us and wait for hunger and thirst to do their fighting for them. The only water in these lava hills is rainwater from last night. It will soon dry up."

"What if it does, great military strategist? How do you know they have more water than us?"

Ki couldn't believe a man who insisted on calling himself a samurai could know so little about basic tactics. "They don't have to get by on the canteens they may have with them. I know for certain of a well less than a day's ride from here. As they were no doubt trailing Yoko and me from that place to here, they have to know about that well, too. Once they have us surrounded and pinned down they'll be able to send riders they can well spare to fetch all the water they may need."

Yoko turned to the others, sobbing, "Can't the rest of you see this is a death trap? I know the way to get over these lava hills. I can lead you all to Sonora and safety. An armed party this big should have no trouble with the Yaqui."

"Hush," Ki told her in English. Nakamura half-drew his katana, hissing like a sidewinder. Ki saw Yoko had let *his* weapons get away from her in all the excitement. His gun rig and bag of throwing stars lay in the grass beyond her. He told her in English, "This is man talk." He told Nakamura in Japanese, "Don't mind her. She's only a child, and half barbarian."

Then he turned his back on Nakamura and moved to pick up his fighting gear before someone told him not to.

He was bending over when Yoko screamed. He dropped and spun on one knee as he heard cold steel bite into warm flesh. He gasped in horror as he saw the girl fall, pierced through the stomach by Nakamura's slashing samurai sword!

Nakamura stood there gripping the katana in both hands.

As Ki rose coldly to his feet, empty-handed but ominous of eye, Nakamura stammered, "She got in the way. I never meant to do that."

Nobody else said anything. It was all too obvious what the treacherous Nakamura had intended to do. But now that he had to face his intended victim, Nakamura took a step backward. "Perhaps it was all for the better, eh? Without a desirable woman to cause trouble we should all get along better now."

Ki was American enough to growl, "Aw, shit!" and Oriental enough to throw caution to the winds and go for Nakamura bare-handed, and to hell with his followers.

Despite his cowardly streak, Nakamura was good, but not good enough, as he slashed again with his bloody blade. Ki slid under it, feet first, locked one boot tip behind Nakamura's right ankle, and kicked the kneecap above, hard, with the heel of his cowboy boot, breaking Nakamura's leg.

As the crippled coward fell beside him, howling in agony, Ki was on him like a wildcat. He twisted the sword from Nakamura's grasp and threw it away. Then he had both hands around Nakamura's throat. It was not the bushi way to kill. It was slower. Ki *wanted* to kill the bastard slowly. But as Nakamura drummed his life away with his one functional boot heel, Ki felt it was not slow enough. It seemed as if the son of a bitch was dead in no time.

As the scarlet-faced young killer died, Ki demolished his dead face with a savage fist. Then Ki shrugged, got up, and waited for the others to move in, knowing at least he had done what he had had to for a girl who'd died to save him.

Miki moved gingerly around Ki to drop to his knees by their supine leader, feel his throat, and announce, *"Nakamura-San wa sinde imasu!"*

Ki tried, "I didn't attack him from behind and you all

232

must have noticed he was sort of a baka."

Miki got warily to his feet, saying, *"Hai,* but he was still our master by birthright."

Nobody else said anything. Ki knew the strength, or weakness, of his mother's people was that Japanese tended to obey orders from an accepted leader blindly, but could only act by general and complete agreement as a group of social equals. Before anyone could offer any suggestions, Ki snapped imperiously, "Listen to me, all of you. Your samurai is dead. Before he died he killed the only reliable guide we had. I still know more than any of you do about this country. I am getting out of here before it's too late. Anyone who finds it desirable to follow me may do so."

He went to strap on his weaponry before they could vote on it. Miki was the first to say, casually, "I am only a bushi. I feel I may live longer following a good fighter than wandering this strange land on my own."

Ki nodded curtly, and it made just as much sense in his mother's language when he said, "Now that we have separated the men from the boys, we'd better start thinking about getting out of here!"

They all got to work packing their gear and saddling their ponies. Ki asked why they had so many and Miki explained, "We stole extra ones, all the way down from San Francisco. We have been able to carry more water and supplies that way."

"A man can't lead a horse and fight well at the same time. Let's pick out the best and shoot the others," Ki suggested.

"Shoot them, Ki-San?"

"Hai, would you leave a poor brute in this country without anyone to look after it? Aside from that, should the others need fresh mounts by the time they get here, let the bastards walk."

★

Chapter 18

Farther to the north but along the same desert range a young Diegueño was having his own troubles or, as he saw it, he'd had his troubles the night before and was waiting for the Long Sleep in the scant shade of a cholla.

The bullet wound in his left thigh was not so bad. But his pony had been killed and even a desert Indian was as good as dead on this desert with no mount, no water, and a broken thighbone.

From time to time a sidewinder, sheltered from the glaring sun in the same cactus clump, buzzed at the wounded warrior, who finally told it, "Hear me, little braggart, you are being silly. If you wish to kill me, do so, without talking about it so much. I am not going to crawl away into the heat of the sun again, no matter how often you may bite me. Perhaps I should. It would take me less time to die of thirst out there in the open. But while I may be a fool to hope, while I still live, I can hope some of my people find me in time."

The snake buzzed again. The Indian sighed. "I know. I said I was a fool. I was trying not to leave sign as I was scouting *los federales* for my nation. Even if *they* miss me, my trail will be difficult for even a Diegueño to cut. But anything is possible while one is still breathing."

He didn't know how long that might be now. His tongue as well as his leg was starting to swell. His throat felt filled with spiderwebs. He knew it would dry him out faster, but some things were more important than mere existence. So he began to sing his death song.

It wasn't easy. The sidewinder didn't like the dismal croaking and rattled ferociously. The young warrior found this dryly amusing and tried to sing louder.

A few minutes later, a quarter of a mile away, Longarm reined in, cocked his head, and asked Lone Star, "Do you hear what I hear, or do I need more water than I've been sipping?"

She listened, too, and decided, "It sounds like a war chant. I hope I'm wrong. I thought we were alone out here."

"It's a death song. It figures. From the way that old boy is croaking he's just about there. It seems to be coming from over that way. Hang back and cover me. I'd best see who's dying around here."

She warned him not to take the advice to heart as she followed with her .38 drawn. Longarm waited a while before he got out his own .44-40. The death song sounded sincere, but Diegueños were said to be sneaky as Yuma, and you couldn't trust a Yuma as far as you could spit or he could shoot.

They finally traced the dismal croaking to a clump of cholla.

Longarm reined in and said, "Might have known he'd bed down in cactus as mean as he is. Cover from this side while I circle for a crossfire before moving any closer."

The wounded Indian knew they were out there. He kept singing, not to tell them where he was but because it was a good way to die, defiant to the end. He had nothing but raw courage left to defy them with. He'd spent his arrows. He couldn't even stand up. But he could still sing.

Longarm moved around to the shady side and spotted the young Diegueño. The boy had his long black hair bound with a red twist of calico. He was wearing a dirty white cotton blouse. But his muscular brown legs were bare, and Longarm had seen men hit that way before. He stared soberly down at the desert pavement the youth had broken through, crawling as far as Longarm could make out the dusty furrow. He said, "Well, old son, your singing ain't much, but you do have guts."

Then he unhooked a water bag and dismounted with it. The Indian knew what a water bag was. He saw that the stranger had holstered his revolver as well. He didn't understand. Strangers always shot at his people. That was why his nation was at war with all strangers. But this one was coming toward him, smiling, with water.

Longarm hunkered down, just outside knife-swing range, and tossed the water bag to the Indian. The youth understood very well that this had to be some cruel trick. Perhaps the stranger meant to kill him just as he had water to his lips.

It didn't matter. Nothing mattered but the gurgling liquid he could feel inside the bag. He twisted off the cap. He put the mouth of the bag to his lips. He drank. The water was warm and flat. It tasted wonderful. As he gulped eagerly, Longarm said in Spanish, "Enough, for now. You'll make yourself sick."

The boy replied in the same language, albeit not as fluently, "Nobody has to tell a Diegueño how to get over dying of thirst. This is good water. Good, good, good. You show you have a good heart by giving an enemy water before you kill him. I feel much better now. I am ready."

Longarm called out, "Jessie? It's all right. Nothing but a sidewinder and a mighty hurt kid under here. You'd best break out that first-aid kit. Don't need nothing for snakebite. He's gunshot."

The Indian didn't understand the words. He was even

more confused when a woman who would have been pretty if she hadn't had such funny hair and eyes came around with a little tin box in her hands. She had a gun, too. It was holstered against her denim-clad hip. It was not at all clear why she had a box instead of her gun in her hands as she knelt beside him.

"Oh, the poor boy. He can't be old enough to deserve getting shot," she said.

As she opened the box, Longarm said, "Hold it. I suspect his leg bone's busted. We'd best get the real pain over before you go lathering him with iodine."

He told the Indian, in Spanish, "I am going to cut some greasewood splints. Then I am going to pull on your ankle. If it's only a bullet in there it won't hurt much. If the bone is broken it will hurt a lot. But not as much as it will later, if you don't let me set it before we splint it."

He didn't ask permission. The Indian was glad. There was a woman present, and the big stranger was talking to him as one man talks to another.

As Longarm cut the splints from a nearby greasewood the young Diegueño said, "I am called Popé and nothing, nothing, nothing can make me show pain."

"We are called Jessica and Custis," Longarm said. "I have heard of a great Pueblo leader called Popé. Back in the Shining Times he drove the Spanish out of the valley of the Rio Bravo."

"I know. We are not Pueblo, but we share their views on your people. Most of the time, that is. Why are you two behaving so strangely?"

Longarm placed a splint on the ground on either side of the downed boy's wounded leg. "We are not Spanish. But this is no time for a geography lecture. You all set, Jessie?"

They were both speaking Spanish now, as common courtesy. She said, "Wait." She cut two lengths of surgical gauze, then picked up the splints. "Now," she said.

Longarm grabbed the ankle of the wounded leg and pulled, hard, as his patient tried not to scream. It hurt even

238

more than he'd expected. His leg felt as if it was an empty wet stocking filled with broken glass that crunched, crunched, and then crunched some more. Then something popped inside his tortured thigh and it only hurt a lot. The yellow-haired woman must have been listening for it. She slapped the splints to either side of his thigh—the inner one too high for a decent woman to poke at a strange man —and then she had both ends tied against him tight, and it was odd how gentle hands capable of inflicting so much pain felt as she wiped the exposed wound in the middle with a wet thing that burned in a way good medicine should. The wound was bleeding again now. It took lots of dust to keep a wound like that from bleeding. As the big man still held his leg straight, the yellow-haired woman stuffed the hole with more of the burning wet cloth and then bandaged it so tight he knew she had to be a witch of great power.

Longarm let go of Popé's ankle and said, "That ought to keep you from bleeding to death before we can get you home. I hope you don't live far from here."

The bewildered Diegueño sat up on his elbows. "My own people are not far enough away for you to feel safe. They are too far away for me to crawl, even now," he told them.

"We can't just leave you here, Popé. How do you think your people would take it if we got you home to them now?" Longarm asked.

"They will probably kill you. I don't think I want to kill you now. But they won't know you are crazy."

Longarm turned to the girl. "He has a good point. How do you feel about forting up here while I see if I can get in and out with all my hair?"

She said, "Lonesome. Besides, if his people are related to Yuma they might not scalp their victims."

Popé said, "That is true. We have heard about scalping, from the Mexicans. Sometimes they scalp us. We think it's a stupid custom. When *we* finish killing people it is a waste of time to try to hurt them any more."

"I don't know, Jessie," Longarm said.

"I've powwowed with Kiowa-Apache, and I'm not bald, am I? Surely no reasonable person would want to hurt someone who'd just helped one of their own, would they?" she argued.

"Depends on how reasonable they might be. I don't like this at all, Jessie. I'd feel awful if I got us *both* killed."

"So would I. I'd never speak to you again. Now are we going to get this poor boy off this hot cactus flat, or are we going to argue some more?"

Longarm sighed. "I can see you're right about two things. This kid needs bed rest, bad, and you're just too damned stubborn to argue with. So help me get him on his feet."

To the south, Ki and his new recruits had not ridden far from the notch in the lava ridge when someone shouted a warning. Ki looked back to see dust, a lot of dust, headed their way, fast. At his side, Miki said, "There is no cover out here on this flat. Our only chance is to outride them!"

Ki looked the other way, at the shimmering mirage farther out on the flat. He made a mental note of one of those carrot-on-its-head trees, growing along the shoreline of the optical illusion as if it thought it was a headless palm along the shore of some tropical island. "We might get away that way," Ki said. "Or we might not. Either way, we'll wear our horses out, and we have far to ride. Listen to me, all of you. I have a plan."

It was a good one. It worked. For as the leader of the Black Dragon ninja troop watched from higher up, he seemed to see a larger party than he'd expected riding across a shallow lake toward the distant shimmering shore. The dragon leader was not fooled by the mirage, of course. He was fooled as the distant dots appeared to keep going, stirring up considerable mustard-colored dust for people who appeared to be fording a vast shallow lake.

He raised his rifle and cried, "After them! Take advantage of this slope to build up speed for the chase across that amusing puddle out there!"

His followers wouldn't have argued even had they thought it desirable. Spreading out in a skirmish line, they charged abreast as, farther out, Miki lay prone next to Ki in what certainly felt like the open and sighed, "They have seen us."

"Not yet. We were just up where they are. I know you can't see a mirage when you're *in* it. But to them we are."

"*Hai*, and all our horses have gone on to perhaps some other imaginary body of water, with the two you detailed to lead them. I feel like a fly on a hot stove, waiting to be swatted before I fry to death," Miki said.

Some of the others were grumbling as they watched the bigger gang bearing down on them at full gallop. Ki raised his voice and commanded, "Hold your fire, all of you, until you hear me open up. I was watching landmarks as we came this far. I know exactly when this open gravel we're on begins to look less like water to a man on horseback!"

It was a good thing they had been trained to unquestioning obedience, Ki thought. He knew what he was doing, but he still felt naked and helpless as he lay out in the middle of what, here, seemed a flat, dry expanse of gravel.

But he held his fire until the first charging horseman passed a greasewood he'd kept track of. Then, as the startled rider saw, too late, what seemed to him a ragged line of prone riflemen along the beach of a big blue lake, Ki fired.

He spilled his target. Other saddles began to empty as his own followers opened up, hurling dares and insults as well as bullets at the bewildered horsemen they had ambushed.

Then someone, on either side, shouted, "Stop yelling and start fighting, you salve-selling sons of noisy peacocks!" and all hell broke loose.

241

Ki blew away man after man, mounted or afoot, as the other gang attempted to make up for surprise with superior numbers. He found himself rolling in the gravel with a cursing, spitting foeman trying to stab him everywhere at once. Ki was too occupied with the other man's wrists to get his own knife out. He sank his teeth into his screaming enemy's throat. Then he rolled away, dug into his knapsack of *shuriken,* and proceeded to make people see stars.

Few of them got to see the spinning steel stars coming at them, of course, but skull after skull was filled for a last few moments with little white lights as cold steel buzz-sawed hotly through skin, bone, and brain. Ki ran out of *shuriken* before he ran out of people to throw them at, so he had to finish off the last few with his guns. They went down just as dead, either way.

As the noise died away and the dust began to settle, Ki got to his feet to tally the results. Miki was rising nearby, his face ash-gray from the desert dust or perhaps from all he'd just been through. Two other men on Ki's side survived. A couple who had been badly hurt had shot themselves to spare Ki embarrassment.

Miki stared in wonder at the torn-up bodies sprawled across acres of bloody gravel. Most were human. Those horses not killed had run away. Miki said, "We seem to be victorious. There are six of us left, counting the boys who led our horses across the mirage. I make it thirty, all right, twenty-eight of them down. I see nobody in uniform, Ki-San. Who could they have been?"

Ki picked up a wicked-looking dagger, saw its hilt was not marked with the Dai Nippon of the government's forces, and decided, "Ninja. Working for someone who didn't like us."

Miki said, "You mean someone who didn't like *you,* Ki-San. They were following *your* trail, as I recall. It was a fight to tell my grandchildren about some day, in any case."

One of the other survivors joined to ask wistfully where

242

the horses might be. "In my stupidity I seem to have stopped a bullet with my hip. It is not a serious wound. But I would feel better about it if I did not think I had to walk too far," he said.

Ki turned to stare thoughtfully to the west. The sun was lower now. The distant desert horizon was a glaring blur. "They must have heard the battle. They must have noticed the gunfire has stopped. They should be back any time now."

Miki sighed. *"Hai,* if they find it desirable to come back at all. They heard gunfire indeed, and they left here knowing we were outnumbered better than two to one."

The wounded man, Yashi, said, "Had it been up to me I would have picked others to take charge of our mounts. I know why Miki-San, here, chose them. I agree they would not have fought as well as the rest of us. It takes a certain courage to stand and fight against superior numbers. It also takes a certain courage to ride back to a quiet battlefield, not knowing just who might have won."

"We'll know in a while," Ki told them. "Since we have the time, we'd better see how much we can salvage here. Don't overload yourselves with food and ammunition, but gather all the canteens you can carry."

It didn't take long. Water weighs eight pounds a gallon. Two or three gallons was about all a man could carry on foot, along with his weapons, if he wanted to move at any speed at all. Ki regathered all but two of his *shuriken.* A steel star with a sprung point would not be worth throwing.

When they had run out of things to do, Miki screened his eyes against the glare to the west with an upraised paw. "The cowards are not coming back," he observed. "How far do you think they can get, alone on this desert, Ki-San?"

"Too far for us to chase on foot. They have over a dozen pony loads of water as well as our ponies. Before we start out, I desire all of you to swallow all the water you can from the canteens we'll be leaving behind, here."

Miki said, "I thought you said it was useless to chase after our mounts on foot."

"It would be worse than useless. It would be suicide," Ki said bluntly. "Even if we somehow managed to cross those cactus flats on foot, the coastal country beyond is where *los federales* should be out patrolling. *Los rurales* are bad enough, but the Mexican Army has new Hotchkiss guns to play with. They don't charge as often as they lob shells at suspicious strangers." Ki glanced up at the sky again. "We'll give them another hour. Once we leave here they'd never be able to find us again even if they wanted to. I do not find it desirable to leave tracks, and that's easy, on foot."

The wounded Yashi sighed and asked, "May one ask how far we have to walk, Ki-San? *Where* does not seem as important to this hip of mine."

"We'll try to take it easy. But we obviously can't stay here. The girl that idiot killed said there was a better pass over that ridge to our east, if we go north. We'll work our way back to the lava scree, where we won't leave foot-prints, and follow the ridge north until we find a way to cross it."

"Did your unfortunate companion say just how far we have to walk?" asked Yashi.

Ki didn't answer. He knew Yashi would feel better if he didn't know.

Lone Star's feminine intuition turned out to be right, but you couldn't tell, at first.

Longarm led the way afoot into the black-walled canyon Popé indicated, leading Old Buck with the wounded Indian aboard. Lone Star covered them from Ribbon's saddle. Dogs commenced to bark, women to howl, and men and boys pegged arrows at them. The Diegueño were terrible bowmen or perhaps just funning. It was hard to tell when an arrow thudded into the ground close.

But as Longarm trudged in the murderous glee faded to

stunned silence. For his people knew who Popé was, and never in the history of his nation had strangers found a real person at their mercy and been so nice to him.

It took Popé some time to explain. His mother, brothers, sisters, aunts, uncles, and cousins helped him down from Longarm's saddle and tried to haul him everywhere at once. When he finally managed to explain, a herd of weeping squaws charged the two whites to hug them, kiss them, sob at them, and try to haul *them* everywhere at once. By the time an older man had made them stop, Popé had been hauled out of sight to rest. The chief led them to his domed wickiup farther up the canyon and chased them inside.

As the three of them found seats around the dead fire in the middle, the chief said to Longarm in Spanish, "I mean no offense, but I don't know what to do about tobacco with you people. It is wrong to smoke with a woman. It seems wrong to insult a woman in pants as good-hearted as this one. I am open to suggestions."

Longarm knew he was expected to speak for both of them. "I think we should just talk, without smoke," he told the chief.

The chief smiled. "That seems very practical. You two already have me confused enough. The son of my daughter tells us he was jumped by a Mexican patrol and almost killed. He says you found him the next day and did not kill him. He says your woman here is a powerful witch who healed him, and I can see she is worth as many ponies as Popé says, even if she did not have such good medicine. May I ask why you were so good to one of my young men? I may be wrong, but you don't *look* crazy."

Longarm said, "We helped Popé for two reasons. We helped him because he needed help and we did not consider him our enemy."

"That is the crazy reason. What was the other?"

"We hoped to be able to have a conversation with you."

The canny old leader nodded. "You deserve more reward than your lives. But my people were poor before they were on the run. We can give you water. We can even spare a little food. We have no money and we need all our ammunition. I have heard some of you gringo men find an Indian girl an interesting novelty. The woman you have with you is more beautiful than any of our young women, but if that's what you want . . ."

Longarm didn't look at his lover. It was important to keep a straight face at times like these. He said soberly, "I don't feel this would be a good day to die. We seek only information natives of the Baja may have. We are searching for a man we like. He has a good heart, but no other friends down here we know of. Would you tell us if you had seen a tall, darker stranger, dressed much like us, traveling alone around here?"

The chief said flatly, "We would be happy to show you his body if any of our young men had noticed such a person. Our scouts have not seen anyone traveling alone out on the flats, and of course it is impossible to travel far among the confusion of this sierra. That is why we hide among its black rocks in the first place."

Longarm nodded. "This *rancherita* is hidden well. We never would have found our way without Popé to guide us. You say you've seen nobody riding alone. Have you scouted others?"

The chief smiled modestly. "Of course. This is wartime. There is a column of *federales* off to the west, screened by patroling *rurales*. They are searching the open desert for us, no doubt to avoid finding us. There are two troops of cavalry and a field artillery battery. Two guns. The *rurales* are nothing, and I have enough young men to deal with the cavalry. Big guns are another matter. Bravery and a swift pony matter little when one is charging cannister shot."

Longarm nodded. "I'd be forted up in these hills if I were in your moccasins, too. Would your scouts have noticed if the Mexicans had a prisoner or more riding along with them?"

"Yes, but how often do the Mexicans take prisoners?"

Lone Star gasped and murmured, "Oh, no!"

The two men ignored her. The old Indian said, "My scouts saw others between us and the military column. They did not attack, on my orders. We have all the enemies a sensible person could want this season."

Longarm waited patiently. The older man went on, "Two bands my young men think must be bandits, since they are not with the *soldados*. One band of thirteen riders, one band of about thirty. The bigger band behaved as if searching for something. They rode slower, as if scouting for a sign. And, oh, yes, I almost forgot, they saw a man and a woman, otherwise alone, wandering about between the two larger bands. They may have been a civilian couple, burned out by *los rurales*, or perhaps our brothers to the north. All the Diegueño are cross with Mexicans this season. The Mexicans started it. They always do. One of our young men was only trying to prove his manhood by stealing a pony. The Mexican who owned the pony shot the boy dead. Is that any way to respond to a harmless joke?"

Longarm said, "Some people have no sense of humor. Things like that happen in El Norte, too. Neither side ever seems to learn. But let's study on that gent riding alone with a woman."

Lone Star knew it was rude. She still had to say, "If that silly Yoko tagged along, it fits, Custis."

He shushed her with a manly frown he'd never have gotten away with in other company. As if he was speaking to their host, he said, "Our friend may have gone first to other friends who have a willful daughter who's often said how fond she was of him. Could you describe them any better, my uncle?"

"I am your father," the old man corrected. "I did not see the couple you ask about. They made a tempting target, but my young men are well behaved and they knew I had said not to attack more than one person without talking about it with me first. By the time they got back and I said two sounded like a nice round number the couple were gone. So we can't show them to you. But, wait, they did say the man was tall and wore a gringo sombrero."

Longarm and Lone Star exchanged glances. "I would like someone to lead us to where we might be able to cut their trail," Longarm said.

"*Heya*, I said you could have anything but our ammunition. But the hour grows late. By the time you could reach the place my scouts last saw the mysterious man and woman, the sun would be down."

Longarm said, "The full moon will rise shortly after sundown tonight, and pony hooves play hell with desert pavement."

The Indian nodded. "True. But even a full moon casts black shadows. A fighting moon is better for ambush than tracking and, forgive me, you seem to have forgotten there are two large bandit gangs out there as well."

Longarm glanced at Lone Star. She shook her head stubbornly. He sighed and said, "To tell the truth, I could use some time in my old bedroll with an old pal. But if that's our friends out there between two bands of who knows what, we have to catch up with 'em first. How soon can we get started?"

"You already have," the chief said. "Wait here, I'll get a guide for you. We were right about you two in the first place. You really *must* be crazy."

★

Chapter 19

Ki drove his bushis without mercy until he felt it safe to call a trail break amid a jumble of black boulders along the base of the lava cliff they were following north. He told the others to go easy on the water as well as their legs and scrambled atop a house-sized lump of lava to see how they were making out so far.

The sun had set far to the west, but the desert sky was still tangerine over that way, and the horizon was now drawn cleanly in a sweeping stroke of India ink. There was enough light left for Ki to see they had left no footprints in the loose black scree they had just walked across. The wounded Yashi had done some complaining about the treacherous footing, but the discomfort to all of them had been worth it. Ki decided they had to be at least ten miles or more from where they had had their big fight. That would have been far enough to matter in less open country. On the desert a man on foot could see for miles. On horseback he could see farther, by daylight. Now that it was getting dark, they could be in the clear.

Ki suddenly sensed a change in the light and turned to ask, "What do you think you're doing, you idiot?"

Miki was building a fire, a big one, below.

"We must boil some water for Yashi's wound," Miki said. "He's been acting too modest about it. We have to get that bullet out of him, unless it's *already* killed him."

Yashi, stretched out by the burning greasewood with his pants down, protested, "It's only a scratch, I tell you."

Ki hesitated. A night fire could be seen for miles, he knew. He also knew Yashi would never make many miles unless his hip was repaired before fever set in. "Make it a smaller fire, then," Ki said. "They call that stuff greasewood because it burns like it's been soaked in lamp oil, and this is no time to leave a light in the window for our long-lost ponies!"

Miki kicked the burning desert scrub into a smaller pile. If anything, it burned brighter, now. Miki placed a canteen cup on the coals. "We'll let the water boil a bit while I have a closer look at that wound," he told Yashi.

Yashi said it was nothing as Miki hunkered over him. "The *bo*-master whistled. "I'd hate to see what you call something. How could you have walked so far with a hole like that in you?"

Yashi shrugged. "A bushi does what he has to. It hasn't been bleeding much, even for a bullet wound."

"*Hai,* you were shot at close range. The powder burns sealed the edges as well as a hot iron could have. You're going to bleed more by the time I dig that bullet out. But we have to get that bullet out. We have no saké, either."

Yashi nodded soberly and took a kerchief from his shirt pocket to tie it in a knot to bite. Miki tore some other rags into strips and dropped them in the boiling water. Then he drew his dagger, passed it through the flames a few times, and let the blade cool. "You may put that knot in your mouth now, if you find it desirable," he said.

While Yashi's unwounded companion watched, ashen-faced, Miki probed for the bullet with a blade designed

250

more for killing. He was more a trained killer than a surgeon, in any case. Yashi's face broke out in beads of sweat. His sobs of pain almost broke through the wet knot between his clenched teeth. Miki had never been noted for his gentle touch, and now he couldn't be gentle. He knew it would hurt more in the end if he fiddled around. He simply went after the bullet as if he'd been shucking an oyster for a pearl. As blood spattered all over his hairy forearms, he got it out. He held it up to the light in his blood-slicked fingers and said, "*Hai*, a .45 pistol round. I said you'd picked it up at close quarters. I hope the other man died well?"

Yashi spat out the knot. "I shot him with my own gun. You were right. I seem to be bleeding like a stuck pig now."

Miki laughed, told Yashi he wasn't pretty enough to be a pig, and began to dress the ghastly wound.

Up atop the boulder, Ki was watching the desert rather than the operation. Something was moving on the horizon, to the south-southwest. Riders that far off would have been outlined clearly against the sunset. Whatever was out there had to be closer. He called down, "Someone's found our old battleground, I think."

"*Yoi!* They *did* come back with our mounts, after all!" the younger bushi shouted.

Before anyone could stop him, he stepped out in the open to yell like hell and fire a signal with his revolver.

Miki as well as Ki called him a stupid bastard. Ki saw that the husky *bo*-master was kicking out the fire without waiting to be told. Ki leaped down from his lookout and slapped the dumb bushi flat just on general principles, since the damage had already been done. "That was really smart, if those are Mexican riders out there," he snapped.

The kid he had knocked down sat up to protest. "It could be our comrades with our mounts, just as well, couldn't it?" he asked.

"Men who panic and ride off are not anyone's

251

comrades, you fool," Miki growled. "You may have noticed the battle we just enjoyed was a noisy one. Gunfire carries for miles across open country, and it takes a little longer to get to the sources of the sounds."

He turned to Ki and bowed stiffly. "We await your orders. A wounded man and two fools. Do we dig in or run?"

Ki said, "We run. This would be a poor place to make a stand even if we didn't have field artillery to worry about. Take the lead. I'll have to carry Yashi."

Yashi was the only one who argued. They all knew he was too chewed up to think straight. Miki headed north along the base of the cliff. Ki slung Yashi on his back and followed, with the noisy kid behind. They hadn't gotten more than a few yards from the now-dead fire before the first ranging rounds came screaming in.

Ki saw his own outline rimmed in bright orange on the scree ahead before the shock wave hit and he went down, Yashi and all. He rolled out from under the man he had been packing and made for the nearest cover, dragging Yashi after him by one limp arm. They were in a cleft of the cliff by the time the distant gunners decided that was close enough and commenced to throw a serious barrage on the target they had heard as well as spotted. During thunderous moments of flame, Ki was able to make out some of the damage. The kid who had been tagging behind was down, either dead or sincerely wishing he was, with both legs off at the hips.

Yashi was dead, too. As he examined the body with his fingers, Ki saw why *he* was still alive. Yashi's back, not his, had soaked up a dozen shards of shell casing. Ki sighed and closed the dead man's eyes. "Oh, well, you were probably a criminal and you'd have never made it far in any case. But I'm sorry you suffered all that pain for nothing," he muttered.

The shell fire died down. Ki knew what that meant. He was up and running. As he passed Miki, huddled behind a

252

boulder, the bushi leaped up to follow, panting, "Where are we going?"

"Anywhere. They'll be charging in to mop up now."

They both heard a distant rooster laugh. "What did I tell you?" Ki added.

Miki didn't answer. There was a time for running and there was a time for conversation. This was not the time for conversation.

They were both hard men, in good shape. Just the same, they were still human, so after they had run a few miles across ankle-twisting scree Ki flopped behind a boulder, drew his gun, and stared back along their moonlit wake, gasping for breath.

Miki took up his own position behind another boulder. "That wasn't fair. You have longer legs. Do you think we shook them off?" he wheezed.

"Not if they think anyone's left. Finding a whole mess of dead Orientals on the same gravel flat must have confused them indeed. But combat patrols are paid to act curious. I don't know what they'll think when they find two more dead Japanese, dressed gringo, near the fire they aimed at next. I hope they'll think both we and those others were one big gang, jumped by bandits or Indians. They may feel sorry about killing two survivors of whatever they think might have happened. They may not give a damn. I don't know whether they'll press on or ride home to put in for more medals and pulque. I don't want to find out the hard way. Are you up to more walking, Miki?"

"No. But a bushi does what he has to. I know we'd leave tracks farther out from this ridge. What if we tried climbing over it?"

Ki rose, ignoring the stitch in his side as he holstered his gun. "The Americans have a saying about frying pans and fires. We could be lucky that way, or we could just as easily trap ourselves in a box canyon. We know nothing about this country. Those troops probably have scouts who know it well."

253

Miki cursed and started walking again, but the code of Bushido allowed reasonable complaints, so he asked, "Which way do we go if they come along this cliff base after us? Neither seems at all desirable."

"Up, as best we can manage. We wouldn't stand a chance in the open to our left. I know you're good with a *bo*, Miki. How good are you at climbing?" he asked.

"Awful. I have a fear of heights. But then I'll no doubt fall off before I can climb high enough to worry about."

The Indian guide reined his paint in and said, "This is where we last saw that man and woman riding together. The trail still leads toward a gap in the sierra we can't see from here, now. In daylight, one can see it from here. I think that must have been what they were making for. They were dumb. The pass only leads to a dumb trail beyond the scablands."

Neither Longarm nor Lone Star had to dismount to read a trail like that, even by moonlight. "No offense, but I make it at least two dozen sets of steel-shod hooves leading off to the southeast," Longarm said.

The Indian said, "I know. I read sign, too. The man and woman were alone when we last saw them out here. Others, many others, seem to have cut their trail before us. If they are *rurales*, they know the pass your friends were making for is no good. I think the larger party must be following them for some other reason."

"I think you're right." Longarm turned to Lone Star to observe. "This is getting to be a big one, Jessie. If Ki and that little gal are still alive, they figure to be boxed by a considerable outfit. I figured Nakamura had about a dozen riders, which would be bad enough, but this is starting to get downright thought-provoking."

She said, "That's all the more reason Ki and Yoko may need help. I don't see why those renegades would be after Ki or Yoko in the first place, since they couldn't *know* either. I think we're scouting dragon tracks here, Custis. Lord knows how they traced Ki this far, but on the other hand it's a secret society, and Yoko's father has all sorts of folk working for him."

The Diegueño wasn't interested in their discussion. "Hear me, I have shown you to the trial you asked about," he said. "Now I must get back to my people. I don't think that was mountain thunder we heard a while ago. We get little rain this time of year, and the sky is cloudless tonight."

Longarm nodded. "Sounded like distant gunfire to me, too. I was sort of wondering about it, but I figured you knew your country better, and since you never mentioned it—"

The Indian cut in, "I go back to my people now. I have done what I was asked to do by my chief. Those big guns were muttering well north of that notch I told you about. You may or may not get through. My own people are closer to those big guns. They may need me."

"If your people have ears they'll have heard that gunfire sooner. Sound takes a while to get this far from that ridge they're hid out in. You'll do better staying with us, old son."

But the Diegueño wasn't listening. He was riding away fast.

Longarm shrugged. "Well, if the *federales* have that sort of friendly band pinned down I feel for 'em both but it ain't our fight. Ki, Yoko, and just about everyone else went *that* way."

They rode on, stirrup to stirrup in the moonlight. Lone Star didn't find it as romantic as she might have under other circumstances. She said, "I thought Count Togo had more sense than to send Marines openly out after Ki, didn't you?"

"It's a dumb way to keep a secret society secret. But it works two ways. We could be trailing military riders trailing our pals, or we could be reading lizard tracks. I can't say how many of the sneaky critters there may be in Southern California, when they ain't in the Baja. But, hell, the average Klan Klavern can mount a fair-sized posse if they allow the kids to tag along. Mayhaps old Togo just told all he had to work with to go after Ki. They sure seem to want him bad."

"Not as much as I do," she said grimly. "For once we're all together again I mean to tie a tin can to that dragon's tail and teach 'em not to mess with me and mine!"

"That sounds like fun. But, Jessie, I hope you understand that once we catch up with Ki and I know you have *him* to protect you, I still have my own wood to split. Lord knows where poor Billy Vail thinks I am tonight, and if I don't come back sooner or later with old Nakamura or his hide, I'll have a hell of a time explaining all this to my boss."

She said, "I know. You've been very sweet about helping me save Ki's hide. Maybe, once we're all together again, we can help you catch Nakamura before we go after the Black Dragon."

He grimaced. "I ain't *that* fond of old Ki, no matter what you say about him being just a devoted admirer you inherited from your dad. I got enough to worry about without him shooting stars past me just for fun. Once we catch up, I want you, him, and that little gal to head straight back to San Diego. You and Ki should have very little trouble making it back to Texas from there, covering for one another as you travel sort of discreet."

"Pooh, once I know Ki's safe by my side again I won't have to sneak about. Starbuck Enterprises keeps railroad cars parked all over the country for my private use. We'll just have the Southern Pacific hook one on for us and travel home in style as well as safety."

He grinned. "Yeah. The Reno brothers and James boys combined would have a time boarding a private car with two such dangerous critters locked up inside it with plenty of guns and ammo."

She said, "There's always room for one more, Custis. You do have to travel east a ways, to get back to Denver, and as I recall the varnish Dad left me in the San Diego

256

yards, there's a shower built into the master bedroom at one end."

He chuckled. "I like to start out clean, but I'll be switched if I can figure out where we'd let *Nakamura* ride. He wasn't last seen traveling alone, either. At least some of his gang figures to give up, and in any case, Billy Vail doesn't want any of 'em in Denver. I'm supposed to turn 'em over to the Frisco consulate, Lord willing and the creeks don't rise."

She shook her head wearily. "Custis Long, you're a mule-headed man and a fool as well if you refuse help from me and mine. You know you'll never be able to take a gang that size all alone."

"Never is a careless word, Jessie. I got five rounds in my Colt, two in my derringer, and a dozen in my Winchester at the time. She'll carry more, if a mere dozen owlhoots want to act testy when I catch up with 'em. So what the hell."

"Going up against odds like that sounds insane, Custis."

"I know. I figure that's about what we're doing at the moment. Add up two dozen against two, don't forget there's *federales* about as well, and I'll agree you're a mule-headed fool, too."

The odds against Ki and the last bushi, Miki, were even worse as they heard at least two cavalry troops thundering along the base of the cliff their way. Miki's first instinct was to run some more. But Ki grabbed his arm and snapped, "No, that cleft we passed just a moment ago."

Miki didn't argue. He just felt stupid, running *toward* the thunder of hooves on scree. Then they were both up the narrow cleft, hoping it was narrow enough for their pursuers to miss in the moonlight.

It wasn't, Ki realized, as he saw how the steep path ahead widened out where the running waters of uncountable rains had been able to bite into softer rock. Worse yet, an obvious trail had been beaten into the black sand and bunchgrass by others, a lot of others, who knew of this route through the sierra as well. As they jogged up the incline, Ki said, "Sorry, Miki. It looked like just a rock shelter."

"Hai," his fellow fugitive said, "but look on the bright side. Every trail has to lead somewhere and now we know, at least, why those others just sounded the charge."

"I was wondering about that, too. We'd left no trail. Their scouts told them this side canyon lay just ahead. They wanted to catch up before we got to it. If we'd only kept going, they might have turned in here and we'd be in the clear!"

Miki grunted. "Maybe. I'd rather fight with my flanks covered than be caught in the open. Where do you think we ought to make our stand, Ki-San?"

Ki said, "Any place will be as bad. Thanks to those cowards who ran off with our mounts, we don't have enough ammunition for a real war."

"I know. That's why I left my carbine behind, too. I'd have never packed this much water had I known I was going to die before sunrise. But at least we can make them *work* at it!"

"Keep going," Ki insisted. "There could be a better place farther up. They won't be able to charge too fast up this steep grade."

As they got near the top and saw the trail dropped off on the other side into total darkness, Miki stopped. "This is as good as it's going to get. *Kiku!* Was that the scrape of steel on stone I just heard back there?"

Ki drew his revolver, stepped behind a flat-topped boulder, and began to deal out his deadly *shuriken* like cards. "They're dismounting, just outside. With luck we may be able to hold them from here a while," he said.

Miki took up his own stand behind a boulder across the trail.

A distant voice echoed up the canyon in Spanish, saying, "We know you are there, *Indios!* I have sent riders to block the other end of your big turn to nowhere. Come out like good little Diegueños and I promise you an honorable, quick death. If you make me waste more valuable shells on you, and we find you at all alive at the end . . . well, you know our customs as well as we know yours, eh?"

Miki chuckled. "They think we are wild Indians."

Ki didn't think it was funny, and it was certainly no great improvement. *Federales* on the prod were hardly apt to ask to see passports. They liked to write simple military reports. Taking any variety of prisoners called for tedious paperwork, and few below the rank of field grade could read or write to begin with.

The same voice called out, "Listen, *muchachos*, we know you are savages, but you have been under our shell fire before. So surely you know it hurts less to die by rifle fire, smoking a good cigar. I promise each of you will get his own last smoke. I shall not cut one cigar in two for you. I can afford to be generous."

"How do they know there are only two of us?" Miki hissed.

"Footprints. Let's hope it makes them brave as well as noisy," Ki muttered.

"*Hai,* he's right about shell splinters bouncing off solid rock all about one."

The standoff continued for a time. When nobody yelled at them again, Ki said, "Brace yourself. They're probably wheeling their Hotchkiss back to train on this slot from the flats."

They were, but before anything happened Ki heard someone clear his throat nervously in the darkness behind them. He casually reached for a *shuriken* but didn't throw it when a small, sad voice asked, "Why are they after you, too?"

Ki replied soberly, "I'm not sure. We haven't done anything to them. But you know how some people are."

The Spanish-speaking Indian stepped into view out of nowhere. He'd have looked more like an elderly Apache to Ki if Ki hadn't known this was not Apacheria. The Indian said, "This certainly has been a most unusual evening.

259

First some total strangers saved one of my young men. Now I find two more have wandered into my ambush, and they sound crazy, too. But let me see if I have this straight in my poor head. Are those Mexicans your enemies?"

"Would *friends* have chased us in here? What was that about an ambush?" Ki asked.

The old chief said, "Speak slower. I am trying to understand. I heard them offering you two tobacco just now. I think you must be their enemies. They are our enemies, too. What do you think that makes us?"

"Friends?" Ki tried.

The old man grimaced. "That can't be. We don't know you. But I don't think it would be right to kill the enemies of enemies. That would be doing enemies a favor, and *that* can't be right."

"Maybe we could be allies, then," Ki suggested.

The Spanish word was unfamiliar to the Diegueño, who only used the language to get along with more reasonable Mexicans in peacetime. Ki explained the term to him twice.

"That is a very practical suggestion, even if our traditions fail to mention such unusual ideas. In any case, they will be firing their big guns, soon. They always aim the same way. We are about to be blown up unless we go somewhere else."

Ki said he didn't want to be blown up. The chief nodded and said, "I didn't think so. Follow me."

Then he vanished again. Ki scooped up his stars and followed. Miki tagged along suspiciously, muttering in Japanese, "I hope you know what we are doing, Ki-San."

Then they were in the lava tube with the old Indian, or with someone padding along in the pitch blackness ahead of them. They hadn't gone far when the glassy walls around them chimed like a huge bell and they could both see the dull cherry glow all around them for a moment. Ki smiled thinly. *"Yoi,* I was wrong, and you have no idea how nice that feels," Miki said.

The chief led them out the far end into an ambush indeed until he told all the other Diegueños atop the flat-topped massif to behave. "We were hoping they would move in this close," he told Ki. "We can't fight them out on the open desert. Here we hold the high ground and have them at some advantage. Watch your step! To your right the cliffs fall sharply away. Behind you, of course, is the rim of the canyon you just followed me out of."

As if to prove it, the slot in the vast flat-top they stood on lit up with a roar and smoke rose even higher than they were now.

Ki eased over to the dreadful dropoff to the west. He stared soberly down at the ant pile gathered around the canyon's narrow entrance. The battery farther out on the flats winked like blood-shot fireflies. There was another crash of exploding shells deep in the now empty canyon to Ki's right. "Nice aim, at least. What are we waiting for, Chief? We have a nice field of fire from up here," he told the Indian.

The old man said, "It will be better once at least some of them dash up into the canyon. I have young men on both sides. We have big rocks to drop on them, too. Alas, the ones out on the flat will run away when they see it is an ambush. They always do. But every little bit helps."

So the fighting men on the flat-top waited patiently as shell after shell was fired harmlessly into the lava at a lower level. The canny old Diegueño had planned as well as he could, and it might have worked out as he'd planned, with a few casualties to one side and none to the other. That was what Indian warfare was all about.

But out on the flats Longarm and Lone Star had other plans. For they'd read enough sign by now to have a better grasp on what might be going on. It was Lone Star who said, "If Ki and Yoko found that pass a blind alley and got out in time, surely they'd have headed north along that ridge, right?"

"That's what I'd have done. And right now said ridge is getting pounded good by Hotchkiss guns. No wheelmarks on this trail we've been following."

She asked, "Oh, what if Ki and Yoko rode into a *federale* ambush?"

"Sure was a noisy one. But the only way to find out is to find out. You stay here. I'll ride on the sound of them guns for a look-see," he told her.

She did no such thing, of course. He was tired of arguing with her. They rode far and fast, abreast, until they topped a gentle rise and Longarm called a halt. "Now just simmer down till I sort this confusion out, Jessie."

He studied the scene ahead until he decided, *"Federales.* Nobody else packs such big guns. As far as the silvery moon gives me the power to make things out, I make it two gun crews just ahead, firing into that black cliff beyond. Don't ask me why. If they knew what they were doing they wouldn't have their dumb rear ends pointed our way with nobody covering 'em."

Lone Star said, "I think I see others, over there, closer to the rocks. If they're out to pound someone loose from the rock wall beyond, why couldn't it be Ki and Yoko?"

"When you're right you're right, and if you're wrong, I never liked *federales* in the first place." He drew his Winchester from its boot with a wolfish grin. "I'd say we got the poor bastards surrounded, wouldn't you?"

He spun his mount and she followed him back down the slope as she got her own saddle gun out. They had some discussion about that point as they tethered their ponies to a bush both Ribbon and Old Buck commenced to nibble, whatever it was. She told him his notions about the weaker sex were silly as they both loaded every chamber of their guns. Then the deadly duo moved in, first afoot and then on their bellies, to make good on his brag.

Lone Star agreed to take out the crew to the north after Longarm grudgingly conceded it was closer to the border if things worked out tedious.

He took on the crew to the south, picking off as many as he could from cover and then charging in to mop up, zigzagging in the moonlight as he threw rapid fire and considerable cursing at the bewildered artillerymen. The two he managed to miss in the tricky light wanted no part of what they saw as a skirmish line coming their way. When they ran like hell, Longarm let them go.

Lone Star had crept in closer before opening up, so she only sent one gunner loping toward the cliff base, screaming something about a horde of savages on his tail.

She levered another round in the chamber of her carbine and leaped gracefully over the trail of the field piece she had captured to dash over and see if Longarm needed a hand.

She saw he had put his Winchester aside and picked up his first Hotchkiss round. As she grasped his intent, she moved gleefully to help him man the gun. But he said, "Not me. Them. Cover us against counterattack while I see how this contraption works. We didn't have such fancy artillery when I was in the army. But what the hell, a big gun's a big gun."

Lone Star moved out to his right flank and dropped into some pear to cover his position as he reloaded. Longarm slammed the deadly but handy-sized round in the breech, cranked the barrel down a lot, and pulled the lanyard.

The Hotchkiss roared and sent his ranging round screaming into the *federales* massed around the canyon mouth. When Longarm saw he had judged the range so neatly, he commenced to load and fire seriously. This gave the confused Mexican troopers three grim choices. They could stand there letting some mysterious someone blow the livers and lights out of them—they could charge what they'd just been assured was a howling horde of whatever —or they could run like hell up a dark and spooky but quiet canyon. Most chose the latter, shoving and cursing to get some cover between them and that captured battery. For, from the way Longarm was firing, it was easy to see two gun crews, good ones, were mad as hell at *los federales*.

The Indians on the rimrocks above the crowded canyon

were as confused as the Mexicans below. But they still proceeded to rain arrows, bullets, and boulders down into the screaming, milling mass of horse and human flesh down there. Little Bighorn hadn't lasted long, either. Having an even greater edge on their enemies, the Diegueños made short work of more troops than Custer had led into a perhaps less stupid mistake.

As the noise died down to a few low moans and the sharper screams of the wounded being finished off by gleeful Diegueños down there, the old chief turned to Ki and said, "I hope that by the time future generations hear the song of this fight, their elders will have some idea of just what has been going on around here tonight. That artillery fire has stopped, too. Why do you think they began to shell their own people, my son?"

"They must have made a mistake with their elevation," Ki replied. "Other *federales* made it out or never rode in to begin with. I think my friend and I had better do some scouting for you."

"Wait. I have many scouts who know this land better than you."

"Do they know how to spike a cannon?"

"No. But be careful. I would not like to lose two sons the same night I adopted them!"

Ki assured his new father that his mother's people could teach some Indians a thing or two about night fighting. Then, together with Miki, he moved back down the lava tube, then down the canyon trail. "We'll circle in from their north," he told Miki.

Miki said, *"Hai.* They'll expect Indians to cut off their line of retreat to the south. How many in all do you think got away?"

"A squad or two of the smarter cavalry. There may be a dozen or so survivors dug in with the guns. Troopers who knew better than to ride up a blind alley would hesitate to ride toward guns that seemed to be firing at them. But we can't count on that. If they assumed the low elevation was

264

a mistake, they may be dug in with the gunners."

"What if all of them have run away?"

"Our mission is to make sure our Indian friends don't have to worry about those field guns, not to kill for the sake of killing."

They stopped talking about it as they got away from the now-silent battle ground to ninja-foot through the scant cover of the flats, moving in a crouch, their weapons ready for anything.

Ki had already judged the position of the field pieces very well. As he was able to make them out as dull black blobs in the moonlight, he whispered, "I see them. They seem to have been left behind, untended. Cover me. I'm still going in to spike them."

He might have, had anyone but Longarm and Lone Star moved back to the rise behind the guns to see what might happen next. Ki might have died, too, had not it been the gentler Lone Star instead of Longarm who spotted movement in the moonlight to the flank she was covering and called out, "I see you, *amigo*. Now don't you want to stand up and grab for some stars?"

Longarm swore. *"Shoot* the rascal, don't *lecture* him, for God's sake!" he snapped.

But Ki had recognized her voice. So as Longarm fired, Ki was flat on the dirt, yelling, "Hold your fire, Jessie!"

Longarm did. Lone Star leaped to her feet, sobbing, "Ki? Is that you?"

Ki assured her it was.

"Lord save us all from impulsive she-males!" Longarm muttered, as she ran to meet her segundo, throwing her arms around him as he got to his feet in the moonlight.

Longarm followed her, of course. He spotted Miki standing a few yards beyond, at least as confused as he was. "If that fat boy's a friend of yours, Ki, he's sure aiming that rifle the wrong way. I want it down. I mean now," Longarm said.

Ki quickly explained the situation to the bushi, who

265

spoke no English. Miki stared thoughtfully at Longarm's impolite gun muzzle and grudgingly lowered his own. "Is he as tough as he looks?" he asked Ki.

"Yes. We keep trying to kill each other, and so far it's never been decided who might be the toughest," Ki said.

Lone Star cut in, "Enough of this bragging. You have to tell me all about it, since I saw you last in Houston, Ki! Is Yoko with you? Is she all right?"

Ki said, "No. She was with me. She was killed saving my worthless life. I'll tell you both all that's happened as we get back to my Indian friends. They'll be getting anxious, and we've all had enough surprises for one night."

By the time they were all seated around the old chief's fire, eating tortillas and sipping pulque, Ki knew as much as Longarm and Lone Star, they knew as much as Ki, and none of them were sure just what had been going on.

"I've been thinking about that other gang we wiped out," Ki said.

"You mean the Black Dragons?" asked Jessie.

"I don't know who else they might have been," Ki said. "I'm more worried about who sent them after me. Count Togo struck me as a cool, calculating politician. The ninjas we tangled with were wild as hell. I'm pretty sure Togo slickered me into doing some dirty work for him back at the consulate. The fire-eater he allowed me to have a sword fight with was his superior, and crazy enough to be a dragon."

Longarm swallowed some pulque. "There are times I wish I could get *my* boss into a gunfight with somebody better, too. Although I can't say I'm as ambitious as old Togo. As I understand them sneaky lizards, they're out to gain control of their government by sneaking into it, right?"

"Yes. Count Togo is already high on the totem pole. Even higher now, thanks to me. He may be smart enough to consolidate his position before he makes any more wild moves, whether he's behind all this or not. On the other hand—"

Longarm cut in, "On the other hand, I find Japanese politics too confusing for a West-by-God-Virginia boy, and we got more sensible matters to settle." He stared thoughtfully at the moon-faced Miki, across from him. "I'm glad you took care of Nakamura so discreet. I imagine the State Department and the Japanese ambassador will be happy to hear they can just forget about the cuss as well. American newspapers hardly ever publish stories about gents eaten by buzzards in the Baja. Just the same, I was sent to round up Nakamura and his gang, plural, and we seem to have one left over."

"Miki and I have fought together, side by side," Ki protested.

Longarm said, "I know. You told me. I ain't finished. I ain't got a warrant with his particular name on it, either. So how in thunder am *I* supposed to tell one fool Oriental from another? Do I word my final report sort of careless, everyone may assume that where I say Nakamura and his gang got wiped out by bandits well outside my jurisdiction, *all* of 'em must be dead."

Lone Star hugged Longarm's arm. "Isn't he sweet?" she asked Ki.

"I'm still waiting for the fine print," Ki said.

Longarm smiled thinly and said, "There ain't none. Since I don't know for certain who your flat-faced pal might be, and couldn't talk to him even if I did, I'm in no position to sign a contract with him. But if I *was* able to talk to him, I might have some good advice for him."

Ki nodded. "He's listening."

"Don't translate in front of us," Longarm said. "I know for a fact that Jessie, here, speaks the lingo, and I wouldn't want her swearing false if my advice don't work out right."

He took another sip of pulque to give himself time to choose his words with care. "Whoever this rascal may be," he went on, "I notice our Indian hosts seem sort of fond of him. It wouldn't take him any longer to learn Diegueño than it would English. All in all, he'd be a lot less likely to wind up rope dancing down this way. Should he ever get picked up by *rurales* they'll no doubt just shoot him out of hand. California vigilantes are likely to treat him meaner, and they're better at catching a lone bandit, in any case. So if I was in whatever position he may be in, I reckon I'd settle down with some nice Diegueño squaw and say no more about it."

Ki stared thoughtfully at Longarm, then nodded grudgingly. "You're all right, Longarm." He rose, beckoned to Miki, and led him away from the fire for a few words of wisdom in private.

Lone Star saw that the old chief had been trying to follow the conversation in English without much luck. She switched to Spanish and said, "Please forgive us, my father. My friends think quicker in English. They were not talking about you or your people."

The old Diegueño looked relieved. "I have known for some time you all have good hearts for strangers, my daughter. May we talk about those big guns we brought back into these hills with us, now? Thanks to you, we have many guns and much ammunition now. If the Mexicans bother us again we mean to slaughter them until they learn to leave us alone. But none of my young men know how to shoot those big guns. Could you teach them how, before you have to leave?"

Longarm could have, but some of his best friends were Mexicans who didn't work for their vicious dictator. "I had to stop when I did because the firing mechanism came loose," he said.

This was true. He'd made sure of that before leaving the guns in the first place. "Your young men can still break open the shells and use the powder for any muzzle loaders you have," he said. "Tell them to use half as much as their older guns are used to. You might find some use for the Hotchkiss wheels, too. I'd just shove the rest where the sun never shines and forget about it."

The old chief said his words were wise. "Since you refuse to stay here and be my children forever, and say you must start back to El Norte so soon, may I show you to your wickiup now? I know the fiesta is still going on, but my people are sure to yell all night, and if you are sleepy..."

Longarm and Lone Star thought it was a grand notion. When they got to their guest quarters up the slope they saw it had been made fresh with sweet-smelling brush and that their own bedrolls and possibles had been left there for them by their thoughtful hosts.

They were both tired enough to sleep at least a weekend away, but as they undressed and bedded down it seemed sleep was out of the question, at least until that fool with the drum got drunk enough to bang it softer outside.

On the other hand, once they had cuddled and stroked a while, neither felt they had to go to sleep quite *this* early, and it wasn't as if they had to worry about anyone hearing them as they commenced to make love in time to the dancing drum outside.

In other guest wickiups a discreet distance away, neither Ki nor the former bushi, Miki, felt like sleeping, either. For, though the pretty little squaws making love with them spoke not a word of Spanish or English, let alone Japanese, the way of a man with a maid required not a word of explanation.

Miki was more surprised by the finer points of Indian lovemaking, since unlike Ki he was new to the American West. But he found his playmate a most enjoyable novelty while she, in turn, was most curious about gringo ways and thought that was what Miki was teaching her. As he drove her wild, the burly killer decided Ki's suggestion he go native made a lot more sense than he'd thought at first.

A few yards away, Ki was regretting the fact that everyone else had to leave so soon. His bedroll partner was even prettier, and had some Indian tricks he'd never encountered before. And, damn it, she only had one night to show them all to him.

269

★

Chapter 20

Getting back across the border was no easier but a lot less dangerous than getting so far south had been. For, sure they were up against a full-scale Indian war now, both the rural police and army troops forted up tight to wait for the full-scale army Mexico City was sending to rescue them.

Lone Star would have felt safer in any case, with both Ki and Longarm covering her from either side as they shot occasional sarcastic comments at one another and wary glances at anything moving anywhere else.

Once they made it back to San Diego they split up, as they'd agreed to on the trail. Jessie felt she had to deliver the bad news about Yoko to her father in person. Longarm felt he had to pay a diplomatic call on the Japanese consulate. When Ki offered to go along and cover for him, Longarm said, "Don't talk dumb. How many times do you think I want to have to rescue you from there? They was never after *me* in the first place. I got to tell *some* infernal official about Nakamura, and Frisco's too far out of my way. You stay with Jessie and don't let the dragons bite."

Ki did, trying not to think about that master bedroom built into the private railroad car they would all be sharing, unless Togo murdered the big bastard. Ki had long resigned himself to the delicate relationship between himself and the woman he loved, and Longarm wasn't as annoying to him as some of her other lovers. But Ki still wasn't looking forward to that long train ride to Texas.

Longarm wasn't too happy about where he was going, as he did what a man just had to do. He strode boldly into the consulate, and found himself explaining the delicate Nakamura matter to a funny little gent in glasses too big for him and a starched collar way too small. The diplomat didn't seem to know what they were talking about. Then a paper wall slid open and Count Togo in the flesh and full dress uniform came in to chase the other one out and take over. As they eyed each other warily across the desk between them, Togo said, "You may forget about the distress Nakamura may have caused our two countries, since, if he is no more, he never existed, understand?"

Longarm shrugged. "He was never our problem in the first place. I told a sheriff called Lopez he could stop looking for the son of a bitch. I never went into details. I'm glad I won't have to file a tedious report on such a tedious rascal. Can we talk about your Black Dragon now?"

Togo sighed. "The dragon is a mythical beast. It does not exist."

"Do tell? Then who the hell's been pestering Jessie Starbuck all this time?"

"You speak of a time that is past," purred Togo. "It is possible that back in the misty times of legend some misguided dreamers dreamt of dragons. Some may, as you suggest, have sought to annoy an American woman of wealth and power. But I ask you to take my word that the matter has been dealt with, and that only men loyal to the will of the Chrysanthemum enjoy any power to cause or not cause trouble in your country at this moment."

Longarm said, "I notice you're sporting another gold stripe on your sleeve. Moments only last moments, and I'm a personal friend of Miss Starbuck's as well as the law. So, legal or not, I ain't leaving here till you convince me she don't have no more lizards to worry about!"

Togo sighed. "I know better than to offer you my word as an officer and a gentleman. But have you not considered my rank as a count of the new Japanese nobility?"

"To tell you the honest truth, I never. What's the difference between a new-fashioned Japanese count and an old-fashioned one?"

"There was no such rank under the shogunate," Togo explained. "When the royal court was restored to full power, a new peerage, modeled on the English peerage, was established. I am a noble of the new aristocracy. Need I say more?"

Longarm shrugged. "I ain't boned up on English nobility, let alone a nobility headed up by a flower. But I follow your drift, and old Ki said you got rid of a superior sort of slick. Is it safe to assume he might have been one of them lizards?"

Togo smiled softly and said, "You may assume whatever you find desirable. The man was my honored and revered master until for some reason he chose to die, bravely if not well. I shall deny this if you ever repeat it, but there may have been other officials attached to this consulate who shared some of his views on early Japanese mythology. For some reason, they all chose to go hunting in the Baja. I tried to tell them the Baja was a dangerous place for sport, but they insisted, and what was I to do? Before I was promoted, I mean?"

Longarm smiled thinly. "Ki's right. You're a real con artist. It was you who told them where Ki and that gal was headed, right?"

"Someone had to. Her father was loyal to the Chrysanthemum."

Longarm nodded, rose, and said, "It sounds so sneaky I

just might buy it. But I warn you, Count . . ."

"Please don't be rude," Togo said. "Neither you nor your friends are in as much danger as certain others are now."

It would be some time before Longarm would know for certain how loyal Count Togo might or might not be to the Chrysanthemum Throne. For the outside world would hear little of him until, as Admiral of the Japanese fleet, he would lead it to a stunning victory over the Russian Navy in the early days of another century. But even as Longarm, Lone Star, and Ki were boarding the train to ride back to Texas that evening, some of Togo's countrymen in Houston had already discovered to their dismay just how the tough young nobleman and military officer felt about the way they felt about his emperor.

The crooked American importer, Posner, stared down in more confusion than fear as he was led into a basement room at the Houston consulate.

The dishonored consular attaché, Yanada, was kneeling before him on a white mat, dressed in a clean white kimono, hair drawn up in a traditional samurai knot, holding a razor sharp ko-dashi by the clean white rice paper wrapped around its glistening steel blade. Another man dressed all in white stood behind the kneeling man, gripping a longer but not duller-looking blade in his own two hands.

Yanada smiled up at Posner and said, "I sent for you because I thought you might like to join me. I have just received a wire from San Diego. It would seem our game did not go well at all. The winners have given us the choice of accepting our defeat gracefully or the more disgusting way. The point of our charade was to restore our traditional honor. I do not find it desirable to stand trial as a common criminal."

Posner gulped and said, "I told you not to mess with Starbuck Enterprises. So what's this shit about *we*? Ameri-

274

can law has nothing on yours truly, and I don't see how any fool Japanese court figures to try me."

By this time the ninja who had escorted Posner in had discreetly backed out of the basement room, leaving just the three of them to discuss the matter.

"I know all too well how you could wriggle off the hook, you worm," Yanada said. "You failed to tell me the Starbuck girl had so many other friends. And now most of my friends are dead. I still don't know how they managed to wipe out so many of us, but the man who wired me does not lie about such matters, even if he is not one of us."

Yanada opened the front of his kimono, exposing his bare belly. He told his assistant, "I desire for him to see how a man must behave at times like these. But get *his* head first. I do not desire him to see my own head roll."

Then Yanada took a deep breath, grasped the papered blade in both hands, and drove it into his belly. Posner groaned as Yanada, face beaded with sweat but otherwise expressionless, cut sideways across his own guts until, human agony getting the better of samurai honor, he hissed, *"Ima!"*

But despite his mousy appearance, or perhaps because of it, Posner was a dangerous man in his own right. He had already learned how fast Japanese blades could move. So, as the swordsman spun and slashed, Posner drew and fired.

They went down together, the Japanese with a bullet in his head and Posner's head grinning back at them from a corner as their bodies landed in a tangled pile.

The disemboweled witness to their mutual destruction realized, sickly, what a dreadful error he'd just made. He tried not to scream. It was dishonorable to scream. But scream he did, long and loud, for quite some time.

About a week later, back in Denver, Longarm had hoped to find his boss in a good mood as he reported in earlier than usual for a Monday morning.

He saw he had hoped in vain when Vail glanced at the

banjo clock on his paneled wall and snapped, "You're late."

Longarm sat down, fished out a smoke, and said, "No, I ain't, Billy. That fool clock and me both agree I beat old Henry to work this morning. Nobody ever beats *you*. You got the key."

"I know what time of day it is, cuss your silly smirk," Vail said. "I was discussing the day of the month, not the time of day. Where in thunder have you been all this time?"

Longarm struck a light for his cheroot. "Just about all over, boss. For this last case was awful. I'd have wired more details but, like you said, the situation was delicate. Suffice it to say, I've been assured the royal flower is satisfied about the way I handled that renegade. I tried to tell them more about the way he wound up dead and eaten by buzzards, but they seem to think he never existed after all, now that they don't have to worry."

"I know all about that," Vail growled. "Washington wired us about how tickled the Japanese are. *Mexico* is mad as hell. I thought I told you not to start no more wars with Mexico, Longarm."

Longarm studied the tip of his cheroot for a thoughtful moment. "They're just guessing. You have my word I left no official record of crossing any borders, and it just ain't fair of them to think of me every time some fun-loving gringo busts a few heads down yonder."

Vail said, "I hear tell it was more like a *rurale* company and a battalion of *federales,* this time. What makes you so mean, old son?"

Longarm took another drag on his cheroot. "I like most Mexicans. It's the ones who work for their rotten government I can't seem to get along with. I know you ordered me direct to stop invading Mexico, Billy, but you ordered me to go after the Nakamura gang, too. It wasn't my fault they jumped the damn border. Anything I might have had to do to others I met in my travels was personal. Nobody left over can prove I was anywhere near the Baja, boss.'"

Vail said grudgingly, "That's what I wired Mexico City after they told me how few survivors you'd left in your wake. But all that fool wiring back and forth took place at least a week ago. So you've got to do better than that, you tardy cuss."

Longarm shrugged. "Well, for openers, the railroad line I spent some of the time on was sort of out of my way. I figured the taxpayers wouldn't mind, since I don't mean to bill 'em the usual six cents a mile I'm allowed."

Vail raised an eyebrow. "I suspicion I know the line you took. But the D&RG up from Texas gets one here in no more than a day, allowing for cows on the track. So 'fess up. You was on the Circle Star all this time, right?"

Longarm looked shocked and protested, "Now, Billy, I was no such place at all for anything like a week! Couple of nights, maybe, but as a matter of fact the Houston police asked my help in clearing up a local mystery that could have been federal, for all we knew. They was suffering an outbreak of Oriental floaters in the Houston ship channel and, knowing I was sort of an expert on Orientals . . ."

Vail cut in to ask, "Don't you mean Jessie Starbuck and that breed of hers helped you and Texas figure out that mass suicide? I read about it in the papers. Quite some time ago, as a matter of fact."

Longarm had heard tobacco ash was good for carpet beetles, so he flicked some on the office rug. "I'm sure glad our own political campaigns ain't as messy as Japan's, ain't you?"

Vail growled, "You're still being evasive and I'm still mad as hell about it. What are you trying to hide from me with that grin and forked tongue, damn you?"

Longarm looked sheepish. "Personal icing on the cake. I don't like to be called a liar and I know you would, if I strayed off the case you sent me on."

"Try me. That's an order. You know I have to dock your pay for time in the field you can't prove to me as line of duty. So that had better be good."

Longarm said, "If you'd be good enough to read the report I filed with old Henry instead of fussing at a deputy so pure of heart, you'd know I ain't asking for the past few days' worth of miserable wages."

"How come? You didn't put in for any bounty money, did you?"

Longarm shook his head. "I know you frown on that. I reckon I'd best backtrack to where we were getting aboard, out in San Diego. We was stocking up on things to read on the way to Houston. You can't look at scenery all the way. They don't publish Japanese papers there, but there was one printed in Chinese. So, as a lark, I bought one for a pal of mine to read."

Vail sighed. "I imagine Ki must find your cow-camp sense of humor as tedious as I do. What's so funny about asking a gent who reads Japanese to read Chinese?"

Longarm chuckled fondly and said, "He can. So the joke was on me when he just thanked me and proceeded to read away once we were in the hills. I figured he might have been just fooling to get even with me. So I asked what he was reading and, when he read me the lead story, I knew he had me. I'd talked enough to real Chinese, passing through Frisco, to know he had to be on the level about the lead story."

"Is there any point to your dumb joke?"

Longarm continued, "There is. I won the Chinese lottery. Not the grand prize, but still enough to thundergast me when I made him read the winning numbers off twice. When we got to Houston I looked up a Chinese I know there, and he paid me off, less a modest percentage for his trouble. So that's the whole tale, and you can believe it or not."

Vail rolled his eyes heavenward. "That sounds so ridiculous it has to be true. How many times do I have to tell you we're supposed to bust up tongs, not gamble with 'em?"

Longarm looked innocent as he explained, "You never

sent me after no tongs. You sent me after Jap renegades. I bought the lottery tickets in the line of duty and, to tell the truth, I'd forgot I had 'em on me till that Chinese paper jogged my memory."

Vail laughed despite himself and said, "That's life. Who else but a gent spending the taxpayers' time with the richest woman in Texas would win a damn lottery?"

Longarm frowned. "Hold on, now. I ain't no gigglebeau. I might have got back even later if the lady you tend to gossip about hadn't insisted on beating me to the draw in fancy French beaneries. Have you ever been out on the town with a gal who kept grabbing for the bill before the fool waiter could lay it on the table, Billy?"

"I know why Jessie Starbuck's still single. So what do you aim to do with all the money you come out ahead with?"

Longarm shrugged. "It's been blowed. All but a few bucks to last me till payday, I hope. I told you I didn't spend all that *time* in Texas, either."

He took a long drag on his cheroot and a cautious stare at his crusty boss before he admitted, "As a matter of fact I got back to Denver last Thursday. But, seeing as the week was about shot, and that another old gal was mad as hell at me, I felt it was only right to show her a better time than usual."

Vail gasped, "Thunderation! You mean to tell me all this time I've had an all-points out on a missing deputy, you was painting Denver red with a painted hussy, right under our noses?"

Longarm looked away. "They don't usually cater to gents like me and you in such places as we was painting red, and she ain't a painted hussy. She's an upright widow woman with money of her own."

Vail snapped, "Well, I hope you enjoyed her. For that's all you'll have to show for your time come payday!"

Longarm shrugged. "I already figured as much. She was a better sport. Never tried once to grab the bill, and when I

279

told her I just plain hated going to the opera, she said a good wining and dining at Romano's would do just as well."

Watch for

LONGARM AND THE DESERT SPIRITS

ninety-ninth novel in the bold
LONGARM
series from Jove

and

LONE STAR AND THE SIERRA SWINDLERS

fifty-fifth novel in the exciting
LONE STAR
series from Jove

coming in March!